SETTLING THE SCORE

CLARE CONNELLY

Boldwood

First published in Great Britain in 2025 by Boldwood Books Ltd.

Copyright © Clare Connelly, 2025

Cover Design by Lisa Horton

Cover Images: Lisa Horton

The moral right of Amy Andrews to be identified as the author of this work has been asserted in accordance with the Copyright, Designs and Patents Act 1988.

Every effort has been made to obtain the necessary permissions with reference to copyright material, both illustrative and quoted. We apologise for any omissions in this respect and will be pleased to make the appropriate acknowledgements in any future edition.

A CIP catalogue record for this book is available from the British Library.

Paperback ISBN 978-1-83633-963-2

Large Print ISBN 978-1-83633-962-5

Hardback ISBN 978-1-83633-961-8

Ebook ISBN 978-1-83633-964-9

Kindle ISBN 978-1-83633-965-6

Audio CD ISBN 978-1-83633-956-4

MP3 CD ISBN 978-1-83633-957-1

Digital audio download ISBN 978-1-83633-960-1

This book is printed on certified sustainable paper. Boldwood Books is dedicated to putting sustainability at the heart of our business. For more information please visit https://www. boldwoodbooks.com/about-us/sustainability/

Boldwood Books Ltd, 23 Bowerdean Street, London, SW6 3TN

www.boldwoodbooks.com

For Amy, Rachael and Pippa. I'm so proud of the stories we've brought to life in The Karma Club, particularly the portrayal of such strong female friendships. Here's to many more collaborations.

IN THE BEGINNING

CHICAGO O'HARE AIRPORT, 21 DECEMBER

It was entirely possible that Sienna was the only person in the airport glorying in the flashing 'delayed' signs showing on every information screen, the only person grinning from ear to ear despite the overwhelming waft of other people's travel fumes and already-stale festive cheer. Maybe, if she got really lucky – and she knew given her track record over the past twenty-four hours (scratch that, the past ten years) that was pretty unlikely – the delays would last so long she'd get to catch a bus back to Ashbury Falls, instead of a sky-high death trap.

Except that would mean being home late, and disappointing her sort of step-daughter, Melanie. No way would she risk that by giving into something as childish as a fear of flying.

Nonetheless, she'd definitely take the reprieve of a slight delay.

Pulling her bag over her shoulder, she made her way deeper into the cavernous airport lounge, way too full of people, Christmas carols, baubles and raised voices. And yes, even here, in delayed-flight hell, there he was.

Aiden 'Perfect Teeth' Carter.

She stared at his bright, shiny picture, illuminated by a thousand LED globes behind it, and had an urge to pull the chewing gum from her mouth and whack it right between his too-perfect eyes. His 'I'll promise you the world then rip it away' eyes. His 'you can trust me with all your secrets' eyes. Or better yet, his 'I'll always be here for you' lying lips. She reached towards her mouth to do just that when the image changed to one of a little girl opening a Christmas present.

Aiden's picture might have been gone, but he was burned into her brain. Though she hadn't seen him in the flesh for a decade, she saw him *every-damned-where* and on this day, of all days, she was sick of it.

Stuff a delayed flight. *That* was the reprieve she really needed: a break from him.

Even now, ten years and a pretty serious (albeit failed) relationship with someone else later, how did this one guy still have the ability to put her in a bad mood?

She forced herself to focus on the falling snow outside, so fast and furious it reminded her of the snow globe she'd got as a kid. She'd loved to shake it as hard as she could and watch the whirling white fuzz surround the little church in the middle. For some reason, it had made her feel cosy. It had made her feel safe.

But even that memory was tainted by Aiden. Aiden in her room, looking at her stuff like it was some kind of museum or tribute to the greatest person on earth, asking her questions that made her feel so special and valued. Aiden shaking the snow globe and studying it, talking about churches and weddings as if that was their future. Aiden who'd lied like most men breathed.

Her gaze drifted to the airline help desk. A queue snaked from one side of the concourse to the other and then back again, and the airline staff looked like they'd happily give their right arms to be anywhere but here, dealing with anything but this.

Everywhere she looked, people were pissed as heck, and not afraid to show it.

As if it was such a shock to be snowed in at Chicago O'Hare in December. What did they think? That if they harassed the staff long enough someone would be able to magic up a snow-safe plane to get them out of here?

Hell no.

The trick in life was knowing what you could change, and what you couldn't, and Sienna had spent a long time honing her understanding of each.

She watched as a generously proportioned woman with a devilish smile and bright magenta hair handed out equally garish, hot pink leaflets to passersby. From where she stood, Sienna couldn't properly see what the flyer was advertising – maybe a massage parlour? Or a nail bar? – but she was fascinated by the woman's selection criteria. Not everyone who walked past received a pamphlet. She'd hand one out, then go back to smiling, looking around the concourse, pretending fascination with a sign, before randomly selecting someone else and pressing a leaflet into their hands.

Such was Sienna's desperate need for distraction – Aiden had cycled back onto the screen, with his perma-tan looking all glowy and golden – that she actually started to make a game of it, trying to guess which of the passersby would be selected for the flyers and which wouldn't make the cut. When she started to lose interest and walk off in search of somewhere to sit for a while, a little girl, around eleven, came out of nowhere and ran right into Sienna's legs. Sienna instinctively reached down and steadied her, smiling.

'You okay, hon?'

The little girl looked embarrassed, just like Melanie would have at that age. 'Yeah, whoops. Sorry. My brother – he's chasing me.'

She had to give credit to anyone who'd try to play tag in an airport as crammed as this. It was more like sardines in a tin. The little girl ran off and a woman rushed by, not connected to the girl, but in just as much of a hurry as if she was also in their game. She stood on Sienna's foot with the spike of her heel – who wore stilettos to an airport? – earning a sharp invective from Sienna.

'Just Desserts?'

Having lost interest in the woman handing out the flyers, the woman had apparently discovered an interest in Sienna, or had at least deemed her worthy of one of the hot pink pieces of paper. What box did she tick? Was it the murderous look in her eyes every time Aiden came up on screen? Did Sienna look as close to breaking point as she felt? The relief of having been granted a reprieve from having to fly had taken a severe dip with the realisation that she was going to be confronted by images of her superstar ex everywhere she went. Of course. Because he was Aiden 'King of Hockey' Carter, beloved the world over. Ugh.

'I'm sorry?'

'Go, grab a table, have some pie.' The woman winked encouragingly.

'Oh.' Sienna looked around at the teeming mess of bodies and pre-Christmas disappointment. 'Thanks, but I doubt there'll be room.' Everywhere she looked, chairs were stuffed, restaurants were flooded. Even the restrooms were like a hot new destination.

'You never know.' The woman shrugged. 'You might get lucky.'

'Yeah, maybe,' she said, because why bother arguing with a woman who was just doing her job? 'Thanks.'

The older woman winked and flashed a smile that could only be categorised as pure cheek, then wandered off.

Sienna shoved the brochure in her pocket and

wandered aimlessly, the strap of her carry-on cutting into her shoulder because she'd chosen not to check baggage and had therefore crammed as much as she could into her bashed up old duffel. As she walked past the sign, Aiden popped up, and in a weird trick of the angle or light, it was like their eyes actually met.

Despite all her anger with him, all her frustration, a shiver ran the length of her spine and she admitted – only for a second and only to herself – that she could never really hate him. No matter what he'd done, no matter how much his desertion had hurt, she'd loved him so much, and with such purity, that it could never really turn to hate. Anger yes, hate no.

'Bastard,' she muttered under her breath as she passed the screen, doing her best not to look at any other signs in the airport – which was about as easy as not getting frostbite in Antarctica. Her mood was going from bad to worse when she turned a corner somewhat against her will, having been caught in the tide of one large, travelling family who were moving... somewhere? Sienna walked along with them, listening to their conversations in a different language – Italian – until a glow of pink almost blinded her and she stopped walking altogether.

Just Desserts, the sign screamed, echoing the writing on the flyer.

Sure enough, the place was full, packed to the brim with people needing sugar, alcohol and a seat, in no particular order. Except... just as she was preparing to keep walking, a table cleared. Hallelujah! Angels at work, surely. She ducked out of the Italian family, head down, beetling towards the table as though her whole life depended on claiming that space and making it hers...

But three other women had the same desperately determined expression on their faces and they'd all arrived at the table at basically the same time.

Sienna wanted to scream.

She wanted to cry.

A huge photo of Aiden eating a strawberry sundae was hanging behind the counter, and in the bottom corner, his signature had been scrawled. Even *here*? Seriously? She glared at the picture then looked back at the women. She didn't want a fight.

She just wanted a seat.

'Fuckity-fuck!' a British woman snapped, and Sienna 100 per cent echoed her thoughts. Fuckity-fuck indeed.

Each of the women held a flyer in their hands just like she did. Sienna was about to leave hers on the table with a statement about her luck pretty much being the worst in the world when one of the women, all short and confident, with fascinating, curly red hair, shrugged one shoulder. 'If none of you are with anyone else, we could share?'

Share? Of course they could share! Why hadn't Sienna thought of that? Because she'd had the day from hell, on top of the year from hell, and lurching from one disappointment to the other had become standard. Somewhere along the way, she'd given up on even looking for an easy solution.

She sighed her relief and smiled a little tightly, scraping back her chair, and removing her dead-weight of a bag with relief, placing it carefully at her feet.

Bella introduced herself first – American like Sienna, except she sounded posh and looked fancy; sleek and untouchable. Sienna instantly felt like a hick despite having worn her favourite outfit for what was meant to have been the most important meeting of her life.

Astrid sat opposite – a brunette with super-model looks and an easy smile. The kind of smile that spoke of always having got your way, always being charmed just for being charming. Sienna ignored the uncharitable thought. Some people got it easy in life, others didn't. That was just the way it was.

Paige was the British redhead, with freckles that danced over her nose and a face that was hyperanimated and expressive, so it seemed to move to illustrate whatever she was thinking and feeling. She'd be a terrible poker player but an excellent friend.

It was Paige who suggested the first bottle of prosecco and Sienna was all too willing to go along with that. She had some sleeping tablets stashed in her purse for the flight, but a couple of glasses of bubbles would go a long way to taking the edge off her altitude anxiety. It might even give her temporary Aiden-blindness.

'Four glasses,' Bella told the waitress. 'And some water for the table, please.' Yep, definitely fancy. Back where Sienna came from, drinking water with your booze was kind of frowned upon.

Except, it turned out, Bella wasn't fancy. She was lovely. A peach. So too were Astrid and Paige. Even though Sienna had made it an artform to keep people at a very firm distance, something about their open natures, the anonymity offered by an airport restaurant and snow-delayed schedule, not to mention a couple of bottles of prosecco, made the time fly. Two hours went in the blink of an eye and she'd only stared daggers at Aiden's strawberry sundae photo a handful of times. Huh. That was progress.

She listened as Paige talked about her VA business, impressed by her obvious myriad skills, then moved onto talking about the wedding she'd been at. 'Pavlova dress. Drunken best man's speech. Smooshing cake into each other's faces. A handsy Uncle Chip.' Sienna stifled a giggle at the imagery, but beside her, Bella was in a totally different mood.

'I'd rather not talk about weddings.' Her voice was tenser than a tightrope. Concerned, Sienna glanced across at her.

'Not a fan?' Paige asked what they were obviously all thinking.

'Absolutely not.' Bella shuddered delicately.

'Don't believe in love?' Paige was persistent and Sienna loved that.

'I did. And then six months ago I stood up in front of 400 guests to let them know that my groom wasn't coming.'

Sienna's jaw dropped.

'Holy mother of... you were jilted?'

'Yup. By text. The morning of.'

'By text? What kind of scumbag does that?' Astrid demanded with an indignation Sienna felt in her soul.

In fact, courtesy of all the stories they'd shared and fizz they'd fuzzed, and maybe just a little bit because of the way Aiden was staring out at all and sundry and daring them not to fall in love with his perfect face, anger exploded through her. 'Who is he?' she heard herself demand. 'Tell me. I'll bring you his head.' Yes! Yes, she damn well would!

Everyone laughed, including Sienna, but inside she was livid.

'He's not a bad person really.'

Sienna almost rolled her eyes. Why did so many women make excuses for these dropkicks? She'd seen it time and time again while volunteering at legal aid. Hell, she'd done it often enough herself, first for Aiden and then for Cory.

'He's just a little clueless,' Bella continued softly. 'Had everything handed to him on a silver platter. He's a bit of a Peter Pan and I made the classic mistake of thinking that it would be different with me. That I could change him.'

Sienna puffed out a defensive sigh and tried to soften her tone, even though she was pretty sure her expression was set to DEFCON 1. 'Doesn't excuse him leaving you standing at the altar.'

'No, it doesn't. That was truly a low act.'

'Yes, it was.'

'Well.' Astrid leaned closer to Sienna. 'You can string mine up.' Maybe she sensed that Sienna was now simply baying for, if not blood, a little payback.

'Were you jilted as well?'

'No. Unbeknownst to me, he'd already trotted up that aisle and merrily said "I do" to someone else.'

'So... he turned you into the other woman?'

'Too right he did. Made me feel like a piece of shit.'

It was like a faucet had been turned on and she didn't know how to control it. Anger was a wide spray nozzle, coursing through Sienna's veins. Her day had gone from bad to worse, but it was the culmination of a pretty shitty decade, and these women were suddenly the receptacle for every feeling she'd absorbed and muted over the years. 'Are you freaking kidding me? He was already married?'

Bella's cheeks had two pink spots. 'What is wrong with these men? Doesn't marriage mean anything any more?'

'I don't think men get the concept of commitment,' Sienna muttered. 'Even the ones who seem to are just faking it.'

Suddenly, three pairs of eyes were turned on her and she began to feel a little hot under the collar. It was all well and good to be outraged on someone else's behalf. That was why she was pretty sure she was going to be a damned good lawyer. But advocating for yourself was way harder. 'Sorry.' Her laugh was tight. 'That's a little dramatic, isn't it?'

But Bella wasn't going to be put off. Like Paige, she was an excellent truth hound. 'What happened?'

Melanie's dad Cory was the one who'd really wronged her. He was the one who'd used her for free childcare, just because she loved his daughter like her own. But Cory had never really hurt her. Even though she could objectively see how badly he'd treated her, it hadn't mattered that much, because she hadn't loved him. Not like she'd loved Aiden.

Her eyes drifted to the poster and something tightened in the region of her heart. Was she really going to open this can of worms? Or was it that it had never been sealed shut before? And when had she ever talked to anyone about it? Never, that was when. She'd kept it all close to her chest, refusing to let anyone see how much he'd hurt her. 'My ex' – she frowned as she looked back to the squad – 'kind of just discarded me.' Her throat stung. 'It wasn't like some big, dramatic break-up.' Like that made a difference. 'I didn't even get the chance to throw plates.' Maybe she'd have felt better if she'd had a chance to fire up at him, to really lose her temper? It was all so long ago, though. 'I mean, we were just kids, but we were each other's firsts, you know?' And now for the really big admission, the one she was loath to share because it showed how stupid and naïve she'd been. 'And I thought we were going to have a life together.' A whole life. A whole, long, happy life. Only, that was his plan for himself, not her. It had never been about her. She dug her nails into her palm beneath the table. 'But he hightailed it out of town without a backwards glance.' *And refused to speak to me, ever again.* 'Like nothing we had mattered.'

And it hadn't.

He'd been dating someone else pretty soon, and his career had lit up like an arena.

Bella's soft, manicured hand reached across to squeeze Sienna's. 'I'm so sorry. That's terrible.'

'Sucks ass,' Astrid agreed in a tone that actually made Sienna laugh despite everything. God, she needed to stop thinking about Aiden.

Her eyes swept across the table, studying her new friends. What was it about these women that had inspired her to open up? Why this group? Why now?

But Paige had been conspicuously quiet during the 'my ex is worse than your ex' conversation, which only made Sienna wonder...

'Can I bring *you* anyone's head?'

She wasn't actually about to go out and hunt these guys down but it was fun to imagine, for a moment, that such power (fuelled by prosecco) was within her grasp.

Paige hesitated, her lips parting a little, and Sienna wondered if she was going to change the subject or say something like, 'I'd rather not talk about it.'

But then she leaned in a little, and lowered her voice.

'I broke up with my ex, Harvey, after a brief, intense relationship and then he posted naked pictures and videos of me online.' Sienna cursed inwardly – the really bad words that her meemaw would have strung her up for saying. 'He'd taken them without my knowledge or consent.'

Sienna gasped then clamped a hand over her mouth when several heads turned their direction. 'Revenge porn?' she hissed, her eyes spitting chips.

Paige nodded, her cheeks pink. 'I've never felt so degraded.' She dropped her gaze to the table. 'I met him at Oxford. He was studying IT and I was a third-year law student. It completely ruined my future career prospects. No prestigious law firm was going to take me on after that. Hell, not even a terrible law firm would. And I couldn't bear staying on at Oxford.

Where everyone had seen the pictures. So I' – she shrugged as she raised her eyes – 'dropped out.'

'What a bastard,' Bella said, a little hesitantly for Sienna's liking so she added:

'Absolute bastard! What's he doing now, do you know?'

'He's some kind of tech bro. Travels between London and Silicon Valley.'

'Ugh.' Sienna rolled her eyes. 'Of course he is.'

It was all just so unfair! Again her eyes shifted to the picture behind the bar, and at the precise moment a couple of women stopped to take a photo with it. Both beautiful and glossy, just the kind of arm candy that superstar NHL player Aiden would no doubt go for. The wave of jealousy surprised Sienna. It had been *ten* years, for God's sake. But Aiden had become a sort of slap-in-the-face for Sienna. He'd gone on to become everything he'd ever hoped, and she'd been left behind, treading water just to get by.

She jerked her attention back to the table with renewed determination. 'They shouldn't be allowed to get away with it.'

Astrid spilled some prosecco as she connected her glass to the tabletop with a little too much gusto. 'Damn right they shouldn't.'

Sienna had felt impotent for a long time, and

she'd felt alone for even longer. What else explained why she'd put up with Cory? He hadn't been much, but at least he'd been someone to do things with, someone to talk to at the end of the day, someone she could pretend cared about her... But these women were like steel being liquified and poured into her spine. For the first time in a long time, she felt strong. She felt empowered. And it was all thanks to them.

'What if we... look, I know this sounds crazy.' Her eyes fell to her empty prosecco glass. 'And I may be a little drunk.' Out of nowhere, she hiccupped and the other women giggled. Sienna laughed too before re-focusing her attention on the idea she'd been about to share. 'What if we took it upon ourselves to exact some... revenge?'

Silence.

Crackly, hard-to-read silence.

Then, Bella queried, with a quiet caution that was very wise, 'How do you mean?'

'I don't mean murdering them or anything,' Sienna clarified quickly. She'd been visiting her dad in prison every Saturday for more than nine years and was determined never to see the inside of a jail cell herself. 'I mean, look. These guys have had everything go their way, right? They got to walk all over us. Or walk out on us. Why should they just get to live their best lives while we're picking up the remnants of ours?'

Astrid's excitement was visible. 'Yes. I like where this is heading.'

Sienna nodded. 'Why not have a little fun at their expense?'

Bella though was still wary. 'What kind of fun?'

'Nothing serious,' Sienna promised, the idea bursting in her mind like fireworks. 'Stuff that would inconvenience them, that we can have a laugh over. Like...' She wracked her brain, trying to think of something suitable. 'Signing them up to hundreds of mailing lists. Or putting a dead fish in their wheel hubs. Buy them a cow and have it delivered. Switch out their clothes for a size or two smaller. Change all the names in their phone contacts to Dr Seuss. That kind of thing.'

She felt the collective stares of the group and wondered if she sounded as though she'd lost the plot.

'Wow.' Paige, though, sounded truly impressed. Scared, but impressed. 'Remind me to never get on your bad side.'

'Some of those things would require us to get close.' Bella picked up the threads of the idea. 'They'll know it was us. There's no way we'd get away with it.' But Sienna, an expert at reading people, could tell from her tone that she was in. She was working out the kinks but in a way that showed how much she wanted this to happen.

Confidence lurched inside Sienna. She hadn't lost the plot, she'd damn well found it for the first time in a decade. In a migraine-inducingly pink bar in an overcrowded airport, but so what? 'That's why we pick someone else's ex!'

The other women went deadly silent. Sienna could almost hear their cogs turning.

'It's an excellent plan.' Astrid was the first to speak. 'So good I wish I'd thought of it.'

Bella nodded. 'Me too. Very Machiavellian.'

Paige was the holdout, the last juror to be convinced. 'Okay,' she said, slowly, evidently still thinking. 'Maybe.'

Astrid though was already taking Paige's acceptance as a foregone conclusion. 'Who would you pick?' Her excitement was contagious and Sienna knew exactly who she wanted to crush like a vile little bug. 'Harvey the Horrible.' That rat deserved to pay, big time. 'If he spends time regularly in the US I'm sure I'll be able to figure out something. You?'

Astrid was also quick to reply. 'I'd take your

heartbreaker. Any guy who'd just walk out on a sweetheart like you deserves to be played a little.'

'And I'd take your cheating, married, bastard ex,' Bella threw out there. 'Which leaves you with Olly.' She turned to Paige, tapping the side of her lip thoughtfully. 'And that's *perfect* because he slunk back to England after the wedding, to his dad's place in Cornwall. How's your sitting schedule for the new year?'

Paige's eyes were deer-in-headlights wide. 'I have a few things lined up in Jan, Feb that aren't set in stone. I have a month-long gig in Edinburgh starting in March.' She looked at the three of them, her lips parting softly. 'Is the place big enough for two?'

'Yes! It's very spacious,' Bella promised. 'And right on the beach.'

Paige tilted her head to the side. 'How would he feel about a guest?'

Bella looked like all her Christmases were coming at once. 'He does like his privacy.'

'I know exactly how he feels,' Paige muttered with a hint of an eye roll before shaking her head, as if to clear the cobwebs. 'I don't know... are we really going to do this? Maybe it's just the alcohol talking...'

'Good point.' Bella's smile slipped.

There was no lack of certainty with Astrid

though. 'Well, I sure as hell am. I don't know about you, but I'll sleep a little better knowing Horrible Harvey is getting his comeuppance.'

Paige's face briefly crumpled with emotion, as though she wasn't used to having people go to bat for her. Which only made Sienna more determined.

'Look,' she said, gently, seriously. 'This only works if we all agree. And nobody should feel pressured into doing it if it doesn't sit right.'

Bella hit her glass to the table a little emphatically. 'Definitely.'

'God, fuck, yes.' Astrid visibly notched her commitment down. 'The last thing I want to do is browbeat my new co-conspirators. Sorry. Besties.'

Sienna didn't look at Paige. She was the one who was struggling and Sienna definitely didn't want her to feel pressured. Instead, she glared at the poster with laser-like anger.

'I do love a cream tea,' Paige blurted out, then glanced at Bella. 'I'd be safe there?'

Sienna's heart damn near broke. What this woman had been through was just beyond – trust once destroyed was almost impossible to rebuild. Sienna would move heaven and earth to exact revenge on the prick who'd done this to her.

'Definitely. For all his commitment-phobe tendencies, he's a true gentleman and I know he feels terribly guilty about the jilting. Which I'm perfectly okay exploiting to get you in there. I still have his number.'

'Oh, yes!' Astrid's enthusiasm was back to off-the-charts. 'That's a *great* plan. You could text him now.' She batted her lashes then glanced at the clocks on the wall. 'It's six in the evening over there.'

Sienna could sense Paige's ambivalence shifting to acceptance. 'Look, how about this?' She pulled her long blonde hair over one shoulder, running her fingers through the ends in a gesture of deep thought. 'What if Bella texts, and then... we leave it up to the universe?'

'The universe?' Astrid looked sceptical.

'Yes, you know. Fate. Kismet. If he texts back while we're all still sitting here at this table we randomly ended up at, then it's a go. If he doesn't? We've all had a laugh and filled in a few hours. No harm, no foul.'

'Oooh.' Astrid's nod underscored her enthusiasm. 'I like that.'

'Me too,' Bella said.

Paige nodded firmly. 'Okay, yeah. Okay.'

Bella set about drafting a text to Olly, reading it

aloud as she wrote, and then they all sat very still, and very silent, and waited.

And waited. Because this felt like a monumental shift, in the middle of pink central, a fork in the road for all of them.

And then, ping.

Bella scrambled for the phone and read to the group, 'Is she a Roger Prendergast groupie?'

Sienna tilted her head, confused by the reference. She'd adored Roger Prendergast even as a young girl.

'The actor that died a little while ago?' Paige asked.

Bella nodded. 'Yep. Roger was his dad.'

A kaleidoscope of butterflies launched inside Sienna. When she thought of Roger Prendergast, she instantly visualised kind eyes and a ready smile. The idea of getting payback on his son made her insides lurch a little. But then she remembered the hell Olly had put Bella through and strengthened her spine.

Paige denied any stalkerish obsession with the late actor and Bella sent word back to Olly. A moment later, with eyes that were round like saucers, Bella gulped. 'He says fine.'

Paige glanced from one woman to the next, a smile twitching the corners of her lips and Sienna *felt* it. A connection, a shared sense of purpose and finally, the hint of fun and mischief. God knew she needed that. 'Okay then. Looks like I'm off to Cornwall.'

Sienna wasn't going to let the moment pass without celebration. She let out a whoop and got the attention of a passing waiter, holding up four fingers and calling for more prosecco. When it arrived, Astrid grinned, holding hers aloft. 'To just desserts.'

To just desserts indeed...

1

EIGHT MONTHS LATER

'Okay, I've been thinking.' Astrid, a hand pressed to her slightly rounded, five-months-pregnant stomach, was the picture of pre-marital bliss, all gorgeous and dewy skinned, hair glossy, cheeks flushed with an overall sense of life-delirium. Even half a continent away, through the pixels of a group video chat, she freaking *glowed* like a bulb.

'*We've* been thinking,' Bella interrupted with a wink.

Paige nodded solicitously, so in the space of a few seconds, Sienna had a sinking sensation that she was on the receiving end of a very well-intentioned good ol' fashioned gang-up.

'Yeah?' she asked, eyes lifting to the clock above

the door. It was almost five. 'Well, spill it quickly, 'cause my shift starts in thirty and I still need to shower.'

'We think you should get your own revenge,' Paige blurted.

Sienna's brows furrowed. 'You know I'm working on that. Harvey the Horrible is well and truly in my sights, believe me.' It was true. She'd been digging. Planning, for months. The problem was, someone like Harvey was almost God-like in Silicon Valley circles. She wasn't sure she had any actual way to get to him, even if she could formulate a perfect revenge plan. But no way was she going to break that to Paige. Or Olly, come to think of it, who'd started a separate side chat with Sienna, to help brainstorm ideas for revenge.

Paige's eyes softened with something like gratitude. 'I know.'

'I mean it. I'm going to get him.' If only she could work out how. This guy was like some kind of digital fortress. Or royalty. Even gaining access to him was almost impossible, but Sienna was determined not to fail. The rat bastard deserved whatever comeuppance Sienna could dish out.

'Anyway,' Paige said. 'That's not what we mean.'

'No?'

'Nope.' Astrid shook her head.

Sienna's brows lifted. 'Then what?'

'In precisely two weeks, you'll be at the wedding.' The wedding of Astrid – who just happened to have fallen head over heels for Blake, AKA Aiden Carter's twin brother – was highlighted on her calendar in big red ink. Not just because she was a bridesmaid and bestie, but because she knew the moment she'd been dreading since Astrid and Blake found their HEA was almost upon her.

She'd have to come face to face with Aiden again. There was no avoiding it.

Sienna blinked. 'And?'

'Annnnnd,' Bella cut in, her clipped socialite accent ever so slightly impatient. 'So will Aiden.'

'Aiden, who broke your heart, Aiden,' Paige said helpfully.

'Thank you for that reminder.' Sienna shook her head, blonde hair flipping softly around her, but one side of her lips lifted with easy affection.

'And we think you should get your own payback. *On Aiden.*'

'Come on, you guys,' Sienna said, rolling her eyes. 'Don't you think he'll work out what's going on?'

'How could he? He has no idea about this.' Bella

did a little circle with her fingers, indicating the Karma Club.

Sienna glanced at Astrid, who nodded her confirmation. She knew Astrid had told Blake everything about their *Strangers on a Train*-style plan for romantic retributions, and that Blake and Astrid had agreed there was no point dredging any of it up to Aiden, that instead they'd simply brushed over Sienna and Astrid being friends as one of life's uncanny coincidences. He knew they'd met at an airport, months before Astrid had met Blake, and for the sake of protecting Sienna, they'd told a white lie: that Astrid hadn't known anything about Sienna's connection to Aiden and Blake until Astrid had gone to Ashbury Falls to meet the twins' father. It was a fudging of the truth, and the only way Astrid had been able to protect Sienna from Aiden knowing the truth about how much his rejection still hurt.

'It's just a bit of harmless fun,' Paige assured her.

'Nothing sinister,' Bella chimed in.

'Blake thinks it's a good idea,' Astrid promised, almost sealing the deal.

Sienna sat up a little straighter as a litany of ideas floated through her mind. Bleaching his wedding tux right before the ceremony, or putting laxatives in his slice of cake, or smearing his shoes with doggie poop, or... 'But it's your *wedding*.' She stopped her thought train hard in its tracks to address the effervescent Astrid. 'I can't do anything that will mess it up. I would never do that to you, or Blake.'

'That's not exactly what we're suggesting,' Bella insisted, leaning a little closer to her screen, coffee cup in hand. 'Let's cut to the chase,' she began, and Sienna couldn't help holding her breath as Bella began to outline their well-developed plan.

* * *

Which was how, almost two weeks later, Sienna found herself in one of Manhattan's premier spas, surrounded by the Karma Club Mayhem Makers, the women she'd randomly met at an airport the December prior, and somehow become ride or die besties with over the space of a few hours (and several bottles of bubbles).

Their bond had only got stronger since that one fateful meeting, despite the fact this was only one of a few times they'd actually been face to face since that night. Travelling wasn't easy for Sienna. She scrimped and saved everything she earned to cover her living expenses and pay off her degree. Without a little help from her friends and their airmiles, she would have struggled to make any of the previous trips. This, though, wasn't just an ordinary trip. It was Astrid's wedding, and there was nothing she wouldn't do for her – or any of these girls.

Even submitting to a total glam up.

So, her hair had been foiled and trimmed, given some kind of weird treatment that smelled like buttercream frosting, so even though she knew she shouldn't and couldn't eat her own hair, it was making her ravenous for all the sweet things anyway. Her face and body had *both* been slathered in mud-like mixtures, her slender limbs had been wrapped in kelp, then exfoliated by an army of women who kept exclaiming over how 'wonderful' everything was making her look. Who needed a fairy godmother when there was the make-over mafia?

It was, Sienna decided, if not precisely torture, pretty damned close to it. For a woman who'd always been more comfortable knocking around in a pair of faded jeans and a tee, this level of beauty preparation made her head spin. Not to mention being glued to a seat for well over an hour while several technicians did her fingers and toes. Even her eyebrows had been whipped into submission. Thank God she was naturally tanned and therefore escaped the 'little bit of bronze' one of the beauticians was determined to administer. Astrid had evidently taken pity on her at that point, and suggested they have a drink by the pool instead, even if her own drink would be a mock-tail owing to her pregnancy.

'Much more my speed,' Sienna confided, admiring the luscious green palms that grew from big white pots, sprinkled around the swimming area.

'I know, it's gruelling,' Bella admitted. 'But totally worth it. You look a million bucks.'

Sienna's lips pulled to the side. She had felt like one of her pseudo step-daughter Melanie's old Barbie dolls for most of the day, but the effects had, she grudgingly admitted, been worth it. Having spent several years pretending – even to herself – not to notice how *glossy* Aiden's girlfriends all looked, she had to admit, she'd sort of morphed into one of them.

'I'm still me.' She shrugged, looking down at the oversized robe that engulfed her petite frame.

'Yes, love, but also kind of new and improved.' Astrid winked, before reaching down beside her seat and pulling out several large bags. Sienna didn't have to be a *Vogue* reader to recognise the couture brands.

'What are those?' She couldn't keep the wariness from her voice.

'Think of them as your costumes.' Astrid encouraged.

Sienna stared at her friends blankly.

'For the wedding.'

'I... don't need a costume.' She glanced from Astrid to Bella to Paige. Three faces looked back at her with 'butter wouldn't melt' expressions. 'It's not themed, right? Tell me it's not themed.'

Bella's laugh was good natured. 'Did we, or did we not, agree that you are going to spend the whole weekend making Aiden absolutely drool at the sight of you?'

'And wish he could go back in time and never walk out on you?' Astrid added.

'And just generally regret every single life decision of his since then?' Paige chimed in.

'And then get him right where you want him, eating out of the palm of your hand, so *you* can be the one to walk away?' Bella finished with a wide-eyed innocence that was all assumed.

'But, you guys, I mean, come on.'

'What?' Paige demanded, indignation on her face. 'I thought you liked the plan?'

'I do. I really do. I love you guys for thinking this could ever work. But I'm nothing to Aiden any more. Just some girl he walked out on about a million years ago.'

Paige snorted. 'More fool him.'

'I'm serious. And haven't we learned that we're not exactly the master revenge getters we thought? I mean, it's taking me forever to get what I need on Horrible Harvey.'

Genuine frustration tinged her voice, because she'd tried so many avenues to get to Harvey and every time reached a dead end. She'd applied for an internship at his company, figuring she'd work out how to make that happen when and if she was accepted – only she hadn't been. She'd applied for a housekeeping role in his building, figuring that would at least get her access to him in shared spaces, like the gym, except she hadn't even got an interview. And her online snooping had drawn a blank: with little wonder. He was a tech genius; of course he could cover his tracks. She needed to be able to make the bastard pay for what he'd done to Paige. Publishing sex videos of her online – that she hadn't even known he'd filmed – had almost ruined her life, and Sienna was determined to make him sorry.

She pushed aside those thoughts for now, returning her attention to the discussion at hand. 'And you all fell in love with your targets.'

'I didn't,' Astrid was quick to supply.

'No, you just fell in love with his brother.'

'And this time, it's different,' Bella said.

Sienna arched a brow. 'How, exactly?'

'Well, for one thing, it's the first time we've done this all together.'

'Yeah.' Paige jumped onto the bandwagon. 'We were all sent out on our own to wage war. No artillery or support. Just us. And we... lost our way a bit.'

'Or found it,' Sienna pointed out archly.

'Or found it.' Astrid's smile glowed as she added her agreement. Bella's eyes were a particularly delightful shade of silver. Paige's cheeks flushed pink.

Sienna bit back a smile. 'And I'm thrilled for you guys. Like, deliriously, over the moon delighted. But there's no way I'm heading for a happy ending with Aiden. That ship sailed when he smashed my heart into a gazillion pieces.'

'We know,' they said in unison, and it was only the smallest flicker of Astrid's lips that made her wonder if they actually believed her. Because they hadn't *seen* her then. Aiden had been the knight in shining armour she hadn't even known she needed, and she'd placed all her teenage trust in him. All of it. He'd thrown it back in her face like it meant nothing when she needed him to be by her side. Only a wound like that could explain why, more than ten years later, she was still seething with rage.

'But you've got us,' Astrid continued. 'We'll help you.'

Sienna bit into her lower lip. It tasted like honeycomb courtesy of some scrub they'd used on it.

'Yeah,' Paige nodded encouragingly. 'We'll make him wish he'd never, ever let you go. Cross my heart and—'

'No, no,' Bella interrupted with a giggle, lifting her drink in the air. 'On red velvet cakes...'

'And Just Desserts,' Astrid finished with a wicked glint in her eyes, as she brought her drink towards Bella's for a cheers.

Part of Sienna wanted to disavow any part of this plan and spend the next week or so determinedly ignoring Aiden except for when she absolutely had to make some kind of attempt at small talk for the sake of good manners. But the girls were *so* invested in their plan, and the way they were looking at Sienna actually made her feel like maybe she could do this, after all.

Of the four of them, maybe she'd be the one who would actually get to avenge her ex? It wasn't exactly prank central, but given the way Aiden had treated her like a big fat zero, perhaps dishing out the same in reverse would finally ease the pain she'd carried around for so long?

'Well, now.' Sienna reached for her bright pink cocktail after several beats, lifting it towards the others. 'That does sound pretty damned good, I'm not going to lie.' Almost eleven years seemed to condense into a whirlwind of memories, like a carnival ride after too much food, so fast and bright they almost nauseated her.

Memories of the first time she and Aiden had met, or held hands, the day he'd made her laugh when she'd felt like her world was crashing down all around her, the way he'd started to walk her home after school, always looking out for her, making her feel safe, making her feel loved. Their first kiss. Their first time. The day he'd told her he was leaving, big, strong hands jammed into his jean pockets, just before she'd need him most of all. *You've got another year of school left, Sienna. And I've gotta get out of here.* How much she'd cried that night. And the next night. And the next. He'd left, anyway. A week later, she'd found out about the baby.

Memories of her trying to call him. His ignoring her calls. Two months later, when she'd lost the baby and felt like she could barely keep going, but Aiden hadn't been there for her. He'd been the toast of the college hockey scene already – she'd been stupid enough to google him, and God, hadn't that felt like a kick in the guts? Even worse was when he actually asked her to stop calling. When he'd texted to tell her he just wanted a clean break, that she needed to understand: they were *over*. He'd moved on, and so should she. That had stung. The idea of him being with other girls hadn't even occurred to her until then, but *of course* he'd moved on. Why shouldn't he?

She blinked quickly, ignoring the familiar stabbing in the region of her heart. His betrayal had hurt like a bitch.

The girls were right. If she could get a little payback, all of her own, maybe she'd finally be able to put Aiden properly in her rear-view mirror, where he deserved to be. It wasn't like she could actually hurt him, but she could maybe dent his oversized ego, just a fraction.

'Astrid? Are you sure you're okay with this? I mean, it's your wedding. And this is Blake's brother...'

'You know how I feel about Aiden,' Astrid said, lifting one slender shoulder. Of course she was one of those women who carried her entire pregnancy like a perfectly neat basketball, right at her front. 'But he hurt you, and you deserve to make him see what a mistake he made back then.'

Sienna nodded slowly. 'And Blake?'

'What about Blake?'

'He's down with this?'

Astrid glanced at Paige and Bella, a hint of pink in her cheeks. 'He doesn't want Aiden to get seriously hurt,' she said. 'But a little bit of harmless fun is fine.'

'Harmless fun,' Sienna repeated.

'It's really not that big of a deal,' Bella encouraged, leaning forward and putting a hand on Sienna's knee. 'You're just going to go to a wedding, frock up, dazzle his socks off, and move on. I don't see anything wrong with that.'

The other two shook their heads in agreement.

Sienna sucked in a deep breath, realising they were right. This was just about levelling the playing field a bit. Who didn't want to knock their ex's socks off when they had the chance? 'Okay.' She leaned forward a little, gesturing towards the bags. 'Show me what you've got.'

2

'You good?'

Aiden felt his brother's eyes on him, their twin connection making it almost impossible to hide any damned thing from Blake. But that didn't mean he'd stop trying. Especially now.

Because this was Blake and Astrid's wedding week – yes, a whole freaking week to celebrate the love of two people who hadn't even been fussed about a big white wedding a few months ago – and Aiden wasn't going to let it be about him. And Sienna.

God, even thinking of her name made his gut churn like he was about to lace up for the playoffs.

He stared straight ahead as the golf cart cut away from the luxurious mansion the owner of their team had insisted Blake use as a wedding venue, and down towards the sparkling Mediterranean. It was a picture-perfect summer's day. The sky was a crystal blue, the palm trees that were abundant on this island huge and green, offering spiky patches of shade. But Aiden's focus was almost entirely on the sleek white sports boat that was bobbing beside the jetty. He could just make it out in the distance, as well as the people – as small as match sticks from here – who were disembarking.

But she was one of them.

Sienna.

His ex.

Could it be called an 'ex' if it had just been a teenage crush? A distant romance, that had ended so badly he'd sworn off ever thinking about it? Because to think about it, to even let his mind go there, was to feel almost on fire with shame at his behaviour.

He knew why he'd broken up with her, what had been at stake, why it had been the right decision for himself, but also for Sienna. He knew that the criminal charges against Blake meant he'd had no choice. But he'd been an asshole, how he'd gone about the whole thing, no doubt about it. He'd purposefully acted as though she was nothing to him. Nothing.

After a year of spending every afternoon together. Sharing secrets, getting to know Sienna better than anyone, and for her to know him, to really know him. Sharing each other. The way they'd made love that first time, and he'd felt like the stars were about to burst out of the sky. How they'd fallen together after that, every moment they could. They hadn't been able to keep their hands off each other. And God, they'd laughed, so much.

For Aiden, who was uneasy at home, and felt the weight of the world on his shoulders out of his need to keep his mom safe from their father, and to get Blake out of the group of lousy friends he'd chosen to waste time with, having someone to simply laugh with had been like a revelation.

An addiction.

Yeah, he'd been addicted to her, all right. Addicted enough that he would have given up everything, if she'd asked it of him. And then what? Risk becoming like his father? Worse, turning Sienna into their mother?

A muscle hammered in his jaw as he tried to make out which one of the women was her. Impossible, at this distance. Except... his eyes narrowed. A blonde lifted her hand and did something to her hair, and there was just something in the gesture, the grace of her movements, that had his heart kicking up a notch in instant, soul-deep recognition.

Sienna.

Here.

On the island.

'Bro. You look like you're about to pass out. Or barf. Please don't barf.'

Fuck.

He turned to Blake and forced a grin. Tried to remember that he'd been nicknamed Ice on the hockey circuit from his first college game, because nothing – and no one – could rile him. He was cold. Untouchable. He'd had to be.

Except with Sienna, who'd been the one person on earth who'd been able to turn ice to fire – the kind that could burn a guy half to death if he wasn't careful.

He modulated his voice, forcing his large frame to relax. He was only a few minutes older than Blake but Aiden had always played that part to perfection. He was the big brother. The guy in charge. The one who kept it all together. He wasn't about to stop now.

'You're the one who's getting married. Aren't pre-wedding jitters meant to be your bag?'

'No jitters here, man.' Blake returned his attention to the path. 'I've never been more sure about a damned thing in my life.'

Aiden expelled a breath. That's how he'd felt then, too. He'd acted like a shit and he was pretty sure Sienna hated him for it, but that didn't mean it had been wrong. All his reasons still stacked up. He'd had to leave. Not just town, but Sienna.

He followed a mantra of absolute control. It was how he lived, how he played, and how he dated. Not once, since Sienna, had he been with a woman that he had anything more than lukewarm feelings for. No one that threatened his equilibrium. No one he would find it hard to walk away from.

'Listen.' Blake's tone was serious. 'I never really knew what happened between you and Sienna when we left, why you stopped seeing her. I was wrapped up in my own stuff at the time, you know? But I remember what you were like afterwards.'

'I was fine,' he insisted flatly.

'You couldn't even hear her name.'

'Because she was my ex.'

Blake expelled a breath. 'Okay. But you're both

going to be here, all week. She's really important to Astrid. I just want—'

Aiden ground his jaw. 'If you're worrying about me, don't. Sienna Mastrangelo is someone I haven't thought about in years. As far as I'm concerned, she's just a friend of your fiancé's – which is fucking weird, I'll admit. For those two to have met, to have become friends...'

Blake grunted. What more could he say? Aiden knew that Sienna and Astrid had met at an airport, but that Astrid hadn't realised Sienna's connection to the twins until she'd gone back to Ashbury Falls to interview their dropkick dad and Sienna had been there, all protective and throwing herself in harm's way to keep Astrid safe. They'd been inseparable ever since. Despite the fact he and Sienna had history. So what? Astrid didn't have to avoid Aiden's one-time girlfriend on his account.

'I'll be as nice to her as I would any other wedding guest.'

'I'm not worried about you being nice,' Blake said. 'I'm worried about you being okay.'

'I dumped her. It was my choice.'

Blake's brows furrowed. 'It's just—'

'Bro!' Aiden's laugh was forced to his own ears, but he reckoned Blake would buy it. 'Chill. This is all good. I swear to you, there's nothing you need to worry about. I mean, it'll be interesting to see her again, you know, in the same way it would be anyone you knew from a different part of your life, but other than that, Sienna is nothing to me. There's nothing there. Can we drop it now?'

* * *

Getting married on a tiny, out-of-the-way island in the middle of the sparkling Mediterranean was both romantic and exciting, Sienna supposed, but it also involved a gruelling day of travel, even with the private charter flights and luxury speedboats. By the time they disembarked on *l'Isola Antica*, with its stunning white sand, coves lined with palm trees and the incredible, huge mansion – more like a five-star hotel – she could see just down the beach a little way, Sienna felt a lot less like the wannabe beauty queen the other girls had morphed her into and more like a creased, frazzled version of her original self.

It wasn't their fault.

It definitely wasn't.

The fact Sienna was scared witless of flying was something only she could control – something she always thought she'd grow out of, but didn't seem able to shake, no matter how many meditations she listened to. Then, there'd been the jetboat ride, across choppy waters, with the sun beating down hard on them the whole time. Which might have been bearable, except her hat had blown into the sea almost the minute they'd set off. She felt more Jack Sparrow than Jackie Onassis, and wild, windswept and woozy.

'Okay, you ready?' Bella asked, leaning closer, nodding towards the mansion.

Sienna pulled a face. 'I need a stiff drink, a hair-brush with the power to undo this' – she gestured to her bird's nest – 'and possibly a vomit bag.'

'You're not a boat person, either?' Paige cooed sympathetically, and when Sienna blinked across at the other woman, she caught sight of Astrid looking ever so slightly stricken. With sympathy for the fact Aiden was somewhere on the island, or because Sienna looked like she'd been dragged backwards through a bush? Or both?

Even though Sienna had warmed to the idea of getting her revenge on Aiden after all this time – and heartbreak – she hadn't forgotten what this week was really about: Astrid's wedding. Having known that the other woman had sworn off marriage, and how much this whole thing meant to her, Sienna definitely wasn't going to tank any part of the experience for her.

She glued a smile to her face. 'I'm fine,' she lied. 'Let's go.' She linked her arm with Bella's, noting that somehow she made it look easier than anything to stroll across the uneven timber jetty in heels. Not a single one of Bella's hairs were out of place, either, Sienna noted with genuine amusement. It was just so like Bella. Even given the million knots they'd travelled at, Bella's hair still wouldn't let her down.

Unlike Sienna's.

But that was fine. She'd have a chance to get her game face on before seeing Aiden. Time to prepare, and feel amazing, so the first time he saw her after all these years, would be like a kick in his guts.

She'd have time—

'Oh, bloody bollocks,' Astrid groaned, turning to face Sienna, eyes running over her face with something like panic.

'What?'

'It's them.'

'Them, who?'

The four would-be queens of relationship karmic retribution, along with Chase and Olly, turned, in unison, at the approach of a golf cart. It was too far away to make out facial features, but even at this distance, Sienna could easily spot their matching, broad shoulders, larger than life frames. Strength. Charisma. Titan Twins, incoming.

She looked around wildly. 'Is it too late to hide in a bush?'

'Yes,' the others answered as one.

Paige threw her a grimace, so Sienna quickly lifted a hand and surreptitiously smoothed her hair down, hating Aiden in that moment. Hating him more than she had all these years, despite everything he'd put her through. Somehow, this was the worst. The lowest ebb. Because he'd snatched even this from her – the moment of victory she'd been determined would finally be hers.

'I told Blake we'd meet them at the house,' Astrid said, apologetically.

'It's fine,' Sienna lied. 'Of course your fiancé wants to see you after a week apart. It's *fine*,' she added, because Astrid still looked concerned.

'Just smile,' Bella encouraged Sienna. 'You have a beautiful smile. No one will be looking at your shirt if you smile.'

Her shirt? What the heck was wrong with her shirt? Sienna glanced down right as she remembered the coffee spilling over her breasts as the plane had taken on a particularly opinionated cloud, causing it to rattle around in the sky for a good minute or so.

'Oh, for heaven's sake,' she groaned, glancing upwards. 'How many bleeping mirrors did I break in a past life? For the record, this is *not* how it's meant to go. Y'all promised me *revenge*.'

'Revenge?' Olly groaned. 'God, please tell me hamsters won't be involved this time.'

'Or salty coffees,' Chase added.

'You both – just don't say a word,' Paige instructed. 'This is secret women's business.'

'This is a *mistake*,' Sienna grimaced, her skin paling.

'Stop.' Bella's voice was calming. She squeezed Sienna's hand. 'And listen to me. You are a knockout, no matter what you're wearing, how your hair looks, or anything else. Smile, act as though you don't have a care in the world, and our plan will still be firmly on track. You've got this.'

'And we've got you,' Paige said, moving closer and putting a hand around Sienna's waist, squeezing her hip. 'You're not alone, honey.'

It was just the right thing to say. Somehow, these women always did that. No matter how Sienna was feeling, they had just the perfect words of encouragement to soothe away the frustrations of her day.

'I love you guys,' she said, with genuine relief.

'The poor sucker has no idea what he's in for,' Chase muttered, grimly.

'You kind of want to warn him, right?' Olly replied.

'Don't you dare,' Paige said.

'You don't think a heads up about the possibility of a stray dog landing in his lap is something he should know?'

Paige slapped his shoulder. 'Like you didn't actually love it.'

Olly grinned.

'Guys, *shhh*,' Bella whispered.

The golf cart was close now. Close enough to see Aiden turn and say something to Blake. In her peripheral vision, she was aware that he nodded in response, but Sienna could hardly take her eyes off Aiden. Nausea rose inside of her at this impending reality. Seeing him – for real – again.

She had been literally bombarded with images of him over the past decade. Photos of him in magazines in skimpy underwear, displaying his package like a man who had never, ever needed the help of a sock. Talk about BDE. She'd seen him on billboards, interviews on TV, ads, he was *everywhere*. But she hadn't actually seen *him* in the flesh since he'd broken up with her. She hadn't seen his smile, his hair, his eyes, his mouth up close and personal, and now that he was bearing down on them just as fast as the golf cart could go, all the oxygen seemed to be getting sucked out of her world all over again. Her lips parted and her eyes widened, because so much of who she'd once been, so long ago, was bound up in this man.

This *man*. Not a boy any more, a teenager on the cusp of adulthood, but a proper, grown-ass man, all sexy square jaw and deep grooves in his cheek, not to mention the burly, broad shape of him, the legs that looked like two solid tree trunks. Her stomach knotted and she blinked away, mouthing, so only Bella could see, 'Kill me now, please.'

'Not a chance,' the sleek blonde replied, so Sienna had no choice but to swallow past the lump in her throat, paste an overbright smile onto her face and channel every bit of advice they'd given her over the past few days. Stand straight, shoulders squared, no emotions, and smile.

'Well, well, if it isn't the future Mrs Carter,' Blake said with a grin, as he jumped out of the golf cart as soon as Aiden had brought it to a stop. Aiden watched his brother go before his attention turned back to the group, and Sienna felt like a whole country's electricity supply had been shunted into her veins. The nauseating feeling rose higher.

His eyes travelled over Bella first, then Paige, and then, with heart-stopping slowness, almost as if he was fighting it, he looked at Sienna.

Really looked at her.

Like he'd been thinking about her.

Wondering about her.

Like he'd even given her a second's thought at some point since he'd left town.

But she knew he hadn't.

She'd accepted that a long time ago. *I've moved on. You should, too.*

His eyes were the most startling shade of blue, like ice and some kind of sparkly gemstone. She'd loved staring at them back then, but now, they filled her with a sort of rage, because *why* should someone be this hot, as well as so insanely talented? It really wasn't fair. From that chiselled jawline to granite-esque cheekbones, symmetrical features and just ridiculously buff body, he was an insult to the entire concept of 'it's what's inside that matters'. Because his outside mattered. It really, really mattered, even when she wished on every star in heaven that it didn't.

He stepped out of the cart with easy athleticism –

hardly surprising, given his profession as one of the highest-paid hockey players in the league – and began to saunter (yes, literally saunter, because *of course* he sauntered) towards their group. Astrid and Blake were hugging like they hadn't seen one another in years, rather than a week, Blake's hand on Astrid's gently rounded stomach. They were a family, Sienna thought, something popping in the region of her heart.

'Aiden Carter,' Aiden said, extending a hand towards Bella and Chase. Sienna felt her friend stiffen in an A-grade loyalty response before she dropped her grip on Sienna's arm and, after a slight hesitation, took Aiden's hand.

'Bella Carmichael and Chase Miller.' Her tone was delightfully crisp; Sienna wasn't sure she'd ever loved her more.

Aiden nodded once, then moved onto Paige, who was eyeing him like something that had just slithered out from under a rock. Bless her. So much for keeping emotion off their faces.

Paige seemed to remember her mission at the last minute. 'Paige,' she said, not willing to offer a last name, apparently. 'And Olly.' She waved towards her boyfriend.

'Pleasure,' Aiden said with a nod. Sienna could have sworn she heard Paige grunt.

A moment later, he was toe to toe with Sienna, and she couldn't put it off any longer. Her stomach squeezed and swirled.

'Hey, stranger,' he said, his voice a note lower, a little drawled and husky.

Flirty.

How fucking dare he? The nausea seemed to throb right in her throat, so she tasted acid and felt the walls of her tummy heave.

She tried to keep a grip on her temper – because wasn't the whole point of this to make him flirt with her? To make him want her, then trample all over his ego, and maybe even a little piece of his heart, just as he'd done with her? As tempted as she might be to tear strips off him then and there, or give him a frigidly cold shoulder, that was *not* what they'd decided Sienna would do. Besides, she'd sworn her past with Aiden wouldn't ruin this moment – Astrid's wedding. That's what they were here for. That's what mattered most.

'Aiden,' she said, her voice carefully controlled, not showing any of the darker feelings that were making her pulse thunder. 'Long time, no see.'

He dragged a hand through his hair, revealing a hint of tanned waist where his dark grey shirt lifted.

She blinked away quickly.

'Yeah, jeez. How long's it been?'

It was like a slug in the guts.

How long's it been?

So casual. Like he barely even remembered. Unconsciously, she pressed a hand to her stomach. Remembering what it had been like to know their baby was in there. To feel that life as a part of her. The absence was something she'd never quite got over.

How long's it been?

Her insides twisted uncomfortably – she felt as though she were still rocking on that damn boat.

'God, I don't know.' She forced a laugh with the lie, suddenly hoping she didn't vomit. 'It feels like a lifetime ago.'

He nodded slowly. 'And now you're here,' he said, a small frown tugging on his lips.

'Of course Sissi is here.' Astrid had separated herself from Blake long enough to catch the last exchange of dialogue. 'She's only one of my best friends.'

'Yeah, so Blake said.' Aiden looked quizzical. As though he still didn't quite understand how this woman from his past had wound up solidly in his present, even when Sienna knew that Astrid and Blake had given him a slightly adjusted version of the truth.

Suddenly, the world was tilting and twisting, and Sienna's stomach wasn't just throbbing but heaving.

'Oh, God,' she groaned, catching a look of surprise from Paige right before she leaned forward and threw up. Right at the feet of Aiden 'Eye Wateringly Expensive Loafers' Carter...

3

JUST DESSERTS WHATSAPP
GROUP. 18.35 EST.

ASTRID

Where are you, S?

PAIGE

Are you here?

SIENNA

No.

PAIGE

Is everything okay?

Okay? Okay? Was everything okay? No, she wanted to shout. She was about to descend the stairs of this impossibly posh mansion to spend the next however many hours it took in close proximity to Aiden 'Heart Destroying Bastard' Carter, and she'd promised her best friends in the whole world that she was going to have fun flirting with him.

Flirting with him!

Him, who she'd prefer to douse in water from one of the elaborate floral arrangements rather than ever have to look at again. Him, who she wanted to push into the koi-filled lake on the edge of the courtyard. Him, who she'd just seen for the first time in ten years and promptly thrown up at the feet of. While her shirt was stained and her hair was a mess, and he just looked all perfect and sports-god like. Him, who...

A knock sounded at her door and she crossed the floor and yanked it open, cheeks flushed with warmth at the irate direction of her thoughts.

Bella stood there, pristine and beautiful, sympathy in her silver eyes.

'Feeling better?'

Sienna pulled a face.

'Okay. I'll take that as a "no". Need a hand?'

She shook her head.

Bella grinned. 'Or a drink?'

She pulled two flutes of champagne from behind her back and passed one to Sienna as she entered the suite.

'Nice view.' She nodded towards the sunset, visible through the balcony doors. 'I got the other side.'

'The garden?'

'It's fine.' She waved a hand in the air, her bangles making a pretty tinkling sound. 'I'm not much interested in looking outside,' she added with a flush, leaving Sienna in no doubt as to how Bella and Chase were planning to spend their wedding-week downtime.

Sienna gulped back a slosh of champagne.

'What's wrong?' Bella asked, perching on the edge of the vanity.

'You mean besides the fact I'm about to spend several hours in a tiny room with a guy I loathe from the very depths of my heart? Or the fact that it's our best friend's wedding and I can't punch him like I'd truly, really love to? Orrrr the fact I'm planning to somehow flirt with him, even when I want to bounce a vase off his stupid, perfect face? Or shall we talk about the whole throwing up right in front of him incident? That is *not* the first impression I was hoping to make, believe me.'

'All excellent points,' Bella cooed, standing straight and ticking one finger off with the other. 'The room is *not* tiny, it's the whole entrance foyer of this palatial mansion. And you'll be spending the next few hours with *us*; we're not going to let anything happen that isn't amazing for you. You would never punch anyone, and we both know it. Nor throw a vase, for that matter. Revenge by seduction really is your only option. As for flirting with him, believe me when I tell you that your dress does *all* the flirting necessary. No way will he remember vomit-gate when he sees you in this.'

Sienna glanced first at Bella and then let her eyes shift sidelong to the full-length mirror, which she'd been avoiding looking at ever since pulling the stunning silk slip over her head. Her breath hitched in her throat a little, because whomever had chosen the dress had chosen very, very well. A shade of shimmering champagne with spaghetti straps, it was cut on the bias and hugged Sienna's curves in all the right places. She'd teamed it with a pair of espadrilles and styled her blonde hair into a voluminous bun, high on her head.

'You look amazing,' Bella reinforced, coming to stand beside Sienna and put an arm around her shoulders. 'And Astrid has something in store, by the way, to get things started.'

'Oh?'

Bella grinned.

'Care to give me a hint?'

'I don't know. Wouldn't it be more fun to have a surprise?'

Sienna held Bella's gaze in the mirror. 'Nope.'

Bella shook her head. 'Let's just say absence is going to make Aiden's heart – or other parts of him – grow a lot, erm, stronger.'

Sienna frowned.

'Okay, so, he might be thinking that you guys are going to get paired up together, right? I mean, he's a groomsman, you're a bridesmaid, you have the whole history thing.'

'Right...' Sienna's skin paled; she hadn't even thought of that.

'But instead, Astrid's partnered you with Chuck Daly.'

Sienna's expression was blank for about the four seconds it took for her to realise who Bella was talking about. '*The* Chuck Daly?'

Bella looked like the cat who'd got the cream. 'The very same.'

'The Chuck Daly who left his record-breaking

career in the NHL to develop that social media site that went gangbusters and now he's worth like a billion trillion dollars?'

Bella nodded sagely.

'The one who looks like Chris Hemsworth, Zac Efron and George Clooney swirled their DNA together and created one edibly, perfect human?'

Another nod, this time with a quirk of her lips. 'The Chuck Daly who's recently single and ready to mingle.'

'Oh, gosh.' Sienna's cheeks flushed. 'So now I'm flirting with two guys?'

'Well, the flirting with Aiden is by the by.' Bella tilted her head. 'You're supposed to be making him regret walking away from you, and having Chuck Daly get a little handsy would definitely help do the trick. Am I right?'

'You're right.' Sienna swallowed back the rest of her bubbles for a hit of Dutch courage, then looked at the empty glass. 'I could never have dreamed that one fateful night in Chicago would have brought us here.'

Bella sighed contentedly – after all, she'd followed the path of revenge to her own sweet little happily ever after. 'But it did, and now we're going to make the most of it. Ready?'

If she was going to back out, this was her chance. She could pretend she had a headache and hide out in her room, reading the third book in the erotic romance Bella had got them all hooked on, courtesy of her random airport granny encounter.

'Come onnnn, Sienna,' Bella said on an impatient groan. 'Let's get this party started.'

'Okay,' she said, before she could three-million-guess herself. 'I'm ready.'

* * *

He hadn't been looking for her. Not really. Okay, he'd *half* been looking for her, but that was natural. It was coming up on eleven years since he'd left Ashbury Falls and Sienna behind, eleven years since he'd slammed the door to her place so he couldn't hear her sob any more. Eleven years, but when he'd climbed out of the golf cart and she'd been standing there, his gut had lurched with shock, because she was so, so familiar to him. As familiar as Blake or his mom, or his own damned reflection.

Which wasn't to say she hadn't changed.

Of course she had. Sienna had been a week shy of her seventeenth birthday when he'd left town; he remembered, because he'd already bought and wrapped her gift, but he never gave it to her, because he hadn't had a chance. He was pretty sure she would have thrown it in his face anyway.

Now, she was a woman.

As if that thought needed to be illustrated, a very grown-up-in-all-the-right-places Sienna appeared at the top of the sweeping staircase, with Astrid's blonde friend by her side – Bella? The blonde said something and Sienna leaned closer, laughed, tilting her head back a little. He couldn't *hear* her laugh, but it filled his veins anyway, because he'd heard it so many times when they were kids.

A squeal came from his left, and he ripped his attention away from Sienna long enough to see Astrid and her other friend – Paige? – fast walking to the bottom of the stairs. Sienna grinned at them and made her way down with so much grace that he couldn't look away, even if the damned building caught fire.

The dress hugged her like a second skin, all rippling golden silk, cut just low enough to offer a hint of tanned cleavage. At the bottom of the stairs, the four women gave each other a group hug and even from where he stood he could see they were talking a mile a minute, clearly so happy and in love that something else shifted in Aiden's gut.

Relief.

Because he'd tortured himself for a long time, worrying about Sienna, hoping she was okay but worrying she wasn't. When clearly, she was *more* than okay. She had tight friendships with – if Astrid was anything to go by – a group of incredible, supportive, kind women.

* * *

'Oh my God, you look hot,' Paige exclaimed on a whistle.

'Seriously hot,' Astrid agreed.

'But you're not happy?' Paige guessed, when Sienna didn't immediately respond.

Before Sienna could open her mouth, Bella replied, 'She's annoyed she doesn't get to throw a vase at him.'

Astrid laughed. 'Definitely not, thank you. That's something Blake would consider to be a line-cross.' She looked casually over her shoulder. 'Now.' Astrid expelled a quick breath. 'Aiden's on his own. Go talk to him a bit, before Blake and I make the welcome toast.'

'Here.' Bella swiped another glass of champagne

from the tray of a passing waitress. 'Think of it as a prop.'

Sienna took a sip. 'Okay.' Then a huge gulp of air. 'Wish me luck.'

'Honey,' Paige cooed. 'You don't need it.'

Sucking in a deep breath and channelling her best impersonation of someone who had a wise inner goddess, Sienna began to stroll across the foyer of the home, to where Aiden was standing. She'd contemplated playing it aloof, but for this to work, she needed to hook him first. Then she could think about torturing him, once he was on the line.

She pushed down all her anger. All her resentment. All her loyalty to the teenager who'd cried so many tears over his departure. She pushed everything aside except the fact she had a plan to get him back, and she was actually sort of looking forward to going through with it.

While Chase and Olly had turned out not to be so bad, in the end, Horrible Harvey – Paige's ex – and Aiden 'So Perfect It Hurts' Carter were truly deserving of some kind of comeuppance and Sienna was determined to serve it to *both* of them. One by one. Starting with Aiden, because he was here, and she had her wing-women making sure she didn't lose her nerve.

The closer she got, the happier she became that it had worked out like this. While the idea of Astrid messing with him was fun, this seemed so much more appropriate. They said revenge was a dish best served cold, but Sienna thought it was actually a dish best served face to face. She was going to relish putting this arrogant, ice-hearted piece of work in his place and seeing him suffer. Through seduction. Hardly torture, but in the right hands...

'Oh, hi.' She smiled as she got close enough, as if to get his attention. But that wasn't necessary, because he'd been tracking her progress across the room. 'I thought I'd come catch up with you before the official proceedings get underway.'

His thick, dark brows drew together a little. 'I was going to offer you a drink but you seem to have come prepared.'

'I sure have,' she said.

If only you knew, buster.

'How about I join you for one,' she said, nodding towards his half-full beer.

He took a sip. 'So, you and Astrid are pretty close, huh?'

She glanced towards the other girls, who were doing an average-at-best job of pretending to be absorbed in conversation with each other, and *not* like they were obsessively watching Sienna and Aiden.

'Uh huh. Kind of weird, right?'

'Yeah. But I mean' – he lifted one shoulder in a gesture of carelessness – 'that's life.'

Not only was he not bothered by their friendship, he wasn't even curious about it. She knew she should be grateful but it got under her skin. She dug her nails into her palms from the sheer effort of keeping her own expression neutral.

'So...' She hunted around for a conversation change. 'You've done well for yourself.' She could have kicked herself for not being able to completely keep the irritation from her tone. Had she wanted him to crash and burn? Sure, at first she had. Partly because he'd deserved it – and she wasn't too proud to admit she had a vengeful streak every bit as developed as the next spurned woman – and partly because it might have brought him back home.

'I guess.' He shrugged dismissively. 'It's just hockey.'

'Just hockey? Careful, don't let any of your gazillion sponsors hear you say that.'

His grin was all perfect teeth, reminding her so much of the poster she'd seen in the airport – and her urge to wallop him with a piece of chewed up gum – that she had to swallow back a laugh.

'I'm pretty sure they wouldn't care, as long as I kept turning up to get my photo taken.'

'Are you trying to make me think you hate it?'

'No,' he answered, quickly.

'I mean, this was always your dream, right?' she asked, careful to keep the accusation from her voice, even when it was raging through her.

Because at one time, she'd thought his dream was different. At one time, she'd thought his dream was her. And not because she was a naïve fantasist, but because he'd said it. About a week before their first time, when they were on the dirt track behind the Meyers' house, and he'd stopped walking to take her hand in his and lifted it to point at the big, old house. It wasn't the fanciest, but they both loved it because it was so full of history.

'Ever think maybe one day that could be us?'

Sienna had looked up to notice the elderly couple on the porch, Mr Meyer kneeling beside a pot of Azaleas, small spade in hand, while Mrs Meyer poured two drinks from a crystal jug.

'I guess so.' Aiden brought her back to the present with his answer. 'I wanted to do this almost my whole life.'

It took a monumental effort to blot her anger. 'Yeah.' Her voice was a little uneven. She sipped her drink. 'I remember.' She remembered everything. That was the problem. She remembered *everything*.

'What about you?' He changed the subject. 'When I left, you were looking at applying to pre-med.'

God, that felt like a lifetime ago. She couldn't even get into the headspace of the young woman she'd been.

She shrugged. 'I changed my mind.'

'Yeah?' He was looking at her so intently now, and she hated it. Her pulse was raging in a way that made all her skin feel hot and sticky, despite the pleasant ocean breeze rustling through the open doors of the high-ceilinged room. 'Why?'

She had to look away then. She couldn't bear to have him ask *why*. As if it had really been a god-damned choice. The weight of pressures that had landed on her in that senior year was like a bag of cement.

'People change, Aiden. I'm not the girl you used to know. I'm pretty sure you're not the guy I used to know. We're different now.'

She turned back to look at him, surprised to see his jaw was held taut. 'In what way?'

She forced an overbright smile, then scrambled for how to reply. 'I mean, apart from the fact we're more than a decade older? Hopefully wiser?'

His smile caught her off guard. If he'd looked tense a minute ago, now he was all sexy and dishevelled, relaxed and charming with those stupid dimples she used to love grooved into his cheeks. 'I'm not so sure about the latter, but I'm trying.'

She opened her mouth to reply but at that moment, Astrid walked up to them, followed closely by a sex god in human form. 'Oh, hi, you two,' Astrid cooed, angling her face to flash a surreptitious wink at Sienna. 'I wasn't sure if you'd had a chance to meet Chuck, Sissi?'

Sienna *couldn't* look at Aiden. She wouldn't. He probably wouldn't care – at all – that Astrid was intentionally throwing Sienna in the path of one of the hottest men who'd ever lived, but Sienna cared, because she knew why Astrid was doing it, and she didn't think she could look at Aiden without bursting into laughter.

So she focused on her friend and her drink, while Astrid put an arm around Chuck and brought him closer to Sienna. Their eyes met and he smiled.

'Chuck, this is one of my favourite people in the whole wide world, Sienna Mastrangelo. Sissi, this is

Chuck. He's a lot of fun,' Astrid added exaggeratedly. 'You're going to *love* each other.'

Sienna bit back a roll of her eyes. When Astrid committed to gilding the lily, she clearly committed with her whole heart.

'Jesus, Astrid, how many hot friends do you have?'

Astrid laughed. 'You behave,' she said, slapping Chuck on the shoulder then turning to Aiden. 'He's terrible. You have to watch him. But of course, you know that – you two have met before.' She gestured from her future brother-in-law to Chuck, who'd moved to stand almost close enough to Sienna to touch.

'Yes.' Aiden's response was a little curt, but Sienna didn't read into it. Astrid had laid it on with a trowel, after all. 'We've played against each other.'

'That's right, we have.' Chuck grinned. 'A couple of times.'

Sienna didn't have to be a mind reader to guess how those games had gone. Despite his own prowess, there was a look on Aiden's face that spoke of crushing defeat. Chuck shot up in her estimation.

She took another sip of her drink then realised it was empty.

'Another champagne?' Aiden asked immediately.

Sienna was about to demur on the basis that she needed to be able to think straight and two quickly consumed glasses on an empty stomach was not the most well-regarded formula for logic and reasoning.

But Chuck was there, too. 'Let me,' he said smoothly, nodding towards the bar. 'If we're going to be partnered together for the wedding, we should get to know each other. Do you mind?' He glanced at Aiden and Astrid. Before either could reply, he was putting a hand lightly on Sienna's back to guide her away – and she let him.

But before they'd gone two steps, she heard Astrid exclaim, 'Gawd, wouldn't that be something? Can you imagine how gorgeous their babies would be?'

Sienna didn't hear Aiden's response over her own soft laugh.

4

There was no dinner, just a heap of canapes being carried around on trays by waiters who seemed to have been trained in the subtle art of not giving out food, because no matter how hard Sienna tried to death stare them into coming her way, they remained relentlessly oblivious.

She was *starving*. And not for tiny circles of quiche, either, but a big, greasy burger. She thought longingly of the way Luke – the chef at the diner she worked at back in Ashbury Falls – had of crisping bacon and her mouth actually exploded with little bubbles of saliva.

Maybe she could distract a waiter and take a whole tray up to her room? Feast on thirty-seven of the delicate pastries before coming back down, ready to continue with Operation Hurt the Heartbreaker.

'You look tired.' She knew Aiden's voice even without turning to face him. Mentally, she winced.

Was looking tired technically something she could incorporate into her plan? Wasn't she meant to be some kind of Diana goddess all weekend? Stunning and indefatigable?

'I'm not,' she lied, thinking of the shifts she'd had in the lead up to this trip, and the paper she'd had due, not to mention it being her weekend with Melanie sleeping over.

'I got you a coffee anyway.'

She bit back an actual groan as she turned to face him now.

'You still drink the stuff?'

'Drink it?' She looked at the mug longingly. 'Not only do I drink it, it would not be an exaggeration to say the most meaningful relationship in my life is pretty much the one I have with coffee. Gimme.' She held out a hand, ignoring the way her stomach went into backflip mode as he passed over the mug. Or the way her fingers tingled with the force of exploding fireworks when their hands brushed at the moment of coffee cup contact. *Screw you, body. Talk about betrayal. We're supposed to be ignoring him. Defi-*

nitely not feeling little zippedy zoos when our fingers brush.

She looked away again quickly, sloshing a little of the coffee onto the tiled floor.

'Sooo,' he said, and out of the corner of her eye, she caught the way his hand jammed into the pocket of his suit pants. 'Apart from coffee,' he said, then trailed off into nothing, as if he realised the inherent awkwardness of asking the supposed one-time love of his life about her current dating situation. He cleared his throat; tried again. 'Are you seeing anyone?'

She wanted to shout at him. She wanted to shove him. She wanted to pour something – though admittedly not the steaming hot coffee – on his head. She wanted to rage and roar and tell him to go to hell, that of *course* she wasn't seeing anyone, because how could she ever, ever trust someone again after the way Aiden had sucked her in then so royally screwed her over?

Once, a long time ago, Bella had kept them up all night reading quotes from *The Art of War* over a video call, and Sienna vaguely remembered there was a line in there about biding your time, some reference to playing the long game. Or maybe she was getting mixed up; maybe it was one of Bella's little bits of war wisdom or something.

Either way, Sienna knew that blurting out her anger at Aiden here and now would be immensely satisfying in the moment, but utterly emptying afterwards. She hadn't walked through the emotional equivalent of the fires of hell for a decade to lose her shit at the first provocation from the arrogant piece of work.

'Not right now,' she said, sweetly, hoping that he took from that some kind of implication that she had been, up until recently. Then, she added, as if as an afterthought, 'At least, no one serious.'

'Cool.'

Cool? *Cool?* She ground her teeth and looked across the room, to where all of her supposed avenging friends were dancing their little hearts out with the loves of their lives. Astrid and Blake, Paige and Olly, Bella and Chase. All so happy. So oblivious to the currents of rage flooding through Sienna.

As if misunderstanding her, he followed her gaze to the dance floor, cleared his throat and said, 'Did you... want to dance?'

Only if it meant she could stamp on his foot, she thought mutinously. 'I mean, you've brought me coffee,' she reminded him, lifting it higher and breathing in the intoxicating fragrance, imitating a smile. 'I should probably drink that first.'

'Coffee will wait,' he said.

She glanced up at him. 'Whereas you won't?' The question came out sharper than she'd intended, reminding them both of the fact that no, he hadn't in fact waited.

He frowned. 'That's not what I meant.'

She took a sip, letting the flavour ride little pleasure waves down to her belly. She was being a coward, she acknowledged. After all, having come this far, why not dance with the man? What was the possible harm in something so perfectly innocuous?

'I thought you hated dancing, anyway,' she said, having another quick sip of her drink.

'You're the one who said we've changed.'

'Are you trying to tell me now you love it?'

His grin pulled at the fabric of her gut. 'I wouldn't go that far. I tolerate it, for the right companion.'

'Companion? Have you also been reading Jane Austen in your spare time?'

He arched a brow. 'Is this whole week going to involve you giving me a hard time?'

'Don't act like you don't secretly love it,' she said with a wink.

He laughed then, the sound raw and husky and

so damned addictive. 'Jeez, Mastrangelo. I've missed you.'

It was *entirely, absolutely* the wrong thing to say. Utterly disastrous. Because it reminded her of just how he'd left her in the lurch, and how long ago that had been, how long it had been since she'd heard from him, how he'd been perfectly happy to walk out of her life when he was her only, *only* friend in the whole wide world. The only person who knew and understood what her life was like. How much he clearly *hadn't* missed her, or he would have come back for her. She blinked quickly, turning away from him on the pretence of putting her coffee cup on a nearby table.

When she turned to face him, she smiled, though it felt stretched and forced. 'Sure, okay. Let's dance.'

They didn't touch as they walked towards the dance floor, but when they stepped onto it, Paige gave Sienna a subtle thumbs up behind Olly's back, and Bella winked at her encouragingly. Sienna drew in a deep breath, turning to face Aiden, expecting him to assume an old-fashioned pose, with one hand on her hip and the other clutching her hand. Instead, he latched both hands behind her back, drawing her close to him, leaving her to put her hands up and wrap them around his neck. Bringing their bodies close. So close she could feel his chest, his strong legs, his taut stomach. All of him. So close she could smell his musky fragrance – a different cologne to what he'd worn back then, but somehow so perfectly him. So close that when she looked up, she could make out each and every piece of stubble, and the silvery scar that ran down his cheek, from when he was sixteen and a puck had cut across his face when he'd been walking off the rink.

She remembered tracing the line with her finger – back then it had been an angry red and purple, but time had faded the wound. Like it was supposed to do with all wounds, she remembered. Only it didn't always work like that, because time had passed and being here with Aiden, his rejection was every bit as cutting to Sienna as it had been back then. Worse, because she'd been through so much, like the baby they'd made and lost, and her father's legal troubles, and her disastrous rebound relationship with Cory. All without him at her side. All because he'd left her.

She tilted her chin, determinedly focusing on a point to the left of his shoulder.

'So, your friend Bella. What's she like?' he asked, conversationally.

'Why?'

'She's my partner for the wedding.'

'Ah.'

'She seems... nice,' he responded after a beat.

Sienna's smile was genuine. 'She's great.'

'How do you know her?'

'Same way I know Astrid.'

'The airport?'

She felt something like guilt tighten in her gut but she ignored it. 'Yep.'

'Seriously?'

'We were snowed in.'

'And Paige?'

'Yep.'

He let out a low whistle. 'How long were you delayed for?'

She laughed softly. 'Long enough. Or maybe it didn't matter,' she said, after a beat. 'I think we knew within minutes that we were like soulmates.'

'Soulmates?'

'What, you don't believe in the concept?'

His eyes probed hers and he shrugged one shoulder. 'Do you?'

She refused to think about *how much* she'd believed in soulmates, once upon a time. 'The friendship variety? Oh, I definitely believe in that.'

He made a gruff noise that could have been acceptance, or dismissal. 'But not romantic?'

Sienna sighed. She contemplated saying some-thing flirty. Teasing him, making him laugh. But he was sailing too close to the wind, and she was only human. 'Aiden, come on,' she said, stopping dancing and slowly dropping her hands.

'What?'

'Do you really want to talk about our love lives? I mean, I know it was a long time ago, but don't you find it kind of *weird* to discuss our other partners with one another?' She leaned forward then, unable to resist adding, 'You were my first lover, after all.'

First. Not only.

He had the grace to look embarrassed. 'I was just showing an interest in your life.'

'You don't have to,' she said with a lift of one shoulder. 'We're nothing to one another now, and that's fine with me. And I presume it's fine with you. We're just here to support two people we love as they get married. Beyond that... we don't need to say or do anything to one another.' It felt like the throwing down of the gauntlet. Or it felt incredibly stupid, given what she was supposed to be doing.

She waited for him to respond. To say anything. But Aiden just stared down at her, an impassive ex-pression on his face.

'Oookay.' She pulled a face, a look of amusement

crossed with irritation. 'Good chat. One for the record books.' She took a step backwards. 'Thanks for the coffee.'

* * *

Blake found him out in the orangery, midway through snapping a twig off a mandarin tree in full bloom.

'What's up, bro?'

'Nothing,' Aiden grunted, then pulled it together as he turned to face his brother. His brother who was about to get married, against all the odds. His brother who'd turned his life around in spectacular fashion, ever since meeting Astrid, and who deserved to be the happiest version of himself.

'Hmm,' Blake mused. 'I know that kind of nothing. Let me guess. About this tall' – he gestured to just beneath his shoulders – 'bright blue eyes. Feisty temper. Someone who knows you almost as well as I do?'

'Sienna doesn't know me any more,' Aiden dismissed, not bothering to pretend he didn't know who his brother was talking about. 'We haven't spoken since you and I left town.'

'So?'

'So?' Aiden shrugged. 'What's your point?'

'I guess just that it must be nice to see her again. You guys were always tight.'

Aiden ground his teeth. Tight didn't begin to describe what Sienna and he had been like. What he'd thought – back then, as a stupid kid – they'd always be like.

'Yeah, well, we're not now.'

'I can see that. How come?'

'Come on, bro. Give it a break.'

'I just mean... you're here for a week. With her.'

'And?'

'And, you're single. So's she.'

'How do you know?' He thought back to the non-committal way Sienna had answered the question with a sense of dissatisfaction.

'There are some things you can't help but glean when your fiancé is in a friendship group like that. They talk *all* the time. You hear things.'

'Like what?'

'Astrid would have my balls in a vice if I told you,' he laughed gruffly. 'But I do know they're always trying to set Sienna up on dates; from which I gather there's no Mr Mastrangelo in the picture.'

Aiden grunted.

'Look.' Blake shrugged. 'It's your life. Your choice.

But she's here, so are you. The cocktails are flowing, the sunsets are amazing, and I reckon you'll kick yourself if you don't make the most of the time you've got.'

Aiden didn't listen. Or rather, he *tried* not to listen. Aiden didn't want to think about Sienna, and the week ahead, and the thought of watching the sun set over the water with her, nor the prospect of sitting side by side, drinking cocktails and shooting the breeze like they'd done countless times all those years ago. He didn't want to think about spending time with her and starting to let her get under his skin again, in that way she had, of making him feel things he never had any intention of feeling. Things that made him vulnerable. Things that scared the hell out of him, because he and Blake both knew what the flip side to love was – they'd seen it. Every time their dad had pounded on their mom when he'd had too much to drink, every time he'd pounded on them. Even before he'd met Sienna, Aiden had known he'd never, ever get into a situation that might lead him down that path.

He wasn't his father.

But he had no intention of putting himself in a situation of needing to prove that to himself.

Then again... it was only *one week*.

She lived in Ashbury Falls. He was just about to sign a new contract, with a shit tonne of pressure to sign for another two after that. After this week, they'd probably go at least another decade without seeing one another. Hell, by then she'd undoubtedly be married with a gaggle of kids. He wasn't an idiot. The fact that someone like Sienna was single didn't seem likely to last. The fact she was here... that they'd been thrown together by the strangest set of life circumstances... would he be an idiot to throw this away?

To let her get away?

Sweat beaded his brow.

Not *away*, away. He wasn't thinking about anything dumb, like forever. But just in terms of this week. A week, seven days, with no pressure to look beyond that. No pressure to think of the future. No pressure to think at all – Sienna always did have a gift when it came to making Aiden simply exist for the moment.

Maybe that was different now. Maybe he'd idealised Sienna in his mind, idealised what they'd once had, because of the time in his life when he'd known her. Because she'd been his first in so many ways. Maybe he'd find out, this week, that she was actually nothing special, and he could take her off the pedestal she'd somehow climbed right up onto...

He made a gruff sound, as if he was dismissing Blake's words, when all he could do was let them roll around and around like waves against the shoreline.

'Now, listen, Mom arrives Wednesday.' Blake changed gears. 'Are you good to meet her off the plane? You know how she feels about boats.'

Aiden looked at Blake as if the question was coming from the moon. 'Huh?'

'Mom. You still good to pick her up? I mean, I can send someone else, like Chuck, maybe, but I know she'd prefer—'

'I'll go,' Aiden said, galvanised into action by the mention of the other man, who'd made it pretty damned obvious that he was also relishing the prospect of having a week to get to know Sienna. 'Just send me the flight details.'

And with that, he went back into the cocktail party; this time, he didn't bother pretending he wasn't looking for her. If they only had a week, he might as well start making the most of it.

5

'Going somewhere, Mastrangelo?'

His voice ran down her spine like sun-warmed butter. She threw a glance over her shoulder, aiming for flirty, but failing, because her heart did a horrible little twist and squeeze and she felt the bottom fall out of her world, momentarily. She feared she was more wide-eyed doe in the headlights of an on-coming semi than siren-y vixen.

'Shhh.' She lifted a finger to her lips, covering the strange blip with determination and moving one hand to the spaghetti strap of her dress. She ran her fingers along the length of it, sure she'd seen some beautiful actress do that in a movie. Only the actress had looked sultry and desirable whereas Sienna suspected she looked as though she were scratching an itch on her ring finger. She dropped her hand. 'Don't let Astrid hear.'

'You're leaving?'

Sienna nodded. 'I am.'

'Can I twist your arm to stay for another coffee?'

She pulled a face.

'Or a cocktail?'

She gnawed on her lower lip, eyes locked to Aiden without really seeing him. Not as he was now. For a minute, she was slipping back through time; he was a teenager and so was she. The world – their lives – were all before them, and the hope of that sparkled like diamond dust.

'Or a walk?'

Her head cocked to the side. Now *that* had appeal. The truth was, what she wanted was fresh air. Between knowing she was in the same room as Aiden, even when he wasn't anywhere near her, and the girls' very, very well-intentioned encouragement to make him suffer, and Chuck Daly hovering in the wings waiting to get her a drink or chat to her about whatever he thought made it more likely to get her into bed, Sienna was feeling ever so slightly suffocated.

But would a walk with Aiden fix that?

'Just down to the beach,' he suggested. 'It's a beautiful night.'

It *was* a beautiful night. Warm and balmy with the slightest hint of a breeze to offer relief, the air was sweet with the smell of honeysuckle and jasmine, and the night was so dark out here that every single star could be seen twinkling up above.

'Okay,' she heard herself agree. Because the whole revenge plan was predicated on this, she reminded herself. How could she make him want her again if she kept running away from him? Wouldn't it be satisfying to make him realise what he'd walked away from – and then tell him he'd lost his chance with her for good?

Teenage Sienna deserved that moment of glory. In fact, now that she thought of it, that had been one of the fantasies that had got her through the darkest nights. The prospect of one day making him regret what he'd done.

She straightened her spine, squared her shoulders and flashed him a bright, uncomplicated smile – a lying smile, if ever there'd been one, because this situation was complicated with a capital C. But it didn't have to be. It was just a week – and no matter what, at the end of the week, she had her one-way ticket back to Ashbury Falls, and her life there.

'Sure.' She shrugged and the spaghetti strap she'd been holding slipped down a little, so his eyes dropped to her shoulder. His hand shifted, as if he was going to reach for it, to lift it back up, but thank heavens for small mercies, he didn't. 'Just... give me a minute.'

'I'll give you two.' He grinned, without a care in the world. Easy. Breezy. Rich. Successful. Living his best liar, liar, pants on fire life. She swallowed down the acid that clawed through her.

'Great.' She turned to make her way to the ladies' room. 'I'll be right back.'

* * *

Once inside the spacious facilities with the forest green tiles and art deco mirrors, she pulled her phone from her clutch and wrote:

JUST DESSERTS WHATSAPP
GROUP. 22.55 EST.

SIENNA

We are going for a moonlit walk.
This is not a drill, people.

PAIGE

Squeeeeee! You've got him, baby.

BELLA

Whoop.

ASTRID

Reel that sucker in!

SIENNA

It's just a walk...

PAIGE

🔥 Def not just a walk.

SIENNA

Nothing's going to happen.

BELLA

He's pacing in the foyer.

SIENNA

LOL, are you spying on him now?

PAIGE

Isn't that our job?

ASTRID

He looks nervous!!

SIENNA

Aiden doesn't get nervous.

PAIGE

Are you hiding out to torture him?

SIENNA

ASTRID

Well, it's working. Keep it up, sister. 👏

Five minutes later, having finished the day's Wordle – no way would even this wedding jeopardise her 237-day streak – and caught up on the news headlines, Sienna took a last glance in the mirror before deciding she was ready. She sucked in a deep breath, expelled it slowly, then did her very best attempt at a wiggly hip walk across the foyer, towards where Aiden did indeed look kind of nervous. Or impatient. Perhaps that had to do with the fact Chuck had come to stand beside him, though.

'There she is.' Chuck grinned as Sienna approached. 'Astrid mentioned you might be heading down to the beach?'

Sienna's heart dropped to her toes, even as she felt an overwhelming urge to giggle in the face of Aiden's response to that – which was to clench his jaw tighter than a drum.

'Yeah, we were going to go for a walk. D'you wanna come too?'

Chuck grinned flirtatiously. 'Always, but after you, of course,' he promised, so Sienna did burst out laughing at the double entendre.

'You really are incorrigible.'

'That's one word for it,' Aiden muttered, earning a raised brow from Chuck and a racing heart from Sienna. If she didn't know better, she'd say he was... jealous. Of Chuck Daly. Who she'd just met. Who flirted like most men breathed. To whom Sienna meant nothing.

Delicious heat flicked in her belly, a portent of what was to come. Victory. Victory over Aiden, victory over the way he'd hurt her and cast her aside, victory over the place he occupied in her mind. This week was going to be an exorcism; he just didn't realise it. He just didn't know that a ghost of him had haunted her for more than ten lousy years and she was finally about to banish him, by giving him his well-deserved just desserts.

'Hey, I'm just speaking the truth,' Chuck said with an exaggerated wink. 'Shall we?'

Sienna's glance flicked from Chuck to Aiden, and then she shrugged. Her spaghetti strap slipped down again; unlike Aiden, Chuck didn't hesitate to reach out and slowly, so slowly his fingers grazed the flesh of her bare arm, littering her skin in goosebumps, slip it back into place. She was sure she heard Aiden growl.

Which only made her mad. How dare he be jealous after all these years? And after the myriad – and by myriad she meant billions – of women he'd been with since Sienna? She wasn't an idiot. And she also didn't have enough will power to be able to resist occasionally drinking a little too much red wine and googling Aiden 'Horn Dog' Carter. The pics online were alternately of him playing hockey, or him out on the town, never alone, though admittedly his reputation was nothing compared to what Blake's had been before Astrid had swept in and tamed him.

Bitterness rose inside of her; she covered it with an ultra-bright smile, which she aimed somewhere between the two men. 'Yeah, let's go.'

The mansion was up a gravelled, winding path from the cove the boat had pulled into earlier that day, and Sienna's shoes crunched underfoot as she walked. Palm trees formed perfect silhouettes against the evening sky, spiky and artistic, and quintessentially beachy.

'So, you guys grew up in the same town, huh?' Chuck said, as they left the din of the party behind.

'Yeah.' Sienna nodded.

'Whereabouts?'

'Ashbury Falls,' she and Aiden said in unison. She glanced up at him and then away again quickly. In the moonlit night, his face in profile was all harsh angles, and somehow it wiped away the years, so she was looking at him as a teenager and her heart skidded in her chest.

'What's it like?'

'A dive,' Aiden said, at the same time Sienna said, 'Small.'

She furrowed her brow as she gave Aiden the full force of her attention. 'It's not a dive.'

He made a noise of disbelief. 'So it's changed since I left?'

'Everything's changed since you left.' She struggled to keep her tone neutral.

'It's a one street town,' he explained to Chuck. 'There's a run-down diner, a grocery store, a gas station, and that's it. Population approximately one thousand.'

Sienna stared straight ahead, ignoring the way his words made her blood boil and bubble. Toil and trouble. Because while he was technically right, his scathing rendition of the town skipped over so many of the best parts of it. 'There's a church and a playground, too,' she said, a little defensively. 'And a small school. Fun fact – the school's been in the same building for over two hundred years.'

Chuck let out a low whistle. 'Sounds kind of quaint, actually. I think you're underselling it, bro.'

'Go check it out for yourself, bro,' Aiden muttered.

'Hey, what gives?' She stared up at Aiden, a hand clenching into a fist at her side. Forgetting about flirting. Forgetting about reeling him in. 'When was the last time you graced Ashbury Falls with your exalted presence, anyway? Someone who hasn't been in the town for more than ten years doesn't get to pass themselves off as any kind of authority.'

'I was there a couple of years ago,' he corrected. 'It hasn't changed.'

Sienna gawped at him. She could hardly breathe. 'A couple of years ago?' she repeated.

'For a night,' he muttered, dragging a hand through his hair. 'Long enough to know it's the same place we grew up in. The same place I left as soon as I could.'

Bitterness flooded every cell in her body.

'But *you* didn't leave.' Chuck addressed Sienna, drawing her attention back to him. She tried to focus on him. On his handsome face, his charming smile, the fact he was clearly into her. She tried to blot out Aiden, but she couldn't. He was like this big, hulking figure just to her left, and even his footsteps were pissing her off. She stopped walking and jammed a hand onto her hip.

'No.' She looked only at Chuck as she spoke. 'We didn't all get headhunted for a scholarship by some huge college. Some of us didn't have any marketable skills,' she finished on a soft laugh, to take the sting out of what she'd said. 'Anyway' – she pointed to the moon – 'I've seen what I came to see, so... goodnight.' She turned before either of them could respond, stalking back to the mansion and forgetting all about wiggling her hips as she went.

* * *

'What happened?' Bella came in first, holding a tray with a teapot and four cups.

Astrid followed with a bottle of champagne and three flutes. 'We thought we'd cover all our bases,' she said with a shrug as Paige followed.

'Aiden looks pissed.'

'Aiden looks pissed?' Sienna demanded. 'That's pretty freakin' rich!'

'What happened?' Bella repeated, holding a

teacup towards Sienna. She took it and cradled it in her hands.

'He just decided it would be a good idea to insult my entire existence, pretty much,' she muttered.

'He didn't!' Paige's eyes were huge as she sat, cross-legged, on the edge of the bed.

'I'm sure he didn't mean it,' Astrid defended, clearly torn between her future brother-in-law and her best friend.

'Oh, he did. He absolutely did. Bitching about our town like it's... like it's... we didn't all get the chance to leave, you know. I mean, even if he thinks that, would it have killed him to pretend...' Anger fizzed inside of her. 'And you know what else? He's been back.'

'What? When?' Paige leaned forward.

'A couple of years ago. He was in Ashbury Falls – I have no idea why – and he didn't so much as *think* to look me up. Which shows precisely how much I mean to him. How much I meant to him.' She stalked to the other side of the room, slamming her teacup down. 'All this time, I've been holding onto—'

'Onto what, love?' Astrid asked gently.

'This!' She pressed her fingers into her chest. 'I can't explain it. I feel like such a fool. I have been so angry with him and he just... nothings me. Nothing!

Like, he doesn't regret me, he doesn't miss me, he doesn't even think about me.'

'You don't know that,' Bella murmured.

'Absolutely,' Paige concurred. 'You can't jump to that conclusion.'

'Oh, really?'

'I know he thinks about you,' Astrid said quietly, her cheeks flushing with a hint of pink.

'What?' Sienna turned on Astrid at the same moment the others did. 'What do you mean?'

'At least, that's what Blake says,' she hurried to add. 'I don't have any details, but Blake reckons your name comes up, you know, from time to time.'

'Well, that just means he has a memory.' She waved her hand dismissively. 'I was a pretty big part of his life for a few years, so at least he hasn't forgotten that. But that doesn't mean he *feels* anything for me.'

'You don't feel anything for him either, do you?' Bella asked, a little breathlessly.

'Of course I do!' Sienna contradicted, reaching for her tea and taking a quick sip. 'I feel hatred and rage and anger and disgust and disappointment and... and...'

'Okay,' Bella laughed softly, lifting her hands in the air. 'I get it.'

'You guys, you don't know what it was like back then,' she whispered, glancing at Astrid, who was the only one of the group she'd told the whole sordid truth to. But maybe that wasn't fair. Because she hated him more than they could possibly understand, given what they knew of the situation, not to mention Aiden 'Charm Your Panties Off' Carter's easy-going schtick.

'You know we always planned for our future together. I know we were just teenagers, but it didn't feel like that. It felt like two people who'd found their soulmates and were just stepping, side by side, into the future they knew they had to share. It all just felt so right.'

Three pairs of eyes were on her.

'We came from kind of similar families. I mean, not completely. My dad was never violent, but... he drank, after Mom died. He was sort of pulled apart by her death. I was alone, and in a lot of ways, so was Aiden. He didn't feel like anyone got him, even Blake. They weren't always as close as they are now.' Her eyes lifted to Astrid's. She wasn't going to go into Blake's past, and the wrong path he'd taken as a teenager. 'Aiden and I were like... it sounds so corny... but just... like bookends.'

She fidgeted her fingers. 'I remember every detail

of the night we... you know. For the first time. It was so... it felt, at the time, so incredible. We were young and in love.' Her smile was self-deprecating. 'And then, a few months later, he and Blake got an amazing scholarship offer from an interstate college, the kind that's too good to turn down. He told me he was leaving.'

'That must have killed you,' Bella murmured.

'No, I was excited for him. I knew how much he wanted that; how much he'd worked for it. I still had a year left of school, I couldn't go with him, but I thought...' She drew in a deep breath. 'Except, he wanted a clean break. To focus on his career. He said he had to give it a good shot, you know? He made out that it was for me – that it wasn't fair to make me commit to a long-distance relationship when he had no intention of coming back to Ashbury Falls, ever, and I had no plans – no ability – to leave. I mean, I used to talk about studying medicine, but the truth is, there was no way we could afford college, and my chances of getting a scholarship were pretty dismal.' She swallowed to banish the threat of tears. How could he still affect her like this?

'He left. I couldn't believe it. I was... numb. It happened so fast, and he just seemed so sure. Like there wasn't a single moment of doubt for him, of wondering if he should stay for me, or if we could somehow make long distance work. He just left...' She shook her head. 'And then, I got sick.'

'Sick?' Bella leaned forward, her experience with her sister Bea's illness something that had left Bella with a particular anxiety around illness.

'Morning sickness,' she muttered, eyes lifting to Astrid's – the only one who knew the truth of how awful that time in Sienna's life had been. 'I was pregnant.'

Paige gasped. 'You weren't.'

'Oh, yeah.' She pressed a hand to her flat stomach, remembering the moment she'd realised and felt an instant connection to their baby. The baby she and Aiden had made. She dug her nails into her palm – hard – to drive away the threat of tears.

'What happened?' Bella asked.

'I tried to tell him, but Aiden wouldn't take my calls. Eventually, he sent me a text reiterating that a clean break was for the best. Telling me not to call again.' She cleared her throat.

'Bastard,' Paige muttered, tears rolling down her cheeks. 'Oh, honey. I'm so sorry.'

Sienna shook her head, unable to take the platitude. 'And then, I lost the baby,' she said, shrugging and dropping her head forward. 'So, he was off the hook anyhow.'

Now it was Bella who gasped. 'And you had to deal with that, all alone?'

She swallowed, looking away. 'Yep.'

'Does he have any idea?' Paige asked.

Sienna shook her head at the same time Astrid said, 'No one does, right?'

'No one but you guys, now,' Sienna agreed.

'Oh, God.' Bella stalked towards Sienna, putting her hands on her friend's arms. 'I hate him, too, now.'

'Me too,' Paige added.

Astrid, perhaps out of loyalty to Blake, didn't pile onto the hatred, but she came to stand beside Sienna, putting a hand between her shoulder blades and rubbing slowly.

'Anyway,' Sienna said into the silence. 'The way he's just moved on, the way he talked about our town – my town – like it was some kind of shit on his shoe, the fact he just cut me out of his life when I could never do that to him...'

'Yeah,' Bella said on a low whistle. 'What a piece of work.'

'We have to take him down,' Paige murmured.

'Paige' – Astrid's voice held a warning – 'what have you got in mind?'

'Nothing that will ruin the wedding, I promise,' she swore.

'On red velvet cakes and just dessert?' Sienna asked and then, despite the heaviness of the mood, they were giggling.

'Fuck this tea,' Bella muttered. 'Let's have some bubbles.'

'Yes, let's,' Sienna agreed.

'Because if we know anything, it's that we do our best work over a bottle,' Bella chimed in.

'And Aiden Carter is worthy of our very best work,' Paige said. 'This time, no one's going to fall in love with him to save his sorry ass, either. He's going to be the first successful victim of the Karma Club.'

'But not the last,' Sienna promised Paige, whose Horrible Harvey was the worst of the worst, in all their opinions. Frustration at her inability to penetrate his cast-iron defences bubbled to the surface anew, but she put it on hold. For this week, her focus was Aiden – and Astrid and Blake, of course. When she got back to Ashbury Falls, she'd resume Operation Make the Scumbag Pay Big Time.

'Okay, members, come to order,' Bella said, lifting the bottle of champagne in the air. 'All those in favour of settling the score with Aiden the Asswipe, say "aye".'

'Aye,' they said in unison, laughing a little as Bella filled up three of the glasses and they set to work, coming up with some foolproof ways to get under the skin of the man who'd not only broken Sienna's heart, but failed to support her when her whole world came crashing down.

6

The Plan: Part One

1. Make Him Green-Eyed with Jealousy...
2. Make Him Suffer.

Guest Appearance: Chuck Daly
Also, Sprinkler System.

It was Astrid who set it up, texting Chuck to let him know that Sienna would be going for an early morning jog and might be looking for a running buddy. It was only a slight stretch of the truth. While Sienna loved to run early, she always ran alone. It was a time to clear her head and listen to the political podcasts she was obsessed with. But for the purposes of making Aiden pay, she supposed she could put up with a bit of Chuck Daly on the side.

And it wasn't like he was bad company, anyway. If anything, he was genuinely fun, and funny. Charming, like he'd been practising since he was knee-high to a grasshopper, and despite the fact he'd been out of professional sports for more than five years, fit AF.

They ran non-stop for three miles, but as they rounded the bend of the cove, Sienna stopped, hands on hips, cheeks flushed.

'Don't tell me I've worn you out. And here I could have sworn you'd have better stamina.'

She poked her tongue out at him. 'Is everything with you an opportunity for a pervy comment?'

He grinned. 'Apparently.'

She held up a hand up in mock surrender. 'I'm fine, anyway. I just wanted to admire this.' She gestured to the view out over the Mediterranean, which sparkled in the early morning light. Each gently rolling wave showed a lattice of silver across the top, half knocking the breath out of Sienna with its beauty.

'Yeah, the view's not bad.'

She rolled her eyes. 'Come on, give it a rest.'

He laughed then. 'You're not interested?'

'In you?'

She glanced back at him, to see if he was serious.

'In having a bit of fun.'

A single brow arched upwards. 'With you?'

He pulled a face. 'Someone else on your mind?'

'No,' she denied, way too hotly.

He made a gruff sound, coming to stand beside her, looking out at the water now. 'Let me guess. You and Aiden have something going on?'

She grimaced. 'No. Believe me, no.'

'You sure? I thought I sensed something between the two of you.'

'You didn't,' she promised.

'I've usually got a pretty good instinct about this stuff.'

'We... used to date. A million years ago. It... wasn't serious.'

'Ahh. That explains it.'

'Explains what?'

'The chemistry.'

'There's *no* chemistry between Aiden Carter and me now. He's got a whole bag of puck bunnies at his disposal for that. Then again, I guess that's true for you, too.'

'Riiiight.' He sounded sceptical. 'If you say so.'

'I do.'

'Sure. Okay.'

'You don't believe me?'

He turned to look at her thoughtfully. 'Let's see what the week brings.' He moved a little closer. 'But, for the record' – he brushed something off her shoulder, his grin carefree and casual – 'I'm interested and available.' He gently curled her hair behind her ear. 'If you're looking for a distraction from whatever your deal is with him.'

'We don't have...' She tapered off into nothing then met his eyes and smiled. 'Thanks. I'll keep it in mind.' She bit into her lip. 'In the meantime, I like spending time with you. So, there's that.'

He held a hand to his chest in a gesture of being mock wounded. '*That* will have to do. For now.'

They turned to head back to the mansion. 'Want to make it interesting?' she asked, as the enormous white building came into view.

'Didn't I already say that?'

She laughed. 'You are *incorrigible.*'

'So you've said.'

'I meant by racing. Loser buys breakfast.'

'Breakfast is free.'

'Okay, loser owes the other one something. A favour.'

'If I win, you owe me a dance,' he said.

She pulled a face. 'That doesn't sound like a hardship.'

He grinned. 'I knew I'd win you over.'

She rolled her eyes. 'That's not what I meant. You're fun. And easy to be around. A dance with you is not exactly going to kill me.'

'And if you win?' he prompted.

'Hmmm.' She tilted her head and pretended to consider that. 'Maybe I'll get you to wear pink to the wedding.'

'I have no problems with wearing pink.'

Her lips pulled to the side as she considered his response. 'Okay, or bleach your hair for it.'

That elicited a slight groan. 'Now I'm starting to regret this.'

'Well, you'd better win then.'

'One step ahead of you,' he said, taking off.

'Hey, no fair!' she called after his retreating back, but with a laugh, she began to run. And she ran hard, too. Sienna hadn't gone to college on a scholarship, but she'd been on the track team, and she'd won a state championship the same year she met Aiden. After the miscarriage, she'd given up running for a while, and with it, any hope of taking her sporting abilities and using them to help her get out of town.

Besides, she hadn't wanted to leave after that. She

couldn't, because of her dad's criminal charges and the relationship she'd formed with Cory and Melanie. Aiden had left such a monumental hole in her life that she'd scrambled to fill it, and Cory had been there, a new neighbour, in his twenties, with a little girl. He'd needed help and Sienna had offered it. Babysitting for him had been a balm she'd needed, as she came to love his daughter as much as she might have loved her own. Besides, she'd needed the money to cover the mortgage.

And just like that, her smile had dropped, her pace had slowed, and she realised she was in danger of losing. 'No way,' she muttered to herself, pushing her legs to pump faster, damn near sprinting the rest of the way, running until her legs were sore and her lungs were burning with the effort of inflating and reinflating so rapidly.

But bit by bit, she gained on him, until, as they reached the front lawn of the mansion, they were almost, almost neck and neck. 'A real gentleman would never cheat, you know,' she called out to him.

'I didn't cheat!' he responded, but he looked over his shoulder and at the sight of her, slowed down ever so slightly.

'You ran ahead of me.'

'It's a race, that's the point.' He reached back and

flicked her arm. 'Besides, don't we both secretly want me to win?' He turned around before she could answer and started running again, this time, showing no mercy.

Sienna ground her teeth and kept going. Dancing with Chuck was hardly going to be a problem, but at the same time, Sienna hated losing, even a silly foot race.

* * *

It was Astrid who'd asked him to come out into the gardens and look at the flowers – as if he knew jack about flowers – and choose which ones their mother would like best on the table arrangements. Flowers were flowers, right? Some of them were pink. Some of them were yellow. How was it possible that Astrid didn't already have this locked down? And what about her sidekicks? Surely Paige, Bella or Sienna would have been a better choice for this job?

Sienna knew his mom. She'd probably have a great idea which flowers she'd like.

Sienna. His mom.

Stricken, he straightened and stared across the lawn, his heart thumping hard against his ribs, like he'd just scored a goal in overtime to win the game.

His mom and Sienna were going to be here. *Together.*
He closed his eyes on a wave of emotions, because
Cynthia Carter had damn well loved Sienna like a
daughter. And Sienna had loved her right back.

He groaned, dragging a hand through his hair,
trying to imagine what that particular reunion would
be like. And as if that mental arithmetic had somehow, *Matrix*-style, caused his perceptions to turn into
reality, Sienna came sprinting into view, a little way
across the lawn. Running with long, tanned legs on
display, courtesy of the bike shorts she wore. An inch
or so of midriff was visible too, because of her
cropped top. Her cheeks were pink, her body
sheened with perspiration, her blonde hair pulled
back into a high ponytail that swished, swished,
swished with each step.

And he didn't notice, at first, that she wasn't
alone. Mainly because he couldn't drag his eyes off
her, and the perfect picture she made. She was so full
of life and vitality, so beautiful and... sensual. Sensual like he'd never really thought of her, because
back then she'd been *his* Sienna. The love of his
teenage life, he thought with a grimace. Sure, hor-
mones had been involved in their relationship, but
there was so much more, because he'd loved just
talking to her, too.

This Sienna was pure goddess. Pure athletic, stunning, vital, glowing goddess, so out of nowhere he had the fantasy of storming across the grass, lifting her in his arms and holding her to his chest, carrying her cave-man style to the ocean and kissing her as the waves pummelled them, stripping her naked, making her his again.

Then, right in that torturously perfect imagining, his eyes wrenched to the left and clocked her running companion, so everything froze. Chuck Dufus Daly.

'I could have got you if you hadn't cheated!'

'So says every loser,' Chuck replied, but he turned around to face her and Sienna stopped running just a few inches away from the other man. Aiden's gut tightened. He stood entirely still, breathlessly watching, hoping that neither of them would turn and see him.

'You're really calling me a loser?' she demanded, hands on hips. Did she *know* how good she looked? Somehow, he doubted it. Sienna was the least vain woman he'd ever known.

Then again, he didn't really know her, now. A teenager was not the same as a woman in her twenties, and Sienna would have every reason to have confidence in her looks.

'As long as I can call you something,' she heard Chuck reply and Sienna laughed, reaching out and playfully punching his arm.

Anger flared in Aiden's stomach, hot and irrepressible. The kind of anger that he hadn't felt in a long time. The kind of anger that scared the living crap out of him, because he knew what that anger was capable of. He felt it in the tingle of his fingers, the need to form a fist and punch something.

Like his father had.

All his life, he'd avoided feeling *anything* strong enough to make him care. He'd become a master at switching off his emotions, on operating like an automaton. He and Blake had both developed their coping techniques – they'd had to.

He couldn't believe that, after all these years, Sienna still had the power to pull at that control. To pull at it until it very nearly snapped.

He took a step backwards, as if he could physically distance himself from his worst fears that way, but the anger didn't subside.

He hated seeing them together.

He hated seeing her with anyone else.

He knew he had no right to feel that way.

She was her own woman, and the day he'd walked out on her was the day he'd stopped having any say whatsoever in how she spent her time, and who she spent it with. He'd been with other women since Sienna. Lots of other women.

What did he care if she'd been with other men? He presumed that to be the case – obviously.

But he'd never had to see it.

He didn't want to see it now.

He particularly didn't want to see it with Chuck 'Perfect Smile' Daly, who was the biggest player in hockey, well after quitting the game. He went through women at a rate of knots. Did grown-up Sienna really go for guys like him?

She laughed again and this time when she punched his arm, her hand lingered. Aiden saw red, but held his ground.

Maybe if he'd moved, he would have been grateful, though. Because a second later, a hissing noise sounded and then the whole garden was deluged by pop-up sprinklers in full flight.

He let out a sound of surprise, a deep groan, and was still staring across at Sienna and Chuck, so saw the moment they turned towards him. And they laughed. His anger – an anger he would have said he was generally an expert at controlling – went from flame to incinerator.

He turned on his heel and, utterly saturated,

stalked away from the garden, his mood truly and totally tanked. Ice was a distant memory.

* * *

JUST DESSERTS WHATSAPP
GROUP. 09.10 EST.

BELLA

Ohmygod. Did you guys see?

PAIGE

Yassssss. So funny.

ASTRID

I almost felt sorry for him

PAIGE

Sod him. I didn't. He looked pissed.

SIENNA

Did you guys plan that?

BELLA

SIENNA

Wow. You really are evil geniuses.
Genii?

BELLA

It's going to be a fun week... just
wait to see what Astrid has in store
for later this morning.

'There are five coloured flags for each team hidden on this side of the island,' Astrid said, holding up a map, so the small group of bridesmaids and grooms-men, as well as Chase and Olly, could see. 'The first team to find all their five flags wins.'

'And what do we win?' Chuck called out.

'Well, we thought about that, long and hard,' Blake said. 'Then we remembered you guys are all competitive enough to be motivated by a simple de-sire to score victory.'

There was a laugh, and a look of amusement be-tween the guests.

'But to make it more interesting, the winning team will also get a massage each.'

'From you, Fury?' Aiden called to Blake, who grinned.

'It's meant to be a prize, not punishment.'

'A masseuse can be here tomorrow,' Astrid said,

then continued, 'We've formed your teams, to make it fair.'

Bella grinned at Sienna and lifted two crossed fingers that they'd be together.

'Okay, first team, Bella and Chuck. You're looking for green flags,' Astrid said, as Bella and Chuck made their way to a golf cart with a green ribbon tied around one of the support struts. Olly and Chase high fived when they were paired together. Paige was with one of the Titan players' moms. Astrid continued to reel off names, until only four people remained.

Blake. Astrid. Sienna. Aiden.

Sienna's mouth was dry as she contemplated the next pairing. *Please* let her be with Astrid. *Please* let her be with...

'Sissi, you're with Aiden, and you're going for gold,' Astrid said, subtly winking at her best friend.

Sienna's skin paled, even as she realised her friend was trying to create the perfect opportunity for her to further the plan.

'Great,' she said, a little weakly, not glancing up at Aiden.

She'd expected him to say something pithy like, '*Game on,*' or whatever, but if anything, his face wore matching thunderclouds to her own.

She sucked in a breath. *Chill out.* This was just a game. A silly pre-wedding game that the happy couple had devised. She was supposed to be making Aiden want her, so Astrid had given her an opportunity for that. Sienna forced herself to lean into gratitude, even when she'd rather douse herself in honey and lie down on top of an ant hill...

7

'I guess this is us.' She gestured to a golf cart with a gold ribbon. On closer inspection, she saw that a couple of piccolos of champagne, as well as some beer, had been stashed in the front glove box, as well as an ice box with sandwiches. Astrid's handwriting was on a sticky note that read, 'In case you get lost!'

Gawd, please let them not get lost.

'I'll drive,' she said, moving behind the steering wheel, glad when Aiden didn't argue. But a second later, he took up the seat beside her and all her senses went into overdrive because he was just so damned big, his huge, muscly, hairy legs man spread wider than a freaking goal net (because: BDE, obviously), his knee just an inch or so from her own. He couldn't sit in the seat without his elbow brushing hers either, even when she was shoved dangerously close to the edge of the golf cart. It wasn't his fault he was built like a bear, but she wished... she wished... for a lot of things, actually.

She suppressed a sigh as she started the cart up. 'Ready?' She made the mistake of turning to face him. Aiden wore reflective sunglasses, but that didn't matter. Just the set of his jaw told her he was dreading this as much as she was, and the part of her that had dreamed of getting some kind of revenge sparked to life. She flashed him an over-bright smile – definitely not an authentic representation of how she felt, but she imagined it might be a little like rubbing salt in the wound.

'Sure,' he said, the lines of his body radiating tension. 'Let's go.'

Before she pulled the cart out though, he was reaching for the cooler and cracking the top off a beer, taking a long, slow drink, so his Adam's apple shifted and his mouth... that mouth...

She looked away again quickly, and accelerated away from Astrid and Blake, the former shouting after them, 'Good luck! Have fun!'

Sienna was starting to think she just might.

*　*　*

'How the hell are we meant to find these damned flags?' Aiden snapped, after fifteen minutes of driving with no luck.

'By looking for them?' Sienna replied sweetly, glancing across at him and enjoying the rigidity of his body. He wasn't enjoying this. He was actually hating it. He didn't want to be near her this morning, yet last night, he'd been all about the moonlit walks and sharing of cocktails. What had changed? The fact she'd gone running with Chuck? Astrid was right: the green-eyed monster was most definitely swirling in Aiden, even though it had been an eon since they'd dated. Even though he'd been with other women since. The hypocrisy of that!

Still, she could most definitely enjoy his discomfort.

'I have been looking,' he said, reaching into the cooler and removing a sandwich. He uncovered it and took a bite.

'Well, keep going.' She shrugged.

'I hate this kind of shit,' he muttered, surprising her with his honesty.

'Weddings?'

'No,' he replied quickly. Then, frowning, 'I meant

idiotic party games. We're not twelve-year-olds playing pin the tail on the donkey.'

'I don't think any twelve-year-old still plays pin the tail on the donkey,' she said serenely. 'Spin the bottle, maybe.'

'Jeez, I haven't thought about that in years,' he said, sounding a little less grumpy. 'And seven minutes in heaven.'

'More your type of game than mine,' Sienna said, her own voice a little clipped.

'You always were a good girl.'

She bristled a little at that. 'Because I didn't go to the kinds of parties where the whole vibe was to swap herpes and glandular fever?'

He laughed. 'Pretty much.'

'I think you used to like that about me.' She looked across at him in time to catch his jaw tightening again, his body stone-like once more. He took a bite of his sandwich, as if to cover it. Sienna turned her attention back to the gravelled path, part of a network of paths that criss-crossed the whole island.

'I liked a lot about you.'

Fuck. So that had backfired.

'Are you still a good girl, Sienna?'

Her hands tightened on the wheel. 'Well, I still don't play spin the bottle, if that's what you mean.'

His grin surprised her, spreading slowly over his face when he turned to look at her. 'Even with Chuck Daly?'

There was something in his voice though, that belied the simplicity of his dimply face. Her breath caught in her throat at the way he'd brought up Chuck. He was sounding her out, seeing how she felt about the other man. And she was not afraid of pressing her fingers right into that big old jealousy bruise he was clearly carrying.

'I think he's a little too impatient for spin the bottle.'

Aiden snorted. 'You're probably right.'

'You don't like him?'

'He's been a good friend to Blake,' Aiden contradicted.

'But you and Blake are separate people,' she drawled, as if speaking to someone who didn't easily comprehend. 'At least, last time I checked.'

Aiden's nostrils flared. 'My point is, it's not my place to like or dislike him. He's been good for Blake.'

Sienna bit the inside of her cheek, considering that. Aiden had always put a premium on what was best for Blake. Only a few minutes separated them in age, yet Aiden had naturally slotted into a sort of protective, older brother role.

'Yeah, but—'

'Stop driving.' Aiden put a hand on her knee to grab her attention, and she was so shocked by the contact – which felt much more intimate than it should have – that she slammed on the brakes, which meant they jerked in their seats.

'What?' she demanded, turning to face him, breath burning in her lungs, eyes huge in the reflection of his glasses.

'Look.' He leaned forward, removing his hand from her knee so he could point at a tree.

'I don't see...' she said, scanning the direction he was pointing in.

'Look.' He reached across and touched her jaw now, tilting her face slightly. 'There.' He pointed now and his arm brushed her whole side. She shivered, despite the balmy heat of the day.

'I don't... Oh!' Her gaze landed on a green flag. 'A flag, finally! It's not one of ours, but at least we know what we're looking for now.'

'Sienna Mastrangelo, you really are a good girl, aren't you?' he said, in a tsk-tsk-tsk tone.

She stiffened. 'What's your point?'

'There's more than one way to win the game.' And with that, he was stepping out of the vehicle, all big, broad strength as he strode easily off the path and into the wooded undergrowth, reaching up and removing a flag that must have been placed by Blake, given how high and well lodged it was in the limbs of the tree.

'What are you doing?' she asked, when he returned to the cart holding the flag as if he'd secured some kind of victory.

'Making sure no one else can win.' He grinned at her. 'It's a solid plan.'

'Aiden, you play dirty,' she marvelled, wondering why she was surprised. He'd promised he loved her – the first person ever to make her feel secure and safe in the world, since her mom had died. He'd promised he'd stay with her. He'd promised they'd be together forever.

And then he'd left.

Just like that.

Because it had served him. Because it had been right for Aiden, and that was the person Aiden cared most about.

Yeah, of course he played dirty. When it came to winning, Aiden would always do whatever it took. Sienna was just glad she'd learned that lesson – she'd never be collateral damage again: not his, not anyone's.

'The point is to win, right? Well, we're going to win, no matter what. Deal?'

She felt as though she were getting into bed with the devil, by double-crossing her friends. But she nodded anyway, because Aiden was smiling, and she realised that her revenge would be all the sweeter if she lulled him into a false sense of security.

'Sure, deal,' she agreed, reaching for the beer he'd been drinking, taking it from the cup holder. 'May I?'

His smile slipped. His back straightened. He stood just beside the cart, clutching the flag until his nails turned white, staring at her, so Sienna figured she might as well make it count. She made a show of wiping one fingertip (perfectly manicured courtesy of the Cinderella treatment the girls had subjected her to) over the condensation on the side of the bottle, before lifting it to softly parted lips and placing the head there. She took her time, tilting the bottle slightly, and angling her head back, letting a sip of liquid land in her mouth, before swallowing exaggeratedly, removing the bottle and gently dabbing at the corner of her lips.

Aiden just stared at her.

Sienna's heart soared.

'You... drink beer?' he asked, his voice a different

pitch to usual. It was an inane question, and Sienna almost laughed.

'Sometimes. It's hot.'

'I just...' His voice trailed off as she lifted the bottle to her lips once more, took another slow, refreshing sip then held the bottle towards him. 'Did you want some? I presume you don't mind sharing,' she purred.

Aiden was frozen to the spot for a couple of seconds before he reached out and took the bottle, but this time, whether by choice or chance, his hand caught hers around the glass, holding it there a moment, and his other hand – with the flag – lifted to his glasses and unhooked them, so his eyes could finally meet hers.

Her temperature spiked. They were so blue, like glaciers. Her whole body reacted to the intimacy of that look, accompanied as it was by the big bear paw being wrapped around her hand.

'Thanks.' The word seemed to reach right inside of her and twist her stomach in a vice.

He repositioned his hand, moving it to the neck of the bottle, then lifted the drink and had some. Sienna dragged her attention to the tropical wilderness in front of them, staring at it, at the trunks of trees, rather than the way Aiden's throat moved as he swallowed, the way his mouth covered the top of the bottle she'd just been drinking from.

She surreptitiously swiped a hand over her brow, wiping at the sweat that had started to pool there.

'So, beer huh?' He came around to his side of the cart and stepped in. This time, he was a little more relaxed, and his legs spread wider than a goddamn rink now, so his knee brushed hers. Her pulse throbbed.

'What about it?'

'I just don't see it.'

'There's a lot about me you probably don't see.'

'Like what?' he asked, the question relaxed, even when it set off a warning tone in her mind.

'You're asking what you don't see about me?'

'I'm asking what's new with you?'

It was so infuriating she laughed, a slightly hysterical sound. 'You... what's new? Aiden, it's been a lifetime...'

'Between drinks?'

'I was a kid back then,' she muttered, starting the cart and continuing down the path.

'Not quite.'

'You know what I mean.'

'But you're not a kid now.'

'No.'

'So, what's changed?'

'Apart from ten or so years?'

'Is there a reason you don't want to answer me straight up?'

'Like what?' she asked.

'Like, you're secretly on the run from Interpol. Or you've gone into witness protection. Or you've robbed a bank. I don't know.'

A smile tugged at one side of her lips. 'No.'

'Then you're still pissed at me,' he said, after a beat.

The whole world seemed to shutter into hyper colour, like some kind of TikTok filter had been applied. Time seemed to slow down, even when Sienna knew that wasn't possible.

'Why would I be pissed at you, Aiden?' She couldn't believe how steady her voice came out, like she was genuinely surprised by his question.

His laugh was almost self-conscious. 'Forget it. It doesn't matter.'

A frown etched its way across her features. 'I'm not still pissed at you,' she lied. 'I keep telling you, what happened between us was a lifetime ago. It's ancient history. We're just here to celebrate the wedding of two people we love, okay?'

'That night,' he said, though, his voice a little hoarse.

'Which night?' She pretended not to follow along.

He glanced across at her, his knuckles white as he gripped the neck of the beer bottle hard. 'When I told you I was leaving—'

'When you dumped me?'

A muscle ticked in his jaw. She spotted a yellow flag and slowed the cart down.

'I know I didn't say it, at the time, but that was one of the hardest things I've ever done.'

Where time seemed to have stopped a moment ago, now it almost went sickeningly fast.

'It was what you'd always wanted,' she pointed out slightly unsteadily. 'Doesn't seem like you had much choice.'

His brow furrowed. 'But the way I did it...'

'You were right,' she said, curtly. 'A clean break was for the best.'

He turned to face her, his whole body almost seeming to frame hers, even when her other side was open and exposed to the world.

'Was it?'

Her skin paled under the force of his scrutiny. She was lying as part of the game. To make him think she was over him. To make it easier to catch him on her line, to reel him in and set him loose, just like he'd done to her. But she *hated* lying, period. She especially hated lying about something that had been one of the most defining moments in her life.

Loss wasn't new to Sienna. She'd lost her mother to cancer, and she'd lost her father to alcoholism and then prison. But Aiden was the first person she'd lost because he'd chosen to walk away from her. Not because of disease, but because she just wasn't enough for him to want to stay for.

She cleared her throat. 'I don't know,' she backpedalled, lifting one shoulder and focusing her attention on the flag as though it were the most riveting thing in the world.

'It was the right decision,' he said, firmly, in a way that might have infuriated her if it weren't so obvious that some form of hesitation underpinned the words.

'Sure,' she said, lifting one shoulder in a half-shrug. 'There's another one.' She pointed to the flag, her tongue feeling strange in her mouth.

He didn't look away from her.

'We had to get out of that place, you know? I always swore we would, then I met you, and everything got kind of complicated. But...'

She tightened her grasp on the steering wheel. 'I get it. I remember.'

'I just—'

Frustration whipped her patience. 'You just what, Aiden? You wish you hadn't done it? That you hadn't taken up a college spot that turned you into a star overnight? That led to you becoming one of the highest-paid players in the pro league? That turned your life into everything you ever wanted?'

His frown deepened. 'It's not everything I ever wanted.'

Her heart skipped a beat and for one world-tilting second she thought he might actually be talking about her. That he might be trying to say he'd also wanted her.

But so what if he did mean that, anyway? He hadn't wanted her *enough*. Not enough to stay, not enough to stay faithful to all the promises he'd made, no matter what distance separated them.

'But it's what I had to do.'

'Yeah, you said that then, too.'

'Did I?' It was his turn to shrug, before taking a long drink of the beer. 'I can hardly remember a thing about that night, to be honest.'

Sienna saw red. She had no idea how she concealed the immediate whiplash reaction of pain but she did. 'It was...'

'A long time ago,' he finished for her, lips compressing in a line, before he turned and stepped out of the golf cart, striding towards the flag and pulling it out of the tree.

'Two down,' he said, as he returned and took up a seat beside her.

'And none are our own.'

'Nah, not yet,' he said. 'But we've got all day, Mastrangelo. Let's keep looking.'

8

It was the heat that made him suggest it. The heat that had started like a balmy warmth that morning had grown into sauna-like and suffocating, even as their golf cart clung to the coastal path, promising hints, occasionally, of a cooling breeze that never actually eventuated. He'd drunk a few beers, trying to keep cool, but if he kept ploughing through the bag, he'd end up starting even more asshole conversations with Sienna – who clearly didn't want to rehash their past any more than he did. Or should have.

So why the hell did he keep bringing it up? Whatever happened to letting sleeping dogs lie?

He had 100 per cent left Ashbury Falls for all the

right reasons. He'd had to get out of there. Not just for himself – and the quicksand that was Sienna – but for Blake and the anger management issues he was having, thanks to their father's abuse. For their mother, who back then had no clue how to stand up for herself. She'd been mentally paralysed by years of living with fear. It was Aiden who'd had to be brave for them, who'd had to rip them out of that life and away from the home that was so chaotic and miserable.

Leaving Sienna had been one of the hardest things he'd ever done, but he'd told himself that the whole 'clean break' narrative would make it easier for both of them. Easier for her to cut ties with him if he made it obvious there was no future for them, after all. That he was going to be putting all of his focus on the game, and the opportunity he had to make a name for himself.

He'd been a coward.

He'd known that if he'd kept in touch with her, he would have weakened.

Quicksand.

Dynamite.

Whatever way you chose to describe their relationship, would probably hold water. For Sienna, he would have done anything. Given up anything.

And then what? He ends up in a relationship with a woman he cares about more than life itself, only to find out that he's just like his father, and winds up hurting her? Aiden had learned from a young age that the way to make sure he *never* went down that path was to ice everyone out, all the time. To keep them at arm's length. Somehow, Sienna had found her way through the cracks and nestled in there good and proper for over a year, until the thought that he might hurt *her* had been like an anvil against his skull, non-stop. He'd needed to escape, not just the town, not just his father, but *her*. Everything about her.

Maybe if it hadn't been for Blake, he might have questioned that, but he hadn't had the luxury of listening to what he wanted. He and Blake were a package deal. Blake staying out of prison was all down to Aiden moving away with him. It had been a predicament with no winning solution; yet it had been one of the hardest decisions of his life.

So why the fuck did he turn to her and grin, like life was so freaking great and easy, and say, 'How about we take a break from hunting down flags and test the water?'

No wonder she'd looked at him like he'd taken leave of his senses, her eyes widening as she slowed the golf cart to a stop, her gaze hitching to his, first, and then to the sparkling Med behind him.

As soon as he'd made the suggestion, he wanted to retract it. Swimming with Sienna right after admitting he should keep his distance from her had every single part of him screaming *withdrawwwww, soldier.* But he held his tongue, and his breath, staring at her as her incredibly sparkly eyes seemed to swirl with a torrent of thoughts and considerations, before slipping back to his face.

'That is kind of tempting.'

Tempting? She didn't know the half of it.

'Is that a yes?'

Her teeth pressed down on that full lower lip of hers, a habit she'd picked up since he'd left, a habit that would drive any red-blooded male to the point of insanity.

'Sure,' she said, looking down at their collection of flags – one or two of every colour except gold, which was proving elusive. 'It's not like the others can claim victory anyway,' she said with a giggle that made his whole body tighten and teeter on the brink of exploding.

'Greeaaat.' He turned to look at the beach with a sinking feeling in his stomach. Then again, it was a beautiful day, a beautiful stretch of beach, and they were just going to go for a swim. It was hardly a commitment to marry, or anything even like it. He was a big boy, who'd spent a long time controlling his emotions, his libido, anything that might come close to a feeling, so he was pretty sure he could restrain himself even in the face of the temptation that was Sienna.

'What are you waiting for?' she asked, stepping from the cart and lifting her hands over her head in a stretch that made her shirt cling a little to her curves, so his pulse started to riot in his body.

'Nothing.' He grabbed the cooler as an afterthought, carrying it as he fell into step just behind her, away from the path and towards the beach, a hint of her sunshiney fragrance teasing his nostrils with every step.

The sand was hot underfoot, so Sienna laughed as she felt it and ran a little way down the beach, to where a large palm created spiky fronds of shade and offered some relief.

'It's like fire,' she said with a shake of her head.

He placed the bag down and simply stared at her. The air seemed to pulsate with something heavy and sultry.

'I don't have bathers,' she said, after a beat. 'So, I'm going to swim in this.' She gestured to her outfit of short shorts and a shirt.

He shrugged, like he didn't care. Like he wasn't relieved as all get-out that she wasn't merrily stripping off her shirt and shorts and getting down to just her underwear.

'Sure,' he said. 'I presume you won't be offended if I take off my shirt?'

'I've seen naked chests before,' she pointed out, in a way that cut him like a mother trucker. 'I've even seen *your* naked chest before,' she added as a reminder, with a hint of a wink that made his stomach feel all lurchy and weird.

He was pretty sure he made something like a growling noise as he lifted the shirt off over his head and dropped it down onto the sand, but it was totally eclipsed by the soft rush of breath he heard escaping Sienna's parted lips. When he looked at her, those enormous eyes were firmly locked to his torso.

She might have seen it before, but not for a long time, and he'd done a lot of filling out since then courtesy of the monumental workout sessions he drove himself to complete every day, sometimes twice a day. He'd also done a fair bit of time in a tattooist's chair.

'Oh,' she said, eyes quickly flicking to his before dropping lower. 'That's quite some ink.'

'Yeah.' A nonsensical, stupid response, because the way she was staring at him was making his mouth all dry and his stomach hollow, not to mention his head as empty as a deserted attic.

She took a half-step closer, one side of her lips tugging into a smile that made it impossible to look anywhere but at her face. 'The Titans,' she said, pointing – and carefully not touching – the team's logo he wore just beneath his left pectoral.

He nodded, not trusting his voice.

'And an eagle?' Her gaze flicked to his and flames seemed to leap against the soles of his feet.

He nodded.

'And this one?' Her hand shifted to the side a little, just above his hip. He didn't need to look down to know what she was pointing at. The red love heart, about the size of his thumb.

'I lost a bet.'

Her lips quirked. 'With who?'

'Who do you think?' he grunted. 'Blake.'

Her laugh was only soft, but she was close enough that her breath buzzed his jaw, making the hair on the back of his neck stand on end.

'Is that all of them?' She glanced back up at his face.

His heart thumped into his ribs. It was a straight-forward question but the answer took them a step closer to a path they'd be idiots to follow. Slowly, activating full idiot mode even when he should have known better, almost against his will, he shook his head.

'Oh.' Her voice was quiet. As though it was just dawning on her that the only part of him that was concealed from her view was the flesh from low on his hips to mid-thighs. 'Never mind,' she rushed, her eyes troubled when they met his, her cheeks flushed pink.

Heat started low in his abdomen, as though a match had been struck, and shot right up his spine.

'You don't want to see?'

It was a challenge, a dare, and a plea. A plea for her to remember and pull away from this; a plea for her to have some common sense.

Her lips parted on a soft breath and her eyes stayed latched to his. He was dimly aware of the sound of crashing waves, the heat of the sun on his back, the sea breeze ruffling his hair. But mostly, he was hyper fixated on Sienna, on this moment, on the humming and buzzing that was flooding his body and brain.

'Okay.' Her voice trembled a little. 'Show me, cowboy.'

Something panged in the very centre of his chest. A memory, slamming into him, hard and fast.

'Come on, cowboy!'

She'd called him that, back then, always with a teasing smile, because Aiden had been wearing a broad-brimmed hat the first day they'd walked home from school together. The hat had been retired long before the nickname.

He half-turned, so she had a better view of his back, and moved his hand to the waistband of his shorts, his fingers brushing low down before sliding the elastic lower, incrementally, until the text was visible.

'*Ad Meliora,*' she said, halting a little over the un-familiar words. Or maybe it was because half his butt was exposed. That was probably just wishful thinking, though, because Sienna hadn't given him any hint that she was as affected by him as he was by her. He swallowed over a lump in his throat, ignoring the way his gut seemed to drop to his feet as he acknowledged that. 'What does it mean?'

Something else sharpened inside of him now. A dim regret. Or concern.

'I don't remember,' he lied. *Towards Better Things.* It had been Blake and his mantra back then, a talisman he'd clung to in the hopes he'd eventually accept that leaving Sienna and Ashbury Falls really was the right thing, for everybody.

'You have a tattoo on your butt and you don't know what it means?'

He shrugged.

'Aw, come on. You got your star sign in Latin, didn't you?'

'Yeah, totally,' he said with a hint of sarcasm.

'Orrrr' – she lifted a finger to the side of her lips and tapped, in a way he found outright distracting – 'a translated lyric from a Britney song?' Her eyes roamed his body, her features showing she was still lost in thought. 'A quote from the Barbie movie?'

His laugh surprised him. 'Nah. It's just something about the future,' he said, after a moment. 'I got it ages ago.'

'You have such a squeaky-clean image,' she said, apparently dropping the meaning of the tattoo. 'Do your sponsors know about all this?'

He eased his shorts back into place, ignoring the part of him that wanted to actually keep sliding them down, all the way down, until he was butt naked. What the hell had got into him?

'Hell nah.' He turned back to her properly, forcing a grin to his face. Sienna's eyes were still troubled though, like she was thinking about something she couldn't comprehend.

'It'd probably add to your cachet, anyhow,' she said after a beat. 'Everything you touch turns to gold, right?'

Her tone was a little sharp. His smile slipped. 'That pisses you off?'

Her eyes flew to his, wariness in her expression. 'Not at all,' she said, the words a little rushed. 'I'm happy for you, Aiden. You're living your best life, right?' She didn't give him a chance to reply. 'Anyway, we came here to swim, didn't we?'

She flashed him a brittle smile then stalked towards the shore, leaving him staring after her, a jumble of feelings he'd have to be a genius to decode.

* * *

She should have abandoned their mission the second he'd stripped out of his shirt. The second her eyes had clung to his chest like an addict faced with a drug den. The second she took a step closer and her fingertips had tingled with a need to reach out and *feel*. The second he'd slipped his shorts down and showed just a hint of his perfectly toned, tanned ass, and her abdomen had clenched with a fierce need to possess and be possessed by him.

Because it was becoming abundantly clear to Sienna that her carefully drawn plan all hinged on *her* having the ability to control herself around Aiden, and that was starting to feel like a Sisyphean task. As a kid, she'd been totally under his spell. He'd entranced her, captivated her. She'd idolised him, worshipped him, adored him and loved him.

But she wasn't a kid any more. The scales were supposed to have fallen from her eyes. She knew he was a selfish a-hole now. She'd seen it for herself.

Surely that should have offered some kind of inoculation against finding him attractive?

Why couldn't her stupid brain take a more prominent role in managing this whole situation? It was like it had set the out-of-office email reply and stepped away from the keyboard of decision making. She was totally on her own.

She didn't want to find him hotter than Hades. She didn't want to feel an almost impossible need to jump his bones, but gawd, standing on the sand, looking at his flawless, caramel skin, remembering the way his body weight had felt pressing down on her, remembering the way his hands had caressed her body, remembering how even then, as a relatively inexperienced teenager, he'd known just what to do, where to touch, to make Sienna soar, made it impossible not to feel tempted.

She looked down the cove a little way, not remotely surprised to see they were completely alone. It was a private island, belonging to the owner of the Titans, loaned to Blake and Astrid for their wedding. Apart from the island staff, there was no one here but the wedding party, and they were all engaged in hunting for flags.

Her toes hit the water, but instead of it providing a cooling splash of relief to her overheated skin, it had the opposite effect. Every cell in her body was hypersensitive, so the sensory overload of cool contrasting with warm made her tingle, especially her nipples. They puckered in response and she was glad she'd resisted the urge to strip out of her own shirt.

She felt the moment Aiden came to stand behind her, even when he didn't say anything. She stepped deeper into the water, moving away from him, running away, just like he did. Except, not just like he did. He'd dropped her like a hot potato the second he'd had a better offer – and for Aiden, that 'better offer' had been all about himself, his future, his prospects.

The water lapped around her thighs. Two more steps and it was at her breasts. She dipped down then, covering herself to her neck, revelling in the feeling of the crystal-clear Mediterranean.

Aiden was right there, though, so much bigger and more powerful, just watching her, thoughtfully, like he had stuff going around in his brain that he was trying to understand. She glared at the shoreline mutinously.

'You know what, Sienna?'

She forced herself, grudgingly, to look up at him. His body was only submerged to his hips, thanks to the fact he was built like half man, half minotaur. She tried not to look at his naked chest, but it was right there, broad and fascinating, between the ridges of his buff abdomen, the tattoos, the line of hair that ran down into the waistband of his shorts.

Shorts that were wet now, and clinging to him just like her clothes were stuck to her.

'What?' she finally said, realising he was waiting for her to ask him something.

'I think you're wrong.'

She glanced at him then looked away again quickly. 'About what?'

'I don't think this is ancient history.'

The blood in her veins seemed to go all turbo charged, rushing through her so fast she could hear it pounding inside her ears.

She stood a little unsteadily, hands on hips, only realising how revealing her wet shirt was when his eyes slid down her to her clearly delineated breasts and still-puckered nipples. Heat exploded, not just in her cheeks, but through her whole body.

'It's been over ten years,' she pointed out, but her voice was husky now. She wasn't even sure if he heard it, because she'd spoken so softly and the ocean was rolling gentle waves towards the coastline.

'I don't care if it's been twenty years, you can't seriously tell me you're not feeling this?'

Everything spun into blinding hyper colour clarity.

Sensation.

Danger.

The goddamned plan.

The stupidity of thinking she could flirt with him and stay enough in control to make sure she won, this time. It had *always* been like this between them. It hadn't just been because they were hormonal teenagers in their first flush of relationship excitement. This was *them,* pure and simple.

'I don't feel anything,' she lied. A terrible lie. One he clearly saw through, because his lips twisted in a mocking smile.

'No?' He took a step closer, something sparking in his eyes when they latched onto hers, probing her face. Studying her. Looking inside of her, deep inside, in that way he'd had way back when.

'So, if I were to touch you... nothing?' he prompted.

Her throat seemed to close over. Desire throbbed between her legs. Despite the cool of the ocean, warm heat slicked there, making her painfully aware of how badly she wanted him to touch her.

'And if I were to kiss you?' He moved closer. Close enough that he could do either of those two things. Touch her. Kiss her. Whatever he wanted.

If she agreed.

If she even hinted that she was okay with that, he'd make a move, and she'd be lost.

As lost as she'd been back then. Because even though so much time had passed, and she was a totally different person now, he was Aiden, and she was Sienna. He clicked, she jumped. That's just how it had always been.

She was dumber than dumb to have thought, for even a second, she could take the upper hand here.

But then, Astrid was in her head. And Paige, and Bella. Reminding her that she was a strong, intelligent woman now, that she'd been through a shit tonne of adversity and was still going, one step after the other. Studying law part time, so she could help people like her dad. Supporting Melanie as best she could. Visiting her dad every weekend. Working to keep a roof over her head. Doing the best she damn well could to live a good life, and contribute to her town, to make the people she loved happy.

She tilted her chin, channelling those women, who'd helped her see what they did, who'd built up her confidence since Chicago, and made her believe she was capable of anything. Her fears and doubts ebbed away, leaving only certainty that she could handle this. She could handle him.

He was just a man, not a god, and no matter what she wanted from him physically, there was one ginormous, vital difference to how things had been between them back then.

Her body was one thing. But her heart and mind were totally another. He could touch her, and kiss her, and drive her completely wild. She'd never be stupid enough to let him anywhere near her heart, and without that, he had absolutely no power to hurt her. Zilch. She was safe.

Whereas he was, she hoped, a bit of a sitting duck this time around, just like she'd been back then.

First step to proving that? Picking up the gauntlet, of course...

'I can't say for sure,' she said with a shrug, aware that it made her breasts shift. 'But it sure sounds like an interesting experiment, cowboy.'

9

Okay. This was happening.

No big deal.

He'd kissed women before.

Heaps of women.

He liked kissing.

He liked it just fine.

He definitely never felt *nervous* about it, like some monumental life outcome was riding on how well he did. On how she felt. On if she liked it.

Kissing was... kissing. Not rocket science.

But this was Sienna, and even the slightest touch with her was loaded with their backstory. Their history. What they'd meant to each other, once upon a time.

How he'd hurt her.

How he'd *known* he was hurting her, how she'd cried, and how that had only hardened his resolve to get the hell out of there. Because if he weakened then, he would weaken forever, and his chance to escape, to get Blake and his mom out of town, to put them on the path to the future they needed to get away from their dad, it would all have disappeared.

But you'd have had Sienna, a voice that had dogged him for over a decade reminded him sharply.

That was the trade-off, back then. Sienna, and his life in Ashbury Falls, or a scholarship at a college with one of the best hockey programmes out there, the kind of programme that all but guaranteed a chance at the big time.

It had ripped him apart to hurt Sienna though, to know that she'd probably hate him forever because of the way his leaving betrayed everything they'd promised each other.

He would never make that mistake again.

'I'm going to kiss you,' he said, slowly, his voice deep. Dark. Gruff. Flooded with all the feelings he usually repressed. 'But here's the deal, Mastrangelo.'

'I'm listening, Carter.'

'We're here a week. A kiss now, a kiss then. Who knows what else might happen? I am not going to hurt you again.' He pressed a finger beneath her chin, tilting her face to his. 'If you think, for even one second, this is getting out of hand, you tell me and we walk away then and there. Got it?'

Her eyes flashed to his, something like a warning in the depths of her gaze. 'You're not going to hurt me,' she promised, inching closer, so it was Sienna who stood onto her tiptoes and pressed her wet, curvaceous body against his. 'You just don't have that power any more.'

He hoped to God she was right. No matter what, wild horses wouldn't hold him back from this. From leaning down, as she pressed up, from letting his lips get closer and closer to hers. The weight of what they were about to do was hard against his chest, making breathing almost impossible. Every other kiss they'd shared fractured inside his mind like a kaleidoscope of multicolour and glitter. Their first kiss had flooded him with nerves. But it was nothing compared to this.

It's just a kiss. Pull yourself together.

But weirdly, it didn't *feel* like just a kiss. It felt important. Weighty. Like their whole past was somehow about to be reignited, in a way he desperately didn't want, yet, despite that, he didn't draw back. Even then, he didn't listen to common sense and tell her this was a damned stupid idea.

How could he?

How could he when kissing her was the thing he wanted most on earth?

* * *

In the end, she had no doubts. No hesitancy. No concerns. She was fatalistic about the need to do this, to taste him, to dip a little way back in time and see how it felt. To see if he still stirred her body to fever pitch, if he kissed the same as she remembered. In the end, it was Sienna who closed the distance between them and claimed his mouth with her own, who pressed her body to his, who lifted a hand to his chest and pressed it there, fingers splayed wide over the Titans tattoo, right beneath his heart.

She was intentional about it, as if to say to him: it's just a kiss, it doesn't matter. But it *did* matter, and she realised that the second he took over, shifting his body weight so he could bring an arm around behind her back and hold her tighter against him, tilting her a little so he had better access to her mouth, so that his kiss wasn't just a touching of lips but an invasion of every single one of her senses, as his tongue slipped into her mouth, flicking her own, teasing her, making her body tremble with the power he clearly still had – if not to hurt her, to stir her desire to an indescribable peak.

A moan rose inside her, but Sienna refused to give it voice. She refused to say *anything*, even his name. She refused to tell him how good this felt, how much she liked being kissed by him, even when those words were spinning around and around and around in her mind.

Rational thought was still a part of Sienna, a lifeline she clung to, when her senses were scattering into disarray. A lifeline, a reminder that she had to control this, even when she wanted to lose control completely, to drag him to the shallows, lie down in the gently lapping waves and beg him to ravish her. To take her. To make her his.

It was an alarming thought, and it burst through her like a lightning bolt might spike the sky. She blinked, and pulled away from him abruptly, her breath ragged even when she tried to control it.

Aiden stared down at her, lips parted, eyes narrowed, cheeks slightly flushed, and where their bodies were still connected, she felt his arousal against her belly – rock-hard proof of his desire for her.

Which was precisely what she wanted, she thought, but without the sense of triumph she would have hoped to experience in such a moment. After all, kissing him and pulling away was step one, wasn't it?

Unfortunately, though, it was a hollow victory. For while Sienna was doing her level best to act as though she'd been completely unfazed by the kiss, she could admit, only to herself, that this was absolutely not the case. The kiss had fazed her. A lot. A lot, a lot, a lot. She was ridiculously, three-phase power fazed. Super fazed. Fazed to the power of a millionty suns.

It had left her weak at the knees and tingling in her veins and eyes flooded with stars and heart – the heart she intended to keep utterly under lock and key – thundering around in her chest so she could hardly hear anything above the frantic, desperate thwomping sound.

But too much was at stake for her to let him see *any* of that. This guy had shredded her self-confidence, her view of men, the world, had walked out on her like she was worthless, like their relationship was worthless. He'd left her pregnant, alone, heartbroken and bereft, all the while going on to live his absolute best life. Screw him. Not literally, she promised herself. Definitely not literally.

'Well,' she drawled, amazed that her voice only

wobbled slightly. 'I guess we've still got chemistry.' She shrugged, like it was neither here nor there for her. 'Who would have thought it, after all these years?'

He frowned, her tone obviously not what he expected. 'Sienna...'

What was he going to say, though? He just stared down at her, face serious, like he'd never seen her before.

In a way that turned her blood to lava and her stomach to mush.

She took a step back, pulling away from him, desperate for some distance, and brain space.

'We should keep looking for those flags,' she said, forcing herself to smile carelessly. 'Or give up and head back to the house. Your call.'

She didn't wait to hear what he decided. Instead, Sienna Mastrangelo turned on her heel and cut through the water, into the shallows, onto the shore, and as far away as she could get from Aiden without letting him realise that she'd found that whole kissing experience as discombobulating as anything.

* * *

'I was about to send out a bloody search party for you lot,' Astrid called, as their cart wheeled back onto the lawn nearest the house. 'Where have you guys been?' She jogged towards them, scanning their still-wet bodies and the assortment of flags that sat on the floor between them. And laughed. 'You did realise your quest was for *gold* flags? And that they were all on land?'

Sienna forced another smile, just like she'd been doing all afternoon, since that damned kiss. Anything Aiden said, she'd smiled serenely, doing her level best to act like she was someone who went around getting kissed every day of the week. NBD. Even when it was a very, very BD. She couldn't let it be.

'We did a little thwarting when we didn't see gold flags.'

'Yeah, someone else did a little thwarting of you,' she said, with an eye roll.

'Who?' Sienna demanded indignantly, as Paige emerged clutching a bunch of flags – a mix of purple, gold and red.

'Paige!' Sienna spluttered.

Astrid grinned. 'It's always the ones who look like butter wouldn't melt.'

Aiden swung out of the golf cart, eyes shifting to

Sienna's for a beat too long before moving to Astrid. 'Who won?'

'No one, you all bloody cheated,' Astrid said with mock impatience. 'Everyone came back with flags they weren't supposed to collect. First ones back were Chuck and Bella though.'

'That doesn't count as a win,' Sienna said, at the same time Aiden answered, 'So, no one won?'

Astrid glanced heavenward. 'You're both as competitive as each other.' She turned to give Aiden the full force of her attention. 'Blake's looking for you. Something about a suit try on.'

But Aiden didn't move. Not right away. He stayed standing there, looking at Astrid, as if trying to think of how to reply, then at Sienna, as if searching for something to say.

Eventually, he nodded once and muttered, 'So, I guess I'll see you later?'

Sienna was *exhausted.* Spending the better part of the day with Aiden had taken a freaking toll, but she wasn't going to show him that. She smiled, nodded, waved, and even managed to chirrup, 'I had fun!' And then, backpedalling abruptly when she thought about how that probably sounded, 'Hunting flags together, I mean.'

'We should do it again some time,' he replied,

and now Sienna had no idea if he was talking about the flags or the kiss, but either way, her cheeks flushed.

'No more hidden flags with you cheaters,' Astrid interjected. 'Next time we plan a party game, I'm gonna draft in some umpires to oversee the rules.'

Aiden grinned then, and Sienna's breath tightened in her throat, because when he smiled, those dimples seemed to groove deep into his cheeks and his eyes crinkled in a way that spoke of humour and happiness, but also of age – lines that weren't there when he was a teenager added to his air of maturity and charisma.

Astrid, beside her, squeezed Sienna's upper arm as soon as Aiden had turned his back.

'Well?' she demanded, as soon as he was out of earshot. 'What happened?'

His mouth on hers. Heat. Desire. His arousal. Need. Sienna's insides slicked with warmth as memory after memory sliced through her, forcing her to recall those passionate few seconds down on the shore. But when she turned to Astrid to confess the whole sordid event, the words just wouldn't come out.

Astrid was one of her best friends in the whole world, the woman who'd put her life on hold to try to mess with Aiden for the way he'd screwed Sienna around. And it was only a kiss. But somehow, the kiss felt private, and if the girls knew about it, they'd presume it was all part of Sienna getting her revenge on Aiden. They'd want to talk about it, to ask her questions, and Sienna didn't know if she could answer those questions yet. Even to herself.

'Nothing,' she said with a shrug. 'We looked for flags, got overheated, had a quick swim, came back.'

'That's it?'

His tongue tangling with hers. His hand on her back, pressing her forward. His tattoo and ass...

'Yep. That's it.'

Astrid pulled a face. 'Ugh. I was sure being together for so long would shake something loose.'

'Nope,' Sienna denied, cheeks heating at the lie. 'Honestly, I'm starting to want to abandon the whole idea of revenge,' she said with a shrug. 'At least, my part in it. I don't think flirting with Aiden then walking away is going to pay him back for what he did then.'

Astrid put an arm around Sienna's shoulders. 'No, but it may make you feel a smidge better about it.'

Sienna's eyes prickled with unshed tears. 'Honestly, seeing him again, maybe I'm more over the whole idea of revenge than I realised.'

And somehow, she wondered if that was true. It had been so easy to demonise Aiden when he'd just disappeared from her life. But seeing him again, and in the context of his relationship with Blake, being here at a family wedding, she couldn't keep seeing him as wholly bad. There was some good there, too.

So he'd run away from Ashbury Falls. What had she expected? That he'd stay there twiddling his thumbs 'til she was finished school? And then what? She'd never had the same college prospects as Aiden. He was always going to get headhunted to one of the big schools.

But they wouldn't have necessarily broken up, she reminded herself.

They could have stayed in touch, even just as friends. It was losing him in that capacity that had hurt her almost more than anything.

'It's just kinda complicated,' she finished with a shrug.

'Hmmm.' Astrid pursed her lips. 'Well, it's up to you, of course, though I will tell you, the others aren't going to want to scale back their operations, you know.'

Sienna stopped walking. 'What operations?'

Astrid's grin was serene. 'You didn't truly think they'd let you have all the fun?'

Fun? Fun? Sienna blinked. 'Oh no. What have they got planned?'

Astrid winked at Sienna. 'The less you know the better, love. Plausible deniability, and all that.'

* * *

In the small slice of time Sienna had alone in her room, she googled his tattoo. *Ad Meliora.*

Hurt twisted around her heart like a boa constrictor. She wouldn't have thought it was possible to feel any more hurt because of this jerk, but discovering that he had the Latin equivalent of 'towards a better future' inked into his skin was like a kick in the teeth.

Better.

Future.

Away from her.

Away from Ashbury Falls.

That's what he'd been thinking back then.

Not missing her.

Not wondering if he'd made a mistake.

But focusing on his sparkly, wondrously bright future. Bastard.

It's better if we stick to a clean break, Sienna. Don't call me again.

Because *Ad Meliora.*

She ground her jaw, adopting the phrase, co-opting it to her own purposes. Aiden 'Jackass' Carter was her past. A horrible part of her past. But after this week, she could put the ghost of him to bed and move on with her own brighter future. Sure, her dad was in prison and she was still stuck in Ashbury Falls – no way would she leave Melanie the same way Aiden left her. But finally, she'd be free of the grasp Aiden had held on her all these years. Finally, she'd be her own person again. She couldn't wait.

10

It wasn't like he was in the midst of the best sleep of his life or anything. How the hell could he sleep when Sienna had permeated his dreams like nothing else? She'd been taking the puck from the minute she'd arrived, and he had no freaking idea how to get it back.

Kissing her had been certifiable.

At least before the kiss he'd been able to pretend he wasn't *that* attracted to her any more.

Or, in his more honest moments of self-reflection, that at least she didn't feel that way about him.

But the kiss had lodged her right in the very middle of his mind, so he'd been lying in bed, tossing and turning for hours, trying to get her the hell out of his head. The problem was, every time he got close to drifting off, bam. There she was. Sexy. Smiling. So desirable he wanted to bust something.

So dangerous.

Because this wasn't just some horny puck bunny hitting him up for a one-night stand, but *Sienna*. Sienna Aria Mastrangelo. The one woman he'd ever *felt* anything for. The one woman who'd made him actually think maybe he could reach out with both hands and grab the whole big happily ever after fantasy Hollywood movies made you think were a guarantee in life.

But Aiden knew otherwise.

Aiden knew what love did to people. He'd seen the way his dad loved his mom. And the way his mom loved his dad, so much she wouldn't leave him, even when they were all in danger, every single damned day they'd stayed.

Love had been a nightmare in Aiden's house.

It was terrifying how many people signed on the dotted line for a future that could easily include that kind of bullshit.

Even Blake.

He made a rough groaning sound, bashing the pillow beside him with one big fist, staring up at the ceiling in the quiet of his room, with only the distant hum of rolling waves through the open French doors for company.

And then, a chirrup.

A cricket? But on acid. High-pitched and droning, it went on for about ten seconds, then stopped, so his mind was free to churn once more.

Blake and Astrid... they were different, he thought, flopping onto his back, staring up at the ceiling, frowning a little, because Blake having fallen in love, and with someone who accepted him so completely as he was, who loved every part of him, who forced Blake to be the best version of himself just by sharing her life with him, had started to puncture the tiniest of holes in the worldview Aiden had formed as a kid.

Because Blake and Astrid were happy. Not like their mom and dad in the peaceful moments, but truly happy. They loved each other, and more than that, they respected one another. Their relationship was... it was good.

It was real good.

But it didn't follow that he could have that with anyone. It didn't follow that the risks were worth it. Especially not if the risk was becoming like his father, and ever hurting Sienna.

So he really needed to not kiss her again. And

definitely to stop thinking about kissing her. As for the very X-rated dreams his subconscious kept trying to force him to endure, well, that was why he couldn't sleep.

Because if kissing her was bad, and thinking about kissing her was worse, then dreaming about having sex with her was the pits.

Even when it really, really wasn't.

He rolled onto his side. *Chirrrrupppp.*

He blinked.

It kept going, for at least ten seconds, like before. Getting any sleep had seemed almost impossible anyway, but with a noisy neighbour? He could just forget about it. He got up and, wearing only his box-ers, slammed on the light, stalked across the French doors and slammed them shut, satisfied by the noise they made.

Take that, cricket.

He spun to go back to bed, but his gaze fell on his reflection in the floor-to-ceiling mirror. He stopped walking. The tattoos. He put a hand on the Titan first, thinking back to the day he'd got it inked. On how it had felt to sign his contract with the club, to know how wanted he and Blake were. To know they really, truly belonged to something special. It was a feeling he'd never known before. Not even at college.

The Titans had gone all out to secure the twins, had made them front and centre of their line-up, promoting them to their fan base, building them in the league as star players. They were all in with the Carters, so the Carters were all in with the Titans.

His hand shifted sideways to the eagle – which he'd chosen to do one Fourth of July, and loved, because of how he felt about this country, and the opportunities he'd been given.

Then, he turned, slowly, pulling down his boxers and looking over his shoulder so he could see the writing.

Ad Meliora.

Towards Better Things.

It had been his first tattoo. He'd got it with his brother about a month after leaving Ashbury Falls. When he'd been closest to weakening and getting the hell out of there. When he'd been most tempted to walk away from the game, the scholarship, from Blake and his mom, and just go home.

Not to his dad. His father, as far as Aiden was concerned, could go to hell.

But Sienna... God, he'd missed her like he'd lost a damned leg.

He'd ached for her in a way he'd never known it was possible to ache for another human.

He'd been desperate to see her again. To be with her.

But Sienna was impossible, the life they'd talked about wanting just a stupid, childish fantasy. Or maybe, maybe it wasn't. But Aiden would never have taken that risk.

Because, what if he'd hurt her?

What if they'd stayed together, and one day, the same monster that lived inside his father had started to take up space in Aiden?

His dad hadn't always been such a pig.

When his parents first got married, they were happy. Normal.

But then, when the twins were born, and his mom went through post-natal depression, their dad couldn't cope. Instead of helping her, he got angry. And then, he got violent.

When he lost his job, and started to drink, he got angrier. And more violent. And then they were locked in a never-ending cycle of the beatings, the remorse, the apologies, the forgiveness, the honeymoon phase and then, bam. The violence again.

The day Aiden realised just how much he loved Sienna was the day he knew he had to leave.

Even without the catalyst of Blake's charges, and his fear for their mom, Aiden had realised that leaving Sienna and making a clean break of it was the right thing for her. Sienna was smart, funny, motivated and gorgeous. She was going to go a long way in life, with or without him. He knew their break-up would hurt in the moment, but she'd be better off down the track.

At least, that's what he'd told himself then.

So why was she still living in Ashbury Falls?

What happened to all her big plans of making a life for herself in a big city?

Chiiiirrrrupppp.

He startled, glancing around the room. Because the sound wasn't coming from outside, as he'd suspected, but rather, inside his damned bedroom.

It didn't chirrup for long enough for him to find it, but he stayed standing perfectly still, listening and waiting.

Another quick chirrup, from somewhere near his bed.

Silence.

He kept waiting.

Silence.

But the moment he flicked the light off, it chirruped again, and he cursed, the noise ripped from his chest. But it wasn't really about the insect, he admitted to himself.

It was Sienna, yet again.

It was their kiss; it was their fight.

It was the way she'd been after the kiss, so nonchalant and unbothered. Like her world hadn't just been shaken to smithereens. Like she went around kissing guys on the beach every day of the week.

Like he was nothing to her.

Which was what you wanted, a voice reminded him stubbornly. But the voice was wrong.

Aiden didn't want to be nothing to her.

He didn't want to hurt her, but he did want her.

He did need her.

He wasn't stupid enough to fantasise about an impossible future.

But he could offer this week, just like Blake had said.

He could ask her to consider spending some time with him.

Not in a golf cart, with everyone waiting on them to return, but here, in his room, or her room, away from the madness of the wedding, and all those prying eyes. Just him, her, and the unfinished business that had exploded into his present-day life and was making it impossible to think about anything else.

He could ask her to let him have this week. Just

one week. And then, this time, when he let her go, it wouldn't just be on his terms, but on theirs, because they'd both be ready for it. They'd both know it was what they had to do, to get on with their lives. No harm, no foul, but quite possibly a shit tonne of fun, if she agreed.

* * *

'You look like death warmed up,' Paige, Astrid's curvy red-haired friend observed cheerily, over a plate of sausages and egg.

'Thanks,' Aiden responded wryly.

'Trouble sleeping?' Bella, with her posh NYC accent, asked next, long blonde hair swooshed over one shoulder.

He grunted across the breakfast table. 'There was a cricket in my room.'

'A cricket?' Edvin Larrson, the Titans' goalie, with his blond hair pulled up into a messy bun, glanced down the table at Aiden. Everyone stopped talking.

He shrugged. 'I had the doors open all day. Fucker must have got in then.'

He nearly missed the way Paige looked at Bella, who dipped her head forward and pressed her lips into her napkin. But he sure as hell didn't miss the way Sienna was staring at him, eyes narrowing thoughtfully, lips pursed, as though hanging off his every word. He was tempted to tell her that the cricket had been the least of his nocturnal worries.

'Did you find it?' Astrid asked conversationally, reaching for some bacon and piling it on her plate.

'Does this look like the face of a man who was able to find – and get rid of – the damned thing?'

'Oy,' Blake cautioned, and Aiden winced, because he had unfairly taken his bad mood out on his future sister-in-law.

'Sorry.' He held up a hand placatingly. 'It drove me crazy,' he muttered, sipping an orange juice. 'I reckon it must have been in the mattress or something.'

Out of the corner of his eyes, he saw Sienna turn and look at Paige, one brow crooked.

'What?' he asked, rounding on them. 'Are you some kind of expert in cricketology or something?'

Paige smiled serenely. 'That's me, chief cricketologist at your disposal.'

He smiled curtly, realising they all thought it was freaking hilarious, and set about attacking his plate, instead of his companions.

'There are other rooms, bro,' Blake said, once they'd finished eating and everything was being cleared away by the staff, and it was just the two of them. 'You can swap.'

'Nah, what are the chances it'll be there again tonight?'

Blake looked sceptical. 'Okay, well, it's up to you. But I'm pretty sure the end room on that floor is free. The one with the door on the right.'

'Thanks. I'll keep it in mind.'

* * *

'A cricket, you guys?' Sienna's big blue eyes roamed from Bella to Astrid to Paige, before settling back on Bella, who looked the guiltiest of them all.

'No, never,' Paige swore, crossing a finger over her chest.

'Definitely not,' Bella promised, but her smile gave her away.

'You guys,' Sienna laughed softly, pulling them further out onto the terrace where they could be sure they were completely alone. 'What did you do?'

'Nothing.' Paige blinked with mock innocence. 'We definitely didn't put a noisy little thing in his mattress.'

'His mattress!' Sienna squawked. 'That's animal cruelty, for one thing.'

'It's not a real cricket,' Paige responded quickly, as if that was super reassuring.

'It's not?'

Bella shook her head. 'It's just a toy. It's remote controlled. It was only meant to go off a few times, but I guess it might have broken or something.' She grimaced, but could barely hold back the smile. 'Poor baby looked pretty wrecked this morning.'

'Yeah, he really did,' Sienna agreed, though in truth, she'd found it hard to look beyond those ridiculously broad shoulders and chiselled cheekbones to notice the bags under his eyes.

The three women were staring back at her with such a combination of emotions that she burst out laughing.

'You're okay with it?' Bella asked in a rush.

'Astrid told us you wanted to call the whole thing off,' Paige added. 'But we didn't think that was really fair.'

Bella nodded. 'He deserves a little bit of messing with.'

Sienna held up her hands. 'I have *no* problem with you guys messing with him a bit. Harmless pranks. That's fine. I just don't want... I don't feel right pretending I'm okay with what happened back then, when the truth is, I'm just not.' She turned to

Astrid. 'I know he's about to become your brother-in-law, and I know you see a whole other side to him, but I just want to get through your beautiful wedding, focusing on you, and Blake, and then move on with my life. With him completely removed from it.'

Astrid nodded sympathetically.

'Has it been at all cathartic to see him again?' Bella asked.

'Well, no. Not really. I mean, I wish I could say that he's not as hot as I remember, or that seeing him again has made me realise it was all just a teenage crush, but that's definitely not true.' She lifted one shoulder. 'I do know it never would have worked out between us, but I think I knew that even before we got to the island.'

'Why do you say that, love?' Astrid asked gently.

'He just didn't want me enough.' She said the words that had been swirling around in her mind for a long, long time. 'And that's okay. He was entitled to make that choice. He was entitled to walk away from me.' She breathed out a long, slow breath. Now *that* felt like an exorcism. 'Come on,' she said, linking an arm through Astrid's. 'I saw on the itinerary that this is a free day. Why don't we go do something together, just us girls?'

11

Aiden waited at the gate of the airport, and saw the moment his mom came off the flight. Slim and tall, she walked with squared shoulders and a relaxed gait. She was a totally different person to the woman who'd been in that godawful marriage in shithole Ashbury Falls.

That woman had cowered.

She'd done her level best to avoid notice and attention, had made fading into the wallpaper an artform. She'd hunched down, avoided eye contact, silently shuffled her feet.

Seeing her stride out into the balmy Mediterranean air with her dark hair coiffed into a glossy style, wearing designer clothes, Aiden found it hard to regret a damned decision he'd made.

Getting her out of Ashbury Falls had been the right thing.

They'd all been born again, in one way or another, after the departure. Hockey had started a whole new life for him and Blake, paving the way for them with riches two poor kids from the country could never have imagined.

'Oh, Aiden.' Cynthia Carter spotted him when she reached the top of the ramp. He reached for her hand luggage on autopilot, before leaning down and giving her a peck on the cheek. 'How are you, darling?'

'Good,' he lied.

She frowned, scanning his face. 'You look tired.'

He arched a brow. 'That seems to be the consensus.'

'What's the matter?'

'A damned bug in my room is all. I'm fine, Mom. Just fine.'

'Hmm. Well, then. Let's get my bag, and on the way to the island, you can tell me everything I've already missed.'

Since following the boys out of Ashbury Falls,

Cynthia Carter had set up a whole new life for herself. As the twins became more and more successful,
and needed her less and less, and the shadows of her
past failed to reach her, Cynthia really came into her
own, forming tight friendships with dozens of
women. She had friends at the gym, where she
worked out each morning, friends in her book club,
friends at the thrift shop she volunteered at. So, the
fact that one of her new-life besties was turning sixty
had caused a scheduling conflict for Cynthia Carter –
hence the delayed arrival to the wedding week of
Blake and Astrid. 'Let's start with Blake. How is he?'

'Walking on air.'

Her smile relaxed. 'I'm glad to hear it. Astrid has
been so good for him, hasn't she?'

'No arguments from me.'

'Now, if only there was someone you could meet.
Have I told you about Judy Sanderson's grand-
daughter?'

He threw her a look. 'Only about a dozen times.'

'She'd be just right for you.' But as his mother set
about extolling the virtues of a woman he'd already
heard described ad nauseum, all he could think
about was Sienna's body, pressed against his, and
how damned great it had felt to kiss her again.

* * *

'Oh, Sienna!' Cynthia Carter's voice was louder than Sienna had ever heard it, but that aside, Sienna recognised it instantly. Three steps from the bottom of the elegant sweeping staircase, making her way to the foyer for their nightly pre-dinner aperitivo before dinner was served on the deck, Sienna's footing almost faltered.

She'd known Cynthia was coming, obviously. This was Blake's mom, and Astrid had mentioned her often enough in the lead up to the wedding for Sienna to have been theoretically prepared for this. But understanding something academically was completely different to being properly ready for the moment of coming to face to face with a ghost from your past.

'Cynthia.' Her voice was a little uneven. She swallowed, to bring moisture back to her mouth. Behind Cynthia, the group of guests milled happily, apparently oblivious to the mental turmoil Sienna was navigating. There was nothing for it; Sienna had to get this over and done with. 'Hello.'

'Hello? Oh, honey love. Come here,' she said with a pretty laugh, wrapping her slender arms around

Sienna and pulling her in for a huge hug. Sienna was not tall, and despite Cynthia's slender build, she had the same ability to simply engulf Sienna as Blake and Aiden did.

Sienna stood there, totally swallowed up, by Aiden's mom, and a thick fog of memories.

'Goodness gracious, my girl, it's been far too long. Aiden tells me you're still in Ashbury Falls?'

'I am.' Sienna unconsciously swept her gaze across the room, until she saw Aiden, over by the door. He held a beer in one hand, and was in conversation with Chuck Daly, but his attention was clearly on Sienna and Cynthia. She wrenched her focus back to the older woman.

'Well, then, you're going to have to sit by me at dinner and tell me everything about it. I haven't been there for a lifetime.' For a moment, something like sadness shadowed Cynthia's expression, but she covered it with a quick smile. 'And what are you up to, darlin'? My son was a little light on the details.'

That was no surprise.

Aiden didn't know anything about Sienna's life now.

Her lips pulled to the side. 'Same old, same old,' she demurred. 'I'm more interested in hearing about you. Why don't we get a drink and you can tell me what you're up to these days?'

'I'd like that,' Cynthia confirmed with a nod.

* * *

Watching his mother and one-time girlfriend gossip over champagne was doing strange things to Aiden's belly. Like making it flip and flop as if he was about to play for the Stanley Cup. More and more guests had been arriving each day, so the foyer that had seemed sparse on the first night was more filled out now, making it hard to keep a clear line of sight on Sienna.

Which shouldn't have bothered him. Not even a little.

Except no matter how much he kept telling himself that, Aiden couldn't stop staring at her.

And it wasn't just because of that dress, though that definitely didn't help.

Since when had she started buying this sort of thing? He couldn't imagine her owning anything like this in Ashbury Falls. Bright red and skintight, it wrapped around her body in a way that his dreams would undoubtedly have fun with later that night.

Not that he'd be getting any sleep anyway, if that damned cricket had anything to say.

He ground his teeth and tried to focus on the investment opportunity Chuck was describing. Ribbing aside, he admired the other man's technological prowess, and this did sound like a great chance to get in on a cool new project at the ground level.

He just didn't exactly have the brain space to devote to it, then and there.

'So, you want to see more info?'

'Yeah.' Thank God, Aiden thought. More information that he could compute at a later date. Not when Sienna was leaning close to his mother and whispering something in her ear, so Cynthia tossed her head back and laughed. Sienna's lips, painted a perfect shade of red, curved into a slow smile, and at that moment, her gaze flicked across the room and landed square on his face, so his heart felt like it was about to jolt out of his chest.

He should definitely not have kissed those lips.

He should definitely not be standing in the middle of this drinks event thinking about what those lips had felt like. Or how damned much he'd like to stride across the room, throw her over his shoulder and drag her back to the beach, or the nearest bed, or hell, even the lawn outside, and finish what they'd started.

He groaned softly.

'All good, bro?' Chuck asked.

'I wish everyone would stop fucking asking me that,' he snapped, then offered a grimace by way of apology. 'Sorry, man. It's been... a weird couple of days.'

Chuck nodded thoughtfully. 'Sienna mentioned you guys used to date.'

Something about that landed strangely for him. He didn't know if he was glad Sienna had mentioned their history, or annoyed, because somehow it trivialised it. 'It was a long time ago.'

Chuck's grin was knowing. 'Yeah, I can tell.'

'What's that supposed to mean?'

'Just that you're staring with definite intent.'

Aiden forced himself to look anywhere *but* at Sienna, grinding his teeth to find the other man laughing.

'Why don't you ask her out and get it over with?'

Alarm bells sounded. Panic slicked his insides. Ask Sienna out? Well, wasn't that just a whole can of worms he'd been spending pretty much every waking moment avoiding peering into? Blake's suggestion of 'hanging out' for a casual week was one thing, but this was a whole other level. Dating meant a promise. The beginning of something Aiden didn't want to ever finish.

'Nah, it's not like that.'

'You sure?'

He swallowed, his throat rough and dry. 'Yeah.'

But his eyes slid back to Sienna and his gut lurched. God damn it, she was the most beautiful woman he'd ever seen, but that didn't even matter. It wasn't about how she looked. It was the way she laughed. The way she talked. The way she listened. The way she...

Fuuuuck.

And thank Christ, at that moment, one of the staff rang the bell that signalled dinner was being served, so Aiden could finally hope for some form of distraction to get Sienna off his mind. There must be someone else he could talk to. Someone else, who wouldn't interrogate him about his failed relationship. And maybe, if he was a really good boy, he could find a seat facing away from her, so he couldn't look at her without craning in his chair. Yes, that's exactly what he'd do. Look for a seat as far away from Sienna as he could possibly get—

'Aiden!' His mother's voice easily cut across to him. He turned without thinking, to find her and Sienna still side by side, like they'd made some kind of blood pact not to part ways. 'Come and sit with us, dear. I'm having such a good time catching up with your old friend.'

Panic flooded his veins once more as his eyes landed on Sienna. To his relief, one side of her lips quirked in a half-smile, and she did a small shrug, as if to say, 'What the hell?' And didn't that just piss him off even more? That she was so totally fine with all this. Like none of it freaking bothered her.

Just like the kiss hadn't bothered her, when it had been bothering the bejeezus out of him ever since.

He grudgingly cut across the room, to the seats they'd chosen. There was an empty one beside his mother, and another beside Sienna. He had to make a split-second decision – did he want to be next to her? Or across from her? Was it better to be conscious of how close they were, or to constantly be able to stare at her?

'There you are, darling.' His mother made the choice for him, nodding at the seat to Sienna's left. 'That will do just fine.'

He ground his teeth as he pulled out the seat, plonking himself down, aware as he had been at each of these damned meals that the spindly chairs were *not* designed for someone of his build in mind. A glance down the table showed a few of them in the same boat. Blake, Edvin, and Danny all seemed to be sitting with the same caution he was.

'Sienna was just telling me about her studies,' his mother said, flagging down a waiter and lifting her hand in a mime of drinking.

The waiter nodded and disappeared.

'You're studying?' The second he asked the question, he realised he'd been avoiding asking her anything like this. If he could keep her to some two-dimensional rendering in his mind, then she'd be that much easier to hold in the tightly sealed box he'd mentally shoved her into all those years ago.

'Law,' she said, reaching for a bread roll and breaking it in half. Her eyes didn't quite meet his though. He wondered about that. Maybe she wasn't as unbothered as he thought.

'What happened to medicine, anyway?'

'I went off the idea.'

'Why?'

The waiter returned with a bottle of Italian white, and began to fill the glasses. He was vaguely aware of Chuck coming to sit opposite him, beside Cynthia.

'Hey, I'm Chuck. Friend of the groom,' Chuck said, grinning at Cynthia.

'Cynthia, mother of the groom,' Cynthia replied,

holding her hand out to shake. 'And I've heard all about you. It's lovely to put a face to the name.' She turned back to Sienna and Aiden. 'Have you met Sienna?'

'They've met,' Aiden responded, gut rolling as he remembered the sight of them coming back from their run, standing close. It had felt like a punch in the gut to see them looking so damned good together. So *right*.

'Chuck's my groomsman, for the wedding,' Sienna responded, smiling easily. Beneath the table, his hand formed a fist on his knee. Conversation moved on, to talk of Chuck, and his work, and Sienna responded to all of it as though they were old, comfortable friends.

He hadn't seen this side of her.

Back then, she'd been a kid, still growing into herself. But now, she was an adult woman. And a knock-out. It was hardly surprising to realise she was comfortable with guys hitting on her. But she was even charming his mother. That wasn't really a shock either, but somehow, he'd expected Sienna might find it hard to connect with the other woman, who was so reminiscent of a time in their lives that maybe – he might have thought – she'd want to forget.

Evidently not.

'Okay, quieten down,' Blake said, scraping back the spindly chair and standing at the head of the table, while a beaming Astrid looked on with pride. 'We're just a few days from the wedding – it's too late to back out now, Twinkle Toes.' He grinned at his clearly loved-up bride.

'It's never too late,' she admonished. 'But I'm not even contemplating it.'

'You have no idea how glad I am to hear that,' he said, voice gruff. Aiden glanced across at his mother; she had a starry look in her eyes, like seeing Blake so happy and in love was the epitome of her wildest dreams. Of their own volition, his eyes roamed further sideways, to Sienna. She was looking at Blake, a beatific smile on her face. But when she sensed Aiden looking at her, and she glanced at him instead, the smile slipped for a moment, and her lips parted on an exhalation of surprise.

'So, we have some more fun and games planned – just think of us as your friendly cruise directors.' He grinned. 'There'll also be an excursion off island, the day after tomorrow. You should all have got the options in the schedule Bella emailed around.' Aiden looked back at Blake in time to see him wink at the blonde friend.

'There's a survey link you can respond to by tomorrow night,' Bella said, her voice cutting across the room with natural authority. 'To get a gauge of numbers.'

'Right.' Blake added.

'But you can also stick around on the island and just chill out,' Astrid said. 'This isn't camp. No compulsory activities.'

'Except the wedding,' Paige interjected.

'Yeah, that would be good.' Blake nodded. 'Anyway, now that everyone's here' – he looked specifically at Cynthia Carter then – 'we just wanted to say – thank you. Thank you for coming and sharing this with us. Thank you for understanding that for two people who never really wanted the big white wedding, the idea of sharing this day not just with each other but with the most important people in our lives, is the icing on the cake of the best damned adventure we'd ever imagined.' He turned to look at Astrid. 'The thing is, I never thought it would be like this.' It was like he'd tuned out everyone in the whole room. She seemed to have as well, if the intense way she was staring at Blake was anything to go by. 'I've been to a million weddings and never really understood it, until I met you. And I realised I'd been living some kind of half-life this whole time. That meeting you really woke me up, made everything make sense.

Astrid, you and this baby are everything to me. I freaking love you.'

Astrid's eyes teared up, and she nodded, apparently lost for words.

He heard a sound and glanced over to see his mother had clapped her hands together and was holding them to her chest. There was a huge cheer, punctuated by a loud 'Whoop!' that had come from Sienna's tiny frame.

Conversation resumed, and Blake negotiated his bulky frame back into the tiny chair.

Chuck let out a low whistle. 'He almost makes it sound appealing, huh?'

'What's that, dear?' Cynthia asked, taking a sip of her wine as she dabbed at the corners of her eyes.

'Marriage.' Chuck's eyes were settled firmly on Aiden then. 'What do you think? Reckon you'll ever sign up for a walk down the aisle?'

Did he imagine Sienna stiffening beside him? On autopilot, he glanced at her, but she was busy toying with the tablecloth.

'Nah.' He found the word strangely hard to say. He cleared his throat. 'It's not for me.'

'Oh, Aiden.' Cynthia tsked. 'Don't be absurd. Marriage can be for anyone.'

He compressed his lips.

'You just haven't met the right person,' Cynthia continued – unhelpfully. Because beside him sat someone who might very well have been the 'right' person if he'd been a little less fucked up about marriage and his ability to *not* turn into his father the asshole.

'It's not that,' he said, reaching for his own wine and taking a gulp. 'I've just always known – I'm not the marrying sort.'

Beside him, Sienna shifted a little. From discomfort? God knew he was feeling it.

'What about you, gorgeous?' Chuck – who Aiden was quickly coming to realise had Blake's shit-stirring personality traits but to the max – addressed Sienna. 'Have you left some aspiring husband back in – where'd you say you were from?'

'Ashbury Falls,' Cynthia said, and for a moment, her features tightened and her shoulders tensed, so all the protective instincts Aiden had honed since boyhood flared to life.

'Right.' Chuck nodded, oblivious to the emotions he was sparking with his questions. 'Is there a lucky guy back there, waiting for you?'

'No one serious,' she said, and Aiden felt a tightening in his gut. She'd said the same thing to him on the first night and it had bothered him as much then as it did now.

'What does that mean?' he heard himself ask, even when he was pretty sure it was none of his business.

'It means I was seeing a guy, for a few years.' She shrugged, but Aiden hardly noticed. He felt like a knife was being plunged into his gut. Was this why she seemed so unfazed by him? She'd been seeing a guy for *a few years* after him? Well, what was that if not the quintessential act of moving on? In contrast to Aiden, who'd dated sparingly and never for long enough to know more than a woman's full name and maybe her place of birth. Relationships that were both superficial and transactional – in the sense that he knew what women saw in him: the ability to find the spotlight. To draw attention to a cause, or bolster their public profile. And he was happy to help – better than creating the impression he was anything other than Ice. 'But it's nothing. It's more – he has a kid, Melanie. I've basically helped raise her, since she was around three. She's like my step-daughter,' Sienna said, lifting a shoulder, a smile on her face, reaching for her phone. 'Look.' She pulled a picture up on the screen, holding it out for Chuck and Cynthia.

Aiden dug his fingers into his thigh, relishing the spark of pain that throbbed through him at the too-hard contact. He felt like the whole world had gone wonky, because Sienna was talking about people that were important to her, and he had no part in that. She had a whole other life, and belonged to them, in a way. She was a part of their lives and family.

'Isn't she gorgeous?'

'Oh, yes,' Cynthia cooed. 'Look, Aiden. What a lovely girl.'

Sienna glanced up at him, biting on her lip. With guilt? She sure *looked* guilty. But why would she? What had she done wrong? Abso-fucking-lutely nothing. They'd been broken up. Not just broken up – he'd walked out on her. So she'd moved on, just like he'd texted her to. Good for Sienna. And all these years he'd been carrying a gut load of guilt, feeling like he'd screwed up her life or something.

Sienna turned the phone then, showing him a photo of a girl at her twelfth birthday, going by the cake in the foreground with lots of candles on it. Sienna stood behind the girl, one arm around her shoulders, and some guy, tall and lanky, stood on the other side.

This guy? This was who she'd hooked up with

after Aiden? It wasn't like he recognised him, but he looked like a loser.

'Who are they?' he grunted, barely acknowledging the waiter who came and placed entrees down in front of each of them.

'No one you know. They moved into town about six months after you left.' Her face paled a little.

'And you started dating him.'

Sienna sipped her wine. 'I started babysitting for him. I needed money.' Her cheeks flushed pink; her tone was defiant. 'We started dating a while after that.'

'Right.'

He speared a tip of asparagus with a bit too much force. Emotions burled through him. Emotions like anger and rage, the kinds of emotions he never, ever let himself feel, because they scared the shit out of him. He didn't want to be like his father. He wouldn't let darkness take over. He would never put anyone at risk.

But Sienna had always been capable of breaking his boundaries down. Whether that meant making him love more fiercely than he wanted to, or fear she was – and always had been – his undoing. He'd been given the nickname 'Ice' for a reason. He was cold.

Cold on the ice, cold off it. Except with her. Even now...

'It's nice that she has you, dear,' Cynthia was saying, returning to the girl in the photograph.

'Maybe. I think it's even nicer that I have her.'

Aiden sat up straighter. His stomach dropped. His insides clenched. Because Sienna's façade slipped, just for a second. Showing that she *was* fazed. She was bothered. And damn it, if the way she said that hadn't been one of the most wistful, loneliest things he'd ever heard.

12

His mood went from bad to worse. Where the fuck was the freaking bug? He slammed his fist into the pillow. The cricket chirruped. He stood up, stormed across the room and flashed on the light. Like the cricket would just jump out at him and announce itself.

He stood completely still. Listening.

Nothing.

But right at the moment he went back to bed, it let out another squeak and he cursed again. *Screw this.*

He reached for a shirt and pulled it over his head, then wrenched the door inwards and strode out of his bug-infested room, down the corridor, to the room at the end his brother had suggested he could use instead.

He needed to sleep.

Then again, sleep was flooded with dreams of Sienna, which was arguably more disruptive than the cricket, but nonetheless... at least he stood a chance of waking up tomorrow a little more rested. If also with a hard-on that wouldn't quit.

Had Blake said the door on the left, or the right? He frowned, knocking on one of the doors at random and hoping for the best. A very male grumble came from within. Not this door, then. Must be the other one.

He opened the door, closed it with a click then flicked on the light switch.

And froze.

Because there on the Juliette balcony with the French doors open stood – unmistakably – Sienna. Even with her back to him, there was no mistaking it was her. Her small, slender body was silhouetted by the moonlight and the floaty cotton nightgown she wore, leaving even less to the imagination than her wet clothes had the other day.

He knew he should leave. Obviously. There'd been some kind of mistake. Blake had thought the room was empty, when it really wasn't.

Sienna was using this room. As if to confirm that, he glanced around and saw little signs of her occupation – a phone charging on the nightstand, a dress hanging up on the bathroom door, a pair of shoes tucked neatly by the en suite.

He stepped forward without meaning to, eyes focused on her with a laser-like intensity.

Leave. Every fibre of his soul was exhorting him to think rationally. At best, this was a stupid mistake they'd laugh about. At worst, she'd be scared shitless. Or think he was stalking her.

He took another step towards her. And another. On the threshold of the balcony, he cleared his throat, so as not to alarm her. And pigs might fly. She spun around, face pale, lips parted as if to scream. At the last minute, she detoured away from that scream and whisper-shouted his name instead. 'What the heck are you doing in my room?'

He held his hands up placatingly. She was gripping a cup of tea; he should be glad he wasn't wearing the contents of it, he supposed.

'A mistake,' he said, truthfully, but her eyes narrowed.

'Oh, yeah? You just happened to wander in here in the middle of the night? What the actual, Aiden?'

'There's some bug in my room,' he explained, a

little defensively to even his own ears. 'Blake told me this room was free.' His brow furrowed. 'Obviously he got it wrong.'

Her face crinkled a little more, with a look of deep concentration. He held his breath, wondering what she was going to say. Tell him to get the hell out of there? That would make sense. That would be smart. For both of them.

Her throat shifted as she swallowed; he didn't move. He didn't offer to leave. He just stared at her. Remembering. Wanting. Freaking out, if he was honest.

'I swear,' he said, voice gruff. 'This was an honest mistake.'

She crossed her arms over her chest.

Don't look down. Don't be a creep. Don't look... fuck. He squeezed his eyes shut the second they landed on her beautiful breasts. Breasts he remembered vividly, despite the passage of time. Breasts that had been flooding his mind since their kiss the other day.

'Yeah, well, I *honestly* think you should go find another room.'

Great idea. Even a chirruping cricket would be better than just standing like a gawping fish in her bedroom, invading her privacy and ruminations. At midnight...

'Why are you up so late?' He opened his eyes and

looked at her, with the self-discipline of a ninja, focusing on her eyes, and nothing below neck level.

'I... couldn't sleep,' she replied. Haltingly. Defensively. *Interesting.*

'Want some company?' He had no idea what possessed him to ask that. He hadn't planned to. But seeing her just standing there with a cup of tea, suddenly, the thing he wanted most in the world was to grab a cup of his own and join her on the small balcony. Just to stand there, side by side, staring out at the moonlit ocean.

'Do you mean *you*?' she squeaked, like he'd suggested they do a nudie run through the hotel.

'I don't see anyone else in your room.'

'That's because it's my room,' she pointed out archly. And then, in a way that made his chest throb with a fast tattoo, 'But whatever. Suit yourself.'

Did that mean he could stay?

'Kettle's over there, if you want something. I brought my own tea bags.'

Relief flooded his chest.

It was like scoring the winning goal in the dying minutes of the game. He grinned as he expelled a long, slow breath. 'You brought your own tea bags?'

Her tone was defensive. 'So?'

'You thought they wouldn't have tea on the island?'

'I didn't know if they'd have the kinds of tea I like.'

He laughed. 'Some kind of fancy tea?'

'Do I seem like a fancy girl?' she replied, pulling a face. 'I thought they'd *only* have fancy tea, and I just like my everyday peppermint. I didn't want it to have weird crap added in.'

'What makes you think it'd have something fancy?' he asked, walking towards the kettle, but glancing across at her. Sienna stood on the threshold of the balcony, one shoulder propped against the door jamb.

'Hello... have you seen where we're staying?'

He looked around the room and shrugged.

'Okay, Moneybags, you're probably used to living in the lap of luxury, but not this girl. I mean – this is a world-famous billionaire's island. This mansion is probably the size of Ashbury Falls. There's an army of staff, four swimming pools, I don't know how many spas, a restaurant, a bar, a golf course... do you really blame me for thinking the peppermint tea might have, I don't know, cinnamon or rooibos or freaking diamond dust?'

'Rooibos?' he repeated.

'Another type of tea.' She waved a hand through the air, then placed it on her hip, making his mouth go instantly dry as he couldn't help but notice – for the millionth time – her slim silhouette and beautiful curves. He turned back to the now-boiled kettle abruptly, throwing a bag into a mug and sloshing some water in.

The mug felt like something out of a doll's house in his hand. Dainty and fine. Like he could break it with the wrong grip.

Like he could break a person.

Except he wouldn't. He'd never get close enough to break anyone.

He wasn't his father.

He was Ice.

In control, always. *Always.* Except when he was around Sienna. Then, his famed control felt like it was constantly slipping away from him. It felt like a damned myth.

'Have you ever been here before?'

He carried the mug towards her. As he approached, as if she wanted to keep some distance between them, she stepped out onto the balcony and rested her elbows against the wrought-iron railing.

Those stunning island palms were silhouetted against the night sky. The moon, high and full, was a

big ball of silver glittering over them, forming a tri-
angle of light that bounced on the ocean's waves. The
sky was a moody black, with hints of pale grey clouds
floating towards the moon every so often.

'Yeah,' he answered, as he positioned himself beside her and looked away from the line of palms and
directly beneath them. 'For a couple of team bonding
things.'

She let out a low whistle. 'So I could have called
and asked about the tea situation,' she said, tilting an
unexpected smile in his direction. His heart popped.
Guilt almost choked him. *Don't call me again, Sienna.*

'Listen, Si, there's something I want to say to you.
Something I should have explained before this.'

The diminutive version of her name just slipped
out; her eyes were instantly wary. 'It's okay.'

'No, it's not. Listen. The whole... not taking your
calls thing. And telling you not to call me again. That
was a bullshit thing to do. I'm sorry.'

She turned away from him, staring out to sea. In
profile, her face was set in serious lines. There was no
sense of relief at having finally apologised. He just
felt... hollowed out. Because no apology could
change what he'd done. Nothing could fix it.

'It's okay,' she repeated, with a lift of her shoulders that only seemed to emphasise her tension.

'You deserved so much more.'

'Aiden, it was—'

'Don't say it.' Frustration made his voice curt. 'Don't tell me it ages ago. I mean, I know it was. But I still feel like an asshole for doing that to you. That didn't go away.'

'You were an asshole,' she said simply, surprising him again, because she followed it up with a short laugh. But her eyes were hollow. Her lips were held in a tight line. 'Did you ever wonder why I was calling?'

His eyes roamed her face. 'I don't know.'

She nodded slowly, though it was hardly an answer. He tried again.

'I just knew that if I picked up that phone and heard your voice, I'd come home again. Stuff my career, Blake's career, stuff our mom getting away from Dad. I'd screw it all up, just to go back to you. You have no idea how much I wanted to do that, Si. How long it took before I stopped feeling that aching pull to you and the town I'd sworn I'd break free of.'

Her lips parted. She stared at him, shaking her head a little. 'I don't believe you.'

How could she not? Wasn't it obvious? 'It took every ounce of my strength to walk away from you. So much was on the line. Not just for me, but for

Blake and Mom. Even for my dad. He'd have ended up killing one of us if we didn't get the hell out of there.'

'Aiden...'

'I never wanted to hurt you.'

'Yeah,' she said, unevenly. 'But you did.'

'I know.'

She turned back to the ocean, taking a sip of her tea, then gripping the railing with one hand. Her skin glowed white at the knuckles, as though she were holding on for dear life. As though she were bracing herself for an inevitable fall.

In the end, though, it was Aiden who fell. Aiden whose whole reality crumbled apart at the seams, when she uttered, so softly the words were almost carried away on the sea breeze, 'I was pregnant, Aiden. That's why I was calling you.'

* * *

'What?' He couldn't have looked more shocked if she'd told him his face had sprouted shimmery golden wings. 'What did you just say?' He moved closer, urgency in the words.

She held her ground, even when she felt all light-headed and dizzy after admitting something to him she'd thought she never would. But somehow, standing there together, reaching back into their shared past and discussing his not taking her calls, she'd felt a need to set the record straight. To make him understand something about what that had been like for her; how badly he'd hurt her. And why she hadn't been able to let him go. They'd created a baby together. They'd lost that baby. And she alone knew it. She alone had known and grieved. Suddenly, it felt like the baby deserved for Aiden to be aware of this important event.

'I wasn't calling to get you back. I was calling to tell you that you were going to be a dad.'

'Holy fuck.' He closed his eyes and reached for the railing. His Adam's apple jerked in his throat and his jaw was perfectly angular. 'I... Sienna. I didn't... you could have... you should have texted me, for Christ's sake.'

She felt her eyes go buggy. 'Please don't tell me what I *should* have done. I was sixteen, alone, scared out of my brain and my boyfriend – who I was still very, very much in love with – had left town, and told me he never wanted to see me again. Told me to move on, just like he had. So... forgive me if I didn't explore absolutely every possible avenue here. I wasn't exactly thinking straight.'

He dipped his head once, his face screwing up in silent apology. 'Fuck.'

'You said that already.'

'I don't understand. Can we just – I need to sit down,' he admitted, looking inside before stalking back through the doors and grabbing the single seat and positioning it so he could swing his big legs across the pad and brace his elbows on the back.

She moved inside gingerly, as if wary now of the can of worms she'd opened into their shared past. A shared past she'd lived and breathed all on her own.

'What happened?'

She hesitated. Her heart hurt. Her stomach twisted. Her breath caught in her throat. Her whole body trembled in a visceral reaction to remembering that awful night. 'I lost the baby.' Somehow, the words emerged stiff. As if her voice box had 100 per cent got the memo on what would happen if she gave into even a hint of weakness and grief.

His curse tore through the room, a violent eruption. An apology. Pain and grief. 'Our baby.'

Our baby.

Tears scratched the back of her throat. She pressed her teeth together, trying not to let that possessive, partnershippy phrase land with a thud in her heart.

'Yeah.'

His skin was so pale beneath his tan she actually thought he might pass out, and out of nowhere, she had the strangest image of a huge, old tree in a forest being felled. Men like Aiden didn't faint as though they were some Regency romance heroine. But his hand shook as he lifted it to his thick dark hair and dragged it through, like he could somehow brush some comprehension into his brain that way.

'I should have known,' he said, after a beat, frowning. 'I should have been there for you.'

More words she didn't want to hear because of how much they had the capacity to bend and fold parts of her heart she'd long ago hardened, especially to Aiden.

'It's okay,' she said with a practised, dismissive shrug. 'It wasn't meant to be. I was okay. I mean, not at the time. But I met Cory and Melanie, and bit by bit, I started getting my life back on track.'

'Without me,' he said, his voice giving nothing away.

'Well, yeah. You were... what's the phrase I'm looking for again? *Ad Meliora*. Onto a brighter future.' She swallowed to clear the acid in her throat. 'I googled it.'

He stared at her and then stood. Again, she thought of the tree being felled and grimaced.

'You should stay sitting down.'

He ignored her. 'Sienna.' He caught her hands and lifted them between their chests. Such a simple act, but somehow, it had the power to totally erase the past – just for a moment – and form a little bubble outside of time. They were just Sienna and Aiden, as incontrovertible and whole, as if they were their own shared being, as they'd ever been. Then, now, him, her, they were just a confluence of cells living outside normal space and time. 'If I had known, I would have come home to you. I would have been there.'

'But you didn't know,' she said, keeping her heart hard as a matter of urgency. 'You wouldn't even speak to me. You'd moved on, I remember.'

His Adam's apple jerked again.

'And Ashbury Falls stopped being your home the moment you left.' Her smile was wistful, dredged right up from inside her heart. 'We both know that.'

A muscle throbbed low in his jaw.

'You were always destined for this. Your bright future. Fame. Riches. You know, global superstar.'

He flinched as though she'd just called him the worst name under the sun. 'I don't know about that.'

'Yeah? Well, I do.'

'Sienna... you must have felt... I wish—'

She pulled at her hands, freeing them from his grip, taking a step backwards. 'Please, don't. It doesn't matter what you wish, now. It's not going to change a damned thing.' For a minute, heat sparked in the words. Angry, frustrated heat. She forced herself to smile, to at least give the appearance of quelling her turbulent emotions.

'Did you – do you know how – why – the baby?'

He was incapable of forming complete sentences, but she understood it. He was in survival mode. Totally overwhelmed by what he'd just learned, and the myriad spinning wheels it sparked as to their versions of the past.

'No,' she whispered. 'It just happened.' She drew her lip between her teeth. 'The doctor said I could run tests, but... I couldn't afford them.'

He swore softly, but with an intensity that sheared the room in two.

'I was in the hospital for a night. I lost a lot of blood.'

'I would have helped.'

'You weren't *you* then, Aiden. I mean, sure, you'd signed with that college, but that was just a scholarship. It's not like you had a couple of thousand bucks sitting in a bank account.'

He shook his head. 'I would have found a way.'

'I found a way.' She tilted her chin defiantly. 'I coped.'

'How?' he pushed. 'You were still in school.'

'Yeah? Well, I got a job.'

'Babysitting,' he murmured.

'What's wrong with that?'

Another visible twist of his throat. 'Nothing.'

But she could sense his tension and disapproval, and it didn't take a genius to figure out why. She'd met Cory through babysitting. And she'd dated him on and off for a few years. It hadn't been serious. They both knew it was more about Mel than anything else, but also, he'd been *someone* for Sienna to cling to as her whole life seemed to spike off into a direction she'd never foreseen. The baby. The miscarriage. Her father's accident. The moment police came to the door and charged him. The court case and pathetic public defender. Her father being found guilty and sent to prison.

Sienna had been solitary, and weak. She'd felt as though a strong breeze might knock her to the ground with enough force to guarantee she'd never get back up again.

But there'd been Cory and Melanie, and for all Cory was not someone she could see herself with long term, he was dependable, and he was there. Even more important, he needed her, and that had been like a balm to her soul. So too losing herself to Melanie's sweet toddler arms and smiles at that time of her life.

'They were a lifeline, you know,' she said, thinking aloud. 'It wasn't just the baby. There was some other stuff, around the same time.' She worried at her lower lip, wondering if he'd heard anything about her dad. She'd always presumed the news must have got to him – if good news travelled fast, in Sienna's experience, bad news was gossiped about way faster – and subconsciously his failure to reach out even over that had been almost the hardest thing to stomach of all. She waited, breath held, for him to nod. To confirm that yeah, he'd heard about the charges. How was the old man?

'Like what?'

Her heart fluttered. 'You really don't know?'

'I think it's pretty fucking clear that your life after the night I left is a total mystery to me.' He sucked in a ragged breath. 'What happened, Si? What else was there?'

13

He listened in complete silence as she matter-of-factly described the night her father had driven into another car, killing a young mom. How the evidence suggested the mother had actually fallen asleep at the wheel and clipped Nico Mastrangelo's car, rather than the other way around. But the fact Nico had a couple of drink driving charges to his name meant he hadn't really got much leeway from the local cops.

It was, what they'd called then, an open-and-shut case.

'After the baby, I couldn't bear the thought of working in medicine. Just the smell of hospitals makes me sick,' she admitted, in a way that just about broke him. 'But my grades were good. You know Mrs

Polanskova? Well, she wouldn't let me get away with not applying to college. I decided I'd study pre-law. I wanted to make a difference. To help people like Dad.'

'You're telling me your father's in jail?'

'He's due out in three years,' she admitted.

He turned his back, stalking across the room to the bureau that housed the tea bags and kettle, and braced his palms against the flat surface. Memories of the man burned his brain. Sure, Sienna's old man hadn't been any kind of paragon of virtue, but he'd been a good guy. Salt of the earth. And he'd doted on Sienna. Aiden thought about him, locked up, and a shudder racked his whole body.

'And you go see him regularly?'

'Every week, when I'm home.'

'How is he?' He couldn't look at her.

'I mean, it's prison,' she muttered. 'But it's low se-curity and he's well-liked.'

Something tightened inside Aiden but one side of his mouth lifted in a half-smile. 'I can imagine that.'

'He's studying, too,' she said. 'He's learning French, if you can believe it.'

At that, Aiden laughed. Nico was not exactly the most cultured guy you'd ever meet.

'And he's sober,' she said, softly. 'I mean, I wish on

every star there is that he hadn't gone away, but at the same time, Aiden... you know what it's like to live with an alcoholic.'

He turned then, bracing the top of his butt on the bureau instead. 'He was never violent with you,' he said, knowing that to be the case but still desperately seeking her reassurance. Because if he found out that the older guy had ever, ever laid a finger on Sienna, and that that had also been because Aiden hadn't been around to keep her safe, then he had no goddamned idea what he'd do with himself.

'Of course not. Dad's as gentle as they come; you know that.'

'Yeah,' he said, eyes locking to hers in a way he couldn't shake. 'I know.'

Silence fell in the room. Heavy and pervasive.

'Do you ever see him?' For a second, she frowned. Like she was confused. 'My dad,' he clarified.

She was very still for a moment, and then she took a few steps towards him. 'Yes.'

He clenched his jaw. It was like prying open the door to a room he'd intended to keep permanently locked shut.

'He disappeared for a spell, but he's back in town, even comes to church, sometimes.'

Aiden made a short, deranged sound. Not quite a laugh, so much as a scoff. 'To save his immortal soul?'

'I mean, he's got about as much right as the rest of us to try.'

'Nah, not by my reckoning.'

'Probably just as well you're not the big guy, then,' she said, then sighed. 'Not that I necessarily disagree with you.' She moved another step closer. 'I take it you don't see him?'

'When I came back to town, a couple of years back, I needed him to sign some papers to do with the house.'

'Your house?'

He shrugged, a bit dismissively. 'It was either buy the house for him or risk him coming back into our lives, asking for money. Contacting Mom. It was a small price to pay to keep him the hell away from us.'

She looked away, staring at a point over his shoulder, aware of how conflicted he must have been about giving his father anything, even when she understood his reasoning. 'I didn't realise you'd been back. I was... surprised.'

'I was in and out in twenty-four hours. I couldn't wait to get out of there.'

'Did you—' She clamped her lips together, physically stopping herself from asking whatever was on her mind.

He waited though, somehow sensing it was important.

'I mean, did you even think about seeing me, Aiden?' The words were heavy with a mix of anguish and accusation.

'Honestly? I mean, I *thought* about it, yeah. But I knew it wouldn't be a good idea. I was heading right back to my life in New York, just as soon as I could.'

'Right,' she said, nodding a little uneasily, then crossing her arms. He wanted to know what she was thinking. Feeling. But he didn't have any right to ask. 'So, how was he?'

He was trying to keep the conversation neutral, avoiding the fact he'd let her down, *again*, by coming to Ashbury Falls and not looking her up. Which was a pretty fair way to feel. Wouldn't it have been normal to go grab a coffee or something with a girl who'd once meant the world to him? It wasn't like she still meant the world to him – he'd moved on, so had she. They could have shared a pot of coffee and some pie and just shot the breeze, for old times' sake.

But Aiden had known she wouldn't want to. Or maybe he'd just been too ashamed of his own behaviour to attempt it. Maybe he'd been scared he'd see Sienna and feel the same desperate pull to her and Ashbury Falls that had damned near grounded him all those years ago.

Only now, he had a career, and a whole team that counted on him to earn the big bucks in order to support them. From his agent to his manager, his assistant, his sponsorship agent. He could hardly just pack it all up and head back to Small Town, Nowhere.

What the hell was he even thinking?

That wasn't remotely on the cards.

At that very moment, his manager and assistant were negotiating his next contract, and it was going to be huge. Going back to Ashbury Falls was nowhere on his bingo card for this year, nor the next, or any other year. He'd left that shithole in his rearview mirror a long time ago.

Hadn't he?

'Aiden?' She put her hand on his forearm and he startled at the unexpected contact. Warmth seemed to simmer just beneath his skin. 'How was your dad, when you saw him?'

He looked right into her eyes and wondered if she could easily read the sadness in his?

'The same as always,' he admitted. 'Drunk as a skunk, angry at the world. I half wished he'd tried to hit me. I fantasised about having to defend myself.' His smirk was angry. 'He didn't. He always was the worst kind of bully – really only went for people who were too small to pose a threat. The day Blake and I outgrew him was the day he stopped giving us a hard time.'

Her nostrils flared as she sighed, and then, to Aiden's absolute shock, she slid her hands around his hips and to his back, pressing her palms flat and holding him against her. She held her head to his chest, her ear over his heart, and he wondered if she could hear how hard and fast it was beating?

'Life can be pretty cruel, huh?'

'Shouldn't I be saying that to you?' And if he'd been surprised by her hug, he was even more surprised to find himself dropping his head lower and pressing a kiss to her hair, holding his lips there, closing his eyes and breathing her in. Unlike their kiss on the beach, this moment wasn't driven by white hot sensual heat. It was a connection of two souls who understood the complexity of family trauma, who'd been through something together, a long time ago, that had somehow bonded them. Even after not seeing each other for so long, he felt the kind of connection to Sienna he hadn't known to anyone else, ever.

It still had the power to scare the crap out of him because connections like this were strong enough to thaw even the thickest ice sheets.

He would pull back from her. In a minute. He just wanted to feel this for a while longer. To smell her, to experience her soft curves against his body.

It was Sienna who pulled away, anyway, just far enough to look up into his eyes. 'Are you tired?'

His heart slammed into the wall of his ribs. He had been. Before he came into this room, he'd been exhausted, courtesy of that cricket, and Dream Sienna.

'I think so.'

'You think so?' She arched a brow, teasing him, breaking through the reflective sadness that had swirled through the room a second earlier.

'I mean, yeah. Probably.'

She laughed then, a sound that reminded him so viscerally of their teenage years he felt the slippage of time once more.

'You?' He returned the question just because he had no idea what else to say.

'I'm okay.' Her lips twisted. 'How bad is this alleged cricket?'

'Hey, I'm not making it up. The thing's a menace. How long do crickets live, anyway?'

'How would I know?'

'Isn't your friend some kind of cricket expert?'

She wrinkled her nose. 'Hamsters are more her jam.'

'Damn it. I was hoping we could get someone to find the damned thing.'

'I think you're going to have to put up with it.'

'There's probably another room,' he said, looking towards the door, wondering at the twisty feeling in his stomach.

'I mean, maybe. The place is pretty full now, but you could always, you know, go door to door.'

He nodded, stepping back from her, keeping his hands firmly at his side.

'Unless you want to stay here.'

He stared at her. Like, really stared. Because he couldn't speak. It was as if every single word in the English language had upped and left his brain, all at once. A mass exodus of verbal language skills. Of thinking skills. Of everything. Like he was having a stroke or something.

'The bed's huge,' she pointed out, dropping her gaze to the floor between them before piercing him once more with her direct gaze.

'It is,' he agreed, glad some words were back, even if they were monosyllabic.

'I just mean to sleep, obviously. And then tomorrow you can go back to your own room and track down the cricket.'

'Right.' He nodded. 'Are you sure?'

She lifted one shoulder. 'Let me think about that. Do you snore?'

He rolled his eyes. 'You know I don't snore.'

'I don't know anything,' she said. 'You might have started snoring in the last ten or so years.'

'If I have, no one's told me.'

Her smile slipped for a nanosecond and he could have killed himself for alluding to having shared a bed with other women.

'Because that wouldn't really be a fair swap,' she recovered quickly, her tone impish once more. 'You getting away from the cricket and me inheriting a snorer.'

'I don't snore.'

'Well, you just said you don't know that definitively.'

'Are you retracting your offer?'

'I'm just making sure I know what I'm getting myself into.'

'No snoring. No sex.'

Her jaw dropped at the brazen statement.

'Unless you want—'

'No,' she hastened to add, cheeks flushed a pretty bright pink. 'I really did just mean for you to share the bed. As in, one side of it. With, like, a big, impermeable line, right down the middle.'

'Got it. Our own Great Wall of China.'

'Or Mariana Trench.'

'As unpassable as the DMZ. Got it.'

She stared at him for a few seconds before gesturing to the door across the room. 'The bathroom's through there. And that's pretty much it.'

'Thanks.' He moved towards the bed. 'Do you have a favourite side?'

'I use the whole thing,' she said, shaking her head. 'I'm like a starfish right in the middle.'

'Not tonight,' he said.

'Yeah, I should probably apologise in advance if I kick you to the ground.'

'Try not to.'

She batted her lashes serenely. 'We'll see.'

His chuckle was low and soft.

'I mean, you kind of deserve it.'

He really couldn't argue with that.

'I'll tell you what, Mastrangelo. I'll sleep here and try to take up as little space as possible.'

She snorted.

'What?'

'It's just, you might not have noticed, but you're kind of...'

'What?'

'Huge.'

He grinned and wiggled his brows, his implication clear.

She rolled her eyes. 'You're a child.'

'Nope.'

'Get in bed.'

He arched a brow, loving the way she blushed. Loving that he could make her blush.

Which scared the crap out of him all over again.

He pushed back the covers and made a show of lying down right on the edge of the mattress, enjoying the way she regarded him sceptically, before moving gingerly to her own side of the bed and peeling back the covers.

She kept watching him as she hopped in, and didn't, in the end, starfish at all, but rather lay right on the edge of her side of the bed, too. With a gulf of mattress and covers as wide as two hockey rinks between them.

It only occurred to him, as he was starting to drift off, that her predilection for starfishing meant she probably didn't share a bed often, and he hated how much that thought pleased him...

* * *

At first, she thought it was a dream. It wouldn't have been the first time her subconscious had conjured Aiden up out of nowhere. But this was *different*. This time, she could *feel* him. Even after her eyes had opened.

His warmth and nearness. His breath on the back of her neck. His hand, heavy and comforting, wrapped around her waist. She could *hear* him too, each exhalation like a deep, throaty rumble.

Aiden.

Carter.

In.

Her.

Bed.

With his arm around her. And his body playing big spoon to her little.

She startled, eyes wide, staring at the wall across the room, but stayed perfectly still, as though she couldn't bear to break the contact, even when she knew it was a mistake, and probably a disaster in the making.

'Morning.' His voice was a deep rumble from behind, close to her ear. She hated the way her insides twisted with something like need.

He moved his hand. She was instantly cold.

'Sorry 'bout that,' he muttered.

'It's fine,' she demurred, voice crisp. 'It doesn't matter.'

'Yeah,' he responded. 'I guess it was just habit or something. Muscle memory.'

She moved then, shifting away from him a bit, towards the edge of the bed, the safety of space, before she flipped onto her other side, so she was facing towards Aiden.

And immediately regretted it.

If feeling his arm around her had been intimate, then this was somehow so much more. The sheet was down around his waist, revealing his tatted-up torso, and his face had creases in it from the pillow. His eyes were sleepy, his lips parted, hair all messy.

It was like being sucked back in time.

And being hit with a sledgehammer of his life since then. His success. His modelling work. His being a spokesperson for so many global brands.

'How did you sleep?' Her voice was softened by the earliness of the morning.

'Better than I have in a while,' he said, one side of his lip twisting upwards in a half-smile.

'No cricket.'

'No cricket.' He lifted one shoulder. 'No dreams.'

'Same,' she said, after a beat. 'And if you snored, I slept right through it.'

'So I was a good house guest?'

'You were acceptable,' she said.

His laugh was deep and rumbly, doing funny things to her stomach. 'That might be the first time I've been described that way.'

Her heart stammered. Anger seared her. No, not anger. At least, not solely anger. But outrage. Jealousy. Irritation. A swirling current of dark, brooding emotions that caught her unawares because of how instant – and unexpected – they were.

'Does that mean you'd invite me back?'

Her heart lurched. Anger – or whatever she was feeling – evaporated, to be replaced by a rushing pulse and a hotness in her lungs. 'I – I'm sure you'll deal with the cricket today.' Mentally, she made a list, and at the top of it? Get the girls to *remove* the noise-making thing from his room, pronto.

'But if not...'

'Aiden.' Her sigh was soft, and final. 'I don't know what last night was.' Her eyes lifted to his. 'A temporary truce, I guess.'

'A truce?' He seemed to shift closer. No, he *definitely* shifted closer, because a second later, his hand was on her hip and his gaze seemed to be probing hers, looking right into her consciousness. 'Are we at war, Sienna?'

His touch was incendiary. His eyes were like a spark, turning her pulse into a livewire.

'Worse. We're nothing,' she forced herself to say. Wishing it were true. Wishing their history wasn't still such a huge part of what she thought and felt.

'It doesn't feel like we're nothing.'

Her breath hitched in her lungs. 'No?'

He shook his head slowly, but something seemed to change in his features, giving him a look of hesitation. He didn't move, but she *felt* like he did. It was almost as if the air between them thickened and grew warm. Almost as if they were stuck in mud. She could hardly breathe.

'Then what are we?' she managed to squeak out.

'Hard to define.'

Her brow furrowed. 'What does that mean?'

'Tell me this,' he said, rather than answering her question. 'On the beach, when we kissed...'

'Yes?' She couldn't believe her voice emerged so steadily.

'You acted like it was nothing.' He laughed uncomfortably. 'Like you go around hooking up with guys all the time, or whatever.'

Her eyes widened instinctively. Her insides

squirmed. She felt like she'd been caught with her hand in the cookie jar. She felt like the worst kind of liar.

'What's your point?' Now there was the slightest tremble.

He stroked her hip and her pulse went haywire. She wished he didn't have such an easy ability to affect her like this.

'I guess... I'm just wondering if that's accurate.'

'Which part?'

'What do you mean?'

'Was the kiss nothing to me? Or do I kiss random guys all the time?'

'I didn't mean random,' he said, shaking his head.

'And why exactly do you think you have any business asking me this?'

'That's the thing, I don't.' He moved closer, his features imploring. Her heart twisted. He was her first love. He would always have a hard-wire into her mind, and annoyingly, into parts of her heart. 'But I still want to know.'

'Why?'

'Because I want to understand you.'

'Why?'

His lips showed the ghost of a smile, but it didn't reach his eyes. 'You don't want to answer?'

'I just... don't know what to say.'

'Is it hard to just be honest?'

'Honest?' She was floored. 'This, coming from you?'

'I never lied to you.'

'Fine, *you* tell me something. Back then, you walked away like I was nothing. Is that how you really felt?'

He stared at her, mouth compressed into a straight line. 'You know you weren't nothing to me.'

'So why did you go out of your way to make me feel like it?'

He flinched then, and she was glad. Because she wanted to hurt him. She *needed* to hurt him. In order to have any kind of closure, she needed to draw blood. Even if just a little.

'I thought it would be better for you, in the long run.'

She rolled her eyes. 'Bullshit.'

'No, I mean it,' he insisted, and this time, when he moved closer, there was no space left between them. Their bodies connected, and her cells danced in giddy shock and delight. 'I knew I was leaving town for good. I had to. Everything with my dad, man, it was so fucked up. I had to get us the hell out of there.

But you, Sienna Mastrangelo, were kind of a sticking point.'

She couldn't speak. He was too close. His words too full of passion and truth, his face showing genuine turmoil, as though he'd actually angsted over what had happened back then, which just didn't fit the narrative she'd lived with all these years. The past was her truth – a talisman she'd lived alongside since that awful night when he'd broken up with her. Now he was asking her to see it differently, and she just didn't know if she could.

'All I'd ever wanted was to leave town. Leave Dad. Save Mom. Start afresh. And then we started hanging out. And suddenly, it was less about what I wanted and more about what everyone else needed from me. They needed me more than you did. That's what it came down to, I guess.'

His words cut through something inside of her, but she still didn't really buy it. They could have done the whole long-distance thing. He hadn't needed to just walk away from her, wholesale. He'd done *that* because he'd wanted to start a new life. Without her in it.

'It doesn't matter.'

'Stop saying that.' A tinge of anger coloured his voice, and he immediately withdrew, his face a blank slate, his chest still as if holding his breath, and then he moved, expelling it long and slow.

'They didn't need you more than I did,' she said, glad that her own tone showed impatience. 'You only justified it that way.'

'I didn't know any of that stuff, Sienna. About the baby, about your dad.'

'Nor did I, when you left. That all came later. I just mean... I needed you, regardless of that. Or I thought I did.' She jutted her chin out defiantly. 'I *loved* you, Aiden. Not like some stupid high school crush. I *loved* you. Every part of me loved every part of you, and if you'd let me, I would have stood by your side while you chased down your dreams, being your biggest cheerleader, your biggest supporter, forever and always.' She blinked quickly to clear the hot sting of tears. 'Just like we promised each other.'

The silence between them was flooded with static electricity. It sparked in the air between them, buzzing around the room.

'Anyway.' She couldn't bear it. She couldn't bear being this close to him, touching him, with the aching wound in her heart wide open and exposed, raw and making her vulnerable in a way she'd fought not to be ever since that night. 'It's done.' She went to lift the sheet and push out of bed but his hand, on her hip, moved quickly, grabbing her wrist and stilling her.

'I'm sorry.' His thumb padded her inner-wrist and sparks shot towards her shoulder then pirouetted inside her body. 'I thought I was doing the right thing.'

He lifted both their hands, holding them between their chests, still stroking her sensitive skin.

'A part of me thought... if you were in my life, I wouldn't be hungry any more.'

Her brow furrowed. 'What does that even mean?'

'Don't you get it?' His voice was gruff. 'You became my whole world, Sienna. I didn't give a shit about hockey once we hooked up.'

She made a scoffing noise. 'That's not how I remember it.'

'I still played, but my heart wasn't in it. My heart... my heart was with you.'

She ground her teeth together, needing the physical act to stop herself from saying something stupid, or from gushing over him.

'That scholarship was my ticket out of town. My mom and Blake's, too.'

'Blake could have gone without you.'

'We were a package deal. Everything was locked in – and it revolved around the both of us.' He expelled a harsh breath. 'Maybe if I'd quit, it all still would have worked out for them. I don't know. I wasn't willing to risk it.'

For the first time, his words made a strange kind of sense, but there was no relief in that. If anything, she felt a weird hollowing out. An emptiness. Because it was all so futile.

'It's fine. I get it,' she said, and in her heart, she did. 'But the thing is, even understanding why you did what you did, I can't... I just can't forgive you for it. The thing is, Aiden, you got wings. You flew away. And I just... I got stuck.'

14

If you'd asked him a month ago what his idea of perfect R&R was, it would have gone a hell of a lot like this. A private beach. Close friends and family. A bonfire right on sunset. Beers. An epic barbecue feast being cooked up by island staff just a dozen or so feet away, filling the air with amazing smells that should have been making his stomach grumble. This should have seemed like bliss. Instead, Aiden felt like he'd been totally scooped out.

That was Sienna's doing.

You grew wings. I got stuck.

Her words had tortured him, all day.

Not just her words, but the way she'd issued them with a perfunctory, polite smile, before pulling her wrist free and stepping out of the bed, her beautiful, slim body backlit by the soft morning light, her long hair loose and tousled.

He'd wanted to go after her. To pull her back against his body and kiss her. Like he had on the beach, but *not* like he had on the beach. Even a few short days had made such a difference. Everything was different.

So he'd just lain there and watched as she'd gathered up some clothes and made her way into the en-suite bathroom. The sound of the shower running gave him a choice. Stay, or go.

He chose the latter.

Not because he was a coward, but because it was her room, and she'd made it clear the conversation was closed. Dismissed. Thank you, counsellor, he thought, as he got out of bed and moved to the door then back to his own room.

He watched as Sienna said something that made the other three women laugh. Aiden knew Astrid and Blake were happy. Like *stupid* happy. The kind of happy he could never have even halfway hoped for for his twin brother, when things were at their worst. But as he looked at the four of them, he couldn't help but wonder if *that* was the real love story. The way these women looked at each other, talked, laughed, supported, it made his heart explode in a weird way, to know Sienna had chicks like this in her life. Things might have gone to hell for her in lots of ways, but these women saw her for who she was. They got the value of her. And they got to be in her life.

Unlike him.

Something stitched in his chest as he faced the reality of that for the first time.

He'd got used to seeing her again. He liked seeing her. But no matter what happened, after the wedding, he'd go back to his life. That was non-negotiable. The contract was being inked, and he was nowhere near ready to quit his game, yet.

Even for Sienna?

It was like an arrow, spearing into his side, and it forced him to glance towards a road not taken, all those years ago.

Out of nowhere, he imagined moving back to Ashbury Falls. Not to her house, but buying that big, run-down old mansion they'd both always loved, fixing it up together, making it *their* home, just like they'd talked about doing back then.

He could afford to never hit another puck again.

He could afford to do whatever the hell he

wanted. His heart jammed against his ribs. He could afford to *be* wherever he wanted.

A decade ago, he'd left their town behind because he'd been shit out of options: for himself, Blake, and their mom. But Blake didn't need him now. He had his life on track, and he had Astrid for good measure. He was a whole different guy to the kid who'd been about three steps from going hard off the rails, without Aiden to keep him on the straight and narrow. And their mom? Same deal. Cynthia Carter had friends, and the kind of self-confidence that settled in under your skin and didn't let up.

His heart began to thunder.

But could he really walk away from the game, when he was at the height of it? Leave his team?

Blake might not need him any more, but the team did. The younger players looked up to him. The coach relied on him. How could he turn his back on them?

And would Sienna even want him to?

His eyes landed on her and stayed there, so he saw the moment Chuck Daly walked up to the group carrying a bottle of champagne, earning a rousing cheer from the women that had a fair few heads turning their way.

Astrid, clutching a mug of tea, shook her head

when Chuck went to walk off, gesturing to a spare patch of sand. Beside Sienna.

And Aiden's not-so-little inner green monster harumphed as the tech billionaire settled down good and close to the woman who'd been single-handedly torturing Aiden's thoughts – waking and sleeping – for longer than he cared to remember.

She smiled at Chuck; Chuck smiled back. It was like another blade, slicing through his side.

Would Sienna want him to move home? To be in her life again?

Or would she rather start fresh with someone else, like Chuck?

She'd obviously been seeing guys in the ten plus years since they'd been a thing, so why hadn't she got married? His heart skipped. Why hadn't she had kids of her own? Because she'd been too cut up, after what had happened to their baby?

He took a long drag of his beer, trying not to think about what that must have been like for her. How devastating. How heart breaking.

How she must have *hated* him for not being there. For not answering her damned calls. For ignoring her, when she was reaching out because she had *needed* him to hold her and make everything better. Or at least to stop it from hurting so much.

He'd failed her.

What right did he have to even contemplate trying to get back in her life? Because wasn't that the crux of his fears, when it came to Sienna? Not that he'd lose his focus on the game, like he'd told her. But that he'd hurt her, one day, like his father had hurt his mother. That he had those same genes, those same emotions, that same volatility bubbling beneath the surface. He might have learned to control it from a young age by being the exact opposite of his father – by answering emotion with ice, by being cold and calculated instead of driven by feeling – but that didn't change the fact those feelings were there.

Just like they were now, as he watched Chuck tuck Sienna's hair behind her ear, earning a shy sideways smile from her, that made one of his hands threaten to form a fist, so he buried it deep in the sand instead and forced himself to look away. To stare deep into the flickering flames while his pulse calmed down and he got a grip, once more.

He had hurt her.

Just like he'd sworn he never would.

He hadn't meant to.

He'd thought leaving her would save them both from the inevitability of that. He'd been wrong.

He wasn't wrong now though. At the end of this

week, he would walk away from her for good – for her sake. No more fantasising about Ashbury Falls and the quiet, contented life they could have, if they were different people. No more wondering what she'd say if he even suggested it.

There was this week, and then, there was nothing. And that was okay by him. It had to be.

* * *

'I know you can run, but I'm wondering,' Chuck said, voice low, face close enough to her that Sienna presumed she was the only one to hear him.

'Wondering what?' she prompted, when he let the sentence taper off.

'When I can collect on that dance you owe me.'

'Dance?'

'I beat you, fair and square. That was the prize, remember?'

She raised a single brow. Their race – and his stipulation for a prize – had completely slipped her mind.

'What's the matter? Don't know how?' he teased.

She arched a brow. 'You've seen me dance.'

'But you haven't danced with me yet,' he pointed out. 'Isn't that an oversight, when we're partners?'

'For the wedding,' she said with a small smile.

'Right.' He grinned, and her smile naturally widened in reply. He was effortlessly, roguishly charming, and super easy to be around. 'So, how about it?' He held out a hand to her, nodding his head in the direction of the makeshift dance floor in the dimly lit space in front of the DJ. Quite a few people had gravitated that way and were dancing to the heavy beat of the song.

'Hmm.' She wrinkled her nose. 'I guess you do raise a good point. I mean, I know I can dance, but you might have two left feet.'

He nodded sagely. 'That's true.'

'And if you do, there's still time to swap you out for a better model.'

'Brutal,' he said with mock offence. 'Are you saying you won't accept me despite my imperfections?'

'Are you actually admitting you have imperfections?'

He laughed. 'You sound surprised.'

'You just seem a little, erm, how do I put this?'

'Full of myself?' he asked, but there was no offence in his features.

'I was thinking *sure* of yourself,' she responded,

with a shake of her head. 'That's a small, but important, difference, you know.'

'Is it?'

'Well, yeah. I mean, my words are kind of a compliment, yours are not.'

'Then let's choose your turn of phrase. I'm sure of
myself, yes.'

'Except when it comes to dancing?'

'How about we go find out,' he said, standing and
holding a hand to her. Sienna looked at it, her heart
shifting a little. Not at the prospect of dancing with
Chuck, but at the prospect of dancing with him in front
of all these people. Or rather, one person in particular.

But that was silly.

Aiden and she were no longer a couple. They'd
both had a lot of water under the bridge since they
had been. Besides, Chuck was just a friend of a
friend. Sure, he flirted like a dog chased its tail, but
that didn't mean anything. It was harmless. Fun.

'Sure.' She put her hand in his and pulled up to
her feet, their bodies almost bumping into each other
courtesy of the uneven sand.

'Where are you two going?' Paige asked with a
wiggle of her brows. Sienna looked down to see that
Olly had come to join their group, and was sitting

behind Paige, arms wrapped around her waist, chin resting on her shoulder. Paige looked blissfully happy. Sienna's heart lifted at the sight of them, just like it did when she saw Astrid and Blake together, or Chase and Bella.

Maybe her friends were showing her that love – even when you've been badly hurt in the past – was something she shouldn't give up hoping for. Not with Aiden, and not with Chuck, but with *someone*. One day. When she was ready.

'Sienna's taking me for a test drive,' Chuck said, arm casually draped around her shoulders.

'On the dance floor,' she clarified, at the shocked expression on Bella's face.

'Riiiight.' Olly laughed, and Sienna's cheeks flushed pink. She thought about reiterating that they were just going to dance, but what would the point have been?

'You are seriously—'

'Incorrigible,' he interrupted with a sideways grin. 'Yeah, you've said that before.'

'And I meant it.'

'I like it when you use big words.'

'You act like such a jock,' she said, stopping when they reached the edge of the sand and letting him link his arms behind her back. He smelled super masculine, all citrussy and spicy. 'But you're so much more.'

'Am I?'

She frowned contemplatively. 'Why do you do that?'

'What do you think I'm doing?'

'Hide behind jokes. You have this whole stupid persona going on. It's like you're trying to keep everyone at a bit of a distance.'

His eyes flicked to hers and for a second – the briefest second – she felt like maybe she was seeing the real Chuck Daly. But then he threw his head back and laughed. 'Leave it to a lawyer to read into things more than necessary.'

'I'm not a lawyer, I'm a law student.'

'Same difference.'

'Not really, and I have the bank balance to prove it.'

Again, something shifted in his gaze, but it was gone in an instant. She could have sworn she saw confusion, or sympathy, or maybe a mix of both.

'How long 'til you graduate?'

'A couple of years. I'm only studying part time – I have a mortgage. A job. A sort of step-daughter,' she said, smiling to think of Melanie. 'But I'll get there.'

'And then what?' he prompted, asking Sienna a

question she hadn't fully formulated an answer to, even for herself.

'I'll be a lawyer, like you said,' she replied, taking a page out of his book and keeping her tone intentionally light.

'What kind of lawyer? Working where?'

'Criminal defence law, but I'd really like to work in a pro bono team. An innocence project, sort of thing. I know how hard it can be to get a fair hearing, for some people. So much of it comes down to money. Circumstance. And it really shouldn't. The law should always be applied reasonably, equally, and fairly.'

He was quiet, absorbing that. The music changed, another mellow, bass-y song filling the salty air.

'As to where,' she said, with a heaviness she'd been wrangling with for some time. 'I don't know. Leaving Ashbury Falls is hard to imagine. I mean, my whole life is there. But the opportunities to do what I want to do are kind of thin on the ground.'

'Yeah,' he said. Thoughtfully, though. Distracted.

She waited, sure he was going to add something else. The music seemed to make the air pulse, the beat of it accentuated by the gentle slapping of the waves against the shoreline. It was a perfect night. The sky was the inkiest of blacks, and the stars glittered and shimmered, almost as if they were, themselves, dancing in the heavens.

'You know, it's not something I make a big deal of, but I have this thing.'

'Thing,' she prompted. 'You know, you make that sound like it might be forewarning me of some kind of venereal disease. Or that you have a foot fetish or something.'

He laughed, holding her a little tighter. Out of the corner of her eye, she caught sight of a movement and glanced that way, almost on autopilot, then shivered when she saw Aiden. He was talking to Blake, but she had a very strong feeling that he'd just been watching her, and had looked away to avoid making eye contact. Her body tingled.

'Nah, I mean, a charity.' Chuck rushed to add, 'It's not a big deal. I don't really advertise it.'

'What kind of charity?'

'We help people escaping domestic violence. Part of that involves offering legal aid – for whatever they need. Could be help with their will, or custody, or separating assets, or it could be more serious, depending on circumstance. I know it's not exactly what you're talking about, but we do offer the opportunity to work from home, provided there's a week every month spent in the office.'

She stared up at him. 'Are you offering me a job?'

'I'm just saying, you could think about it.'

She blinked quickly. 'Why don't you advertise the fact you do this?'

He shrugged.

'That's not an answer.'

He smiled, but for once, it was lacking his trademark carelessness. 'Then I become the story. I don't want that. This isn't something that needs to be spotlighted. We do good work, behind the scenes. We help people that need to be helped. I have other ways of grandstanding and getting my ego stroked.'

'Wow.' She stopped dancing so she could stare up at him. 'You've really surprised me, Chuck Daly.'

'I aim to please.'

She ignored the double entendre. 'It's an incredible cause.'

'Yeah.' His voice was rough. 'I mean, I know a bit about it.'

She frowned. 'The law?'

'DV. It's – something Blake and I, you know, have in common.'

The penny dropped and a burst of sympathy exploded through her as she understood what he was admitting.

'You grew up in an abusive house?'

He nodded once.

'I'm so sorry to hear it.'

He lifted his shoulders. 'I got out.'

'Still,' she said, a little unevenly. 'I know that kind of thing can leave scars for a lifetime.'

Unbidden, her gaze drifted across to Aiden and Blake, locked in conversation. They were both smiling though, looking happy. Content. Only a handful of people could understand the pain that was just beneath the surface. The hypervigilance that had arisen because of the way their father had been to them, as small boys, and their mother, all their lives, until Aiden and Blake had used their God-given talents to flee to safety.

'I'm okay,' he said. 'I dealt with it. First team I joined in the majors got me to see a shrink. I hated the idea at first. Talk about a waste of time. Except, it probably saved my life.'

'How so?'

'There's a lot to deal with, when you come out of that. The guilt, at not being able to stop it. The grief, because even when someone hurts you, or hurts someone you love, you still kind of love them. It's crazy, but you can hate and love someone all at once, and you have to just kind of learn to sit with that. Accept it, don't fight it, don't try to change it.'

She nodded slowly, and of course, thought of Aiden, and how for years, she had loved and hated him. Different circumstances, similar outcome.

'There's fear, too, of turning into what you hate most in the world. And a few defensive mechanisms, like humour,' he said with a droll smile, 'used to cover up whatever you might actually be feeling.'

'Well, I'm glad you told me,' she said.

'You're easy to talk to. Blake thinks the world of you, you know.' He looked over his shoulder, then back at Sienna. 'I suspect his brother does, too.'

She pulled a face. She did *not* want to talk about Aiden with Chuck. Or anyone. It was too complicated.

'Hey.' She changed the subject swiftly, because her insides were feeling all jammed up by this conversation, her skin starting to get clammy when she thought about how long she'd known Blake and Aiden for, and what both men meant to her. 'I've got a question.'

'Okay.' He shrugged. Another song started to play. 'Shoot.'

'How does it work, the whole tech bro thing?'

He laughed. 'That's your question?'

'What's wrong with it?'

'Well, it's a bit nebulous.'

'Oooh, look at the dumb jock using big words.' She grinned. 'Careful.' She lowered her voice to a whisper. 'You're starting to sound like you have more than two brain cells to rub together.'

'Well, we can't have that now, can we?'

'So?'

'I mean, it's not like there's a club. It's business. I run a business. I just happen to invest in tech start-ups.'

The hairs on the back of Sienna's neck stood on end. 'Yeah, I thought so. And do you know other guys who do the same thing?'

'Well, yeah, obviously.'

'Have you ever heard of someone called Harvey Peterson?'

Chuck stopped dancing for a minute, then started up again. 'Yeah. Why? Do you know him?' A frown flitted across his face briefly.

'Not personally.'

He let out a low whistle. 'I'm glad.'

'Why?'

'He's an A-grade asshole,' Chuck said, confirming everything Sienna already knew and felt about the guy.

'Why?' she asked urgently, leaning forward a little, because she *needed* to hear this.

'Apart from the fact he stiffed me on a deal a few years ago?'

She shook her head.

'I've just heard… some things. He's not a good guy.'

'That much I know.'

He stopped dancing again. But it didn't matter. Inside, Sienna was all swirly, the possibilities opening up before her like a freaking rainbow bridge. After spending almost a year trying to work out *how* to get revenge on a rich, privileged, Silicon Valley tech genius, and drawing a complete and utter blank, she felt like she might actually have the beginnings of a way in. She just had to work out *how* to capitalise on that.

'How do you know?'

Her eyes were rounded and reflected the glow of the moon when they met his. 'I can't say right now,' she admitted softly. 'It's not my story to tell,' she explained, 'and I need to check with the person whose story it is before I go into it with you. But… can I count on your help, if I can think of a way to take the bastard down a peg or two? And make him pay for some of the very not nice things he's done in the past?'

'Nothing illegal?' he prompted. 'No daggers at midnight? Shovels by morning?'

She rolled her eyes. 'If I wanted to do something illegal, I probably would have done it by now.'

'Okay,' he said, shrugging, like it was easy. 'Count me in.'

And Sienna's heart could have damn near burst out of her chest. The way Paige had been wronged was one of the worst, most violating things that could happen to a person, and Sienna would be damned if she'd let the guy get away with it. She couldn't wait to tell the others. Not tonight – they'd all had too much champagne. And maybe not even tomorrow. The focus needed to be on the wedding. But as soon as possible, she'd call an emergency meeting of the Karma Club and plotting would begin, in earnest.

15

'I just think we should call a spade a spade,' Astrid said softly, as the flames raged and the dancing continued, close to the shore. 'He can't stop looking at you.'

Sienna glanced across at Aiden who was, in fact, *not* looking at her. He was standing on his own, eating a hot dog, and just the sight of that – this big guy on the fringes of the group, for all his success, fame, money, looking kind of... lost – made her whole body ache in the strangest way.

'I haven't noticed.' Sienna shrugged. It was true. She'd spent the whole night locked in a silent battle of wills, determined not to look anywhere even remotely in his direction. She was partly worried that if she looked, she wouldn't be able to look away.

Something had shifted inside of her, or maybe between them, last night. Something had made her feel differently towards him. Less angry, more sad. Less hurt, more disappointed – not in him, but in the future that should have been theirs, and how they'd somehow failed that future.

'Oh, come on,' Paige said with a wagging finger. 'You're kidding, right? When you were dancing with Chuck, he looked like he wanted to explode. Surely you felt two hot spots on your body thanks to his laser vision.'

Bella giggled. 'He's not a superhero.'

'You know what I mean. He's like literally staring at you as if he can see *through* you.'

Sienna stood, brushing the sand from her butt with one spare hand, champagne flute – now empty – in the other. 'You guys are imagining it.'

The three other women shared a look that only frustrated Sienna more. They *weren't* imagining it, necessarily, but she had no idea what to say, nor how much she could confess. To herself, let alone them. It wasn't like anything physical had really happened with her and Aiden, but last night, they'd shared moments that somehow seemed more intimate than anything they could have done in bed. She felt torn between her loyalty to her Just Desserts buddies, and what she knew to be their good wishes for her, and a loyalty to whatever she and Aiden had once shared.

She felt torn, period.

'I'm going to get a drink. Anyone else?'

Paige held up a still half-full bottle but Sienna shook her head. 'I think I'm done with bubbles.' She smiled brightly and blew a kiss. 'I'll be back,' she promised, and she meant it. Once conversation shifted away from Aiden and his supposed burning eyes.

At the bar, she looked over the list and selected a diet soda, watching as the waiter opened a small bottle and decanted it into a glass with ice. When she turned around, to survey the bonfire and the party that was still raging despite the fact it was getting close to midnight, she came face to face with Aiden.

Aiden 'Can't Stop Staring at You' Carter.

The first – and only – love of her life.

Top three buttons undone, revealing his tanned chest and a sprinkling of hair, reminding her of the tattoos he wore on his skin. Shorts. Bare feet. Dark hair brushed back from his brow. Eyes, indeed, boring into her.

'Hey.' Voice, deep, gruff, pouring over her frazzled nerves like treacle.

Conscious that her friends would undoubtedly be watching and speculating at a fever pitch, she gave him a curt smile. 'Hello.'

His brow furrowed. 'Having fun?'

'Sure. It's a great party.'

'Right.' He nodded once, his head bobbing mechanically. 'It's kind of loud, though.'

Her insides felt all squishy. It was kind of loud, down near the water, but where they were standing was okay. Which meant either he had supersonic hearing to go with his laser vision, or he was trying out a pick-up line? Surely not.

'Are you about to suggest we go somewhere quieter and talk?' she asked with a hint of a smile – a smile that slipped as dark colour ran over his cheekbones, embarrassment clearly written on his features.

'Oh, come on, Aiden. Surely you've got better lines than that?'

His Adam's apple jerked visibly as he swallowed, and she had a sudden urge to save face, because his flirtation, no matter how practised, had made her heart thump hard and fast.

'I mean, you've dated half of New York. Or are

you just famous enough to be able to get away with lame lines regardless?'

'Hey,' he said, shaking his head a little, frowning in a way she hated to admit she found adorable. 'I didn't mean it like that. I just wanted to... talk, I guess.'

'We talked last night,' she reminded him, a self-preservation instinct making her want to maintain some space from Aiden. 'And this morning. Is there anything more you want to say?'

His dark brows knitted together. 'I think there might be.'

Where did she go next?

'Well, this is my best friend's wedding.' She shrugged, hating how confused she felt. 'That's my focus.'

'It's not their wedding tonight.'

Sienna's laugh was ever so slightly brittle. 'The whole week is their wedding.'

'Okay,' he said, expelling a breath, reaching behind her to the champagne bowl of beers and plucking one out of the ice. His arm brushed her side on the way back and she nearly jumped out of her skin. She realised how hard she was fighting to hold herself together. How tempted she was by him. How much she wanted to go somewhere quiet and talk, after all. But she was conscious of the three pairs of eyes watching her, and of how she could explain all of this to them. So she shook her head a little.

'I have to go back over there,' she said, nodding towards the others. 'I'll catch you later, okay?'

* * *

Though the party was still in full flight, by twelve thirty, Sienna was ready for a cup of tea and bed. Or maybe she was ready for something else. Space? Or a lack of space... either way, she was ready to get back to her own room.

'You're sure you won't stay for another dance?' Astrid called, arms looped around Blake's neck, goofy, happy, loved-up smile locked in place.

Sienna waved a hand. 'Have fun, kids.'

The path was illuminated by the full, silvery moon, and low-set lights that glowed with a golden warmth, so she made it to the mansion easily, stepping inside and avoiding making eye contact with the few groups of revellers who'd strayed inside and were set up in small groups in the foyer, drinking, chatting, having a more subdued kind of party. She took the steps to her own room, her walk slowing down briefly as she approached Aiden's, until she stopped walking altogether and held her breath, her skin prickling in goosebumps.

It was madness to even think of knocking.

To think of seeing him again. To think of... yet, of its own volition, her hand lifted and her fist pumped on the door a couple of times. She took a rushed step back, as if she couldn't quite believe what she'd done.

Thank God he didn't answer.

Thank God she was spared at least that mortification. She closed her eyes and began to walk much, much faster, to the sanctity of her own room, pushing open the door just as she could have sworn she heard the clicking of another door, a little way down the corridor.

Heart in her throat, she closed her door and pressed her back against it, breath coming in rushed fits and spurts, like she'd just sprinted the last mile of a marathon.

Holy crapola. What had she been thinking?

'Sienna?'

Her heart slammed out of its nook in her chest cavity and rammed into her throat. She could *feel* it there, a hard thumping hammer. Aiden's voice was so deep and growly, gruff and familiar, even when it wasn't. Just like him. Familiar and not, all at once.

Her Aiden, but *not* her Aiden.

She squeezed her eyes shut, as though that might somehow magically transport her out of this situation.

It didn't.

'Sienna?'

She jumped forward, off the door, then whirled around to stare at it accusingly.

'Did you need something?'

She was being a baby.

Slowly, she reached out and opened the door, drawing it inwards to reveal Aiden's big – really big – frame, and a face that showed hints of concern.

'You okay?'

'I'm fine,' she said, one hand behind her back, fingers fidgeting.

'Did you knock on my door?'

She squeezed her eyes again before remembering that she wasn't three and that wasn't how you hid from someone.

The door clicked and she opened her eyes to see Aiden had stepped into her room and shut it.

And he was close to her.

So close that all she could really focus on was the wall of pectorals she knew to be behind his grey T-shirt.

'I...'

Great. Great start, she thought, with an inward eye roll. *How poetic.*

'I don't know.'

Much better.

'Sienna.' Another growl. Deep and husky, giving her name – from his mouth – the power to snake out and wrap around her, like a silk rope. She shivered at the imagery of that. The idea of him tying her up.

'You're the one who wanted to talk,' she said, defensively.

He frowned. 'That's why you knocked on my door?'

She shrugged one shoulder.

He expelled a breath. 'Because you didn't seem interested in talking down there. At least, not to me. You seemed fine talking to anyone else,' he muttered.

'It's a party, that's kind of the point.'

He crossed his arms over his chest, so she couldn't help but stare hungrily at the way his shirt strained over his muscles. Her mouth felt all dry and dusty.

'But you want to talk now?' There was the slightest hint of a challenge in those words. A question he hadn't put into words lingered between them. She felt it. Heat flickered through her, challenging her, daring her to do something reckless and stupid, for once in her life. To put herself, and her needs and wants first.

To take a little something, just for herself.

How long had it been since she'd made a decision purely because she wanted to?

'Nope,' she answered, and as if to underscore her meaning, she took a step towards him, effectively closing the remaining distance between them.

'Sienna.' Now her name was both a growl and a plea. And a promise?

She lifted a hand towards his chest and he unfolded his arms but stood perfectly, completely still.

'You know what, Aiden?'

'What?' Another plea. For sanity? Salvation?

'I don't think you want to talk, either.'

His Adam's apple jerked as he swallowed. She lifted a finger and pressed it to the hair-roughened flesh there, then ran her pointer finger higher, towards the curve of his lips. He closed his eyes, swaying a little.

'You've been drinking,' he said, opening his eyes and staring right into hers.

'Mostly soda for the last few hours.'

His eyes roamed her face, as if needing to ascertain the truth of that, and her stomach went all twisty at the small but unmistakably decent hesitation he was expressing. Of course Aiden wasn't the kind of guy who'd take advantage of a woman who'd been slamming back alcoholic drinks. Why would he need to, anyway? She was pretty sure women weren't thin on the ground for him.

'What do you want, Sienna?'

'I think I want this,' she said, lifting up onto the tips of her toes, pressing one palm to his chest and curving her other hand around behind his neck. He was so much taller than her, but when she stretched, she could reach. Just.

Her lips brushed his; the feeling was electric and immediate. It zapped between them, a spark, a seismic shift.

He pulled back. 'You *think* you want this?' he demanded gruffly. 'Or you *know*?'

Another excellent point.

'I know,' she answered, any last doubt as to what she was doing evaporating in the face of the heat that was blasting through her in response to the slightest kiss.

'You don't think this is unnecessarily complicated?' But as he asked the question, he was putting both his big, burly hands on her hips, holding her close against his body, so she shivered.

'Oh, it's definitely that.' He was hard. She could

feel it and her body was trembling. 'But it doesn't need to be.'

He made a noise, deep and low. She didn't think it was a word, but it was at least an acknowledgement of her statement.

'After the wedding, I doubt we'll see each other again. I mean, maybe at one of Astrid and Blake's kids' things or a milestone birthday or whatever, but we're never going to spend this kind of time in the same space again, right?'

It felt good to say those words. To make it clear to him she had no issues with that, whatsoever.

She wasn't pining over him. She'd never do that again.

'Right.'

Still, the searing disappointment at his ready agreement caught her unawares. She hardened herself against it.

'But we're both here now, and clearly, there's something between us. So? Why not do something about it?'

'I thought you were doing something about it,' he replied, but his fingers were stroking her sides now, sending her into something like a meltdown. 'Ignoring me?' he prompted.

'Turns out, you're hard to ignore.'

His grin made her heart go mushy. 'I'm glad to hear it.'

She rolled her eyes. 'I just mean you're big, and kind of everywhere I go.'

'Riiiight,' he laughed, pulling her hard against him again. The air seemed to whoosh out of her lungs.

'This is probably going to be more effective.'

'And by this, you mean...'

'Do you need me to spell it out?'

'Kind of. Just to be sure there's no misunderstanding. I mean, that could be kind of awkward.'

'I think we're both on the same page.'

'Which is?'

She wrapped her arms around his waist and stared right up into his eyes. 'Take me to bed, Aiden. And this time, not to sleep.'

He grinned, but there was something in the depths of his eyes that she didn't immediately comprehend. A look of concern, or hesitation. But a moment later, he was scooping her up and saying, 'I thought you'd never ask, Mastrangelo.'

Held cradled against his chest like that, she felt so petite and fragile, so protected and cossetted, that she had to immediately tamp down a sense of how much she *liked* feeling protected. It reminded her of how he'd made her feel as a teenager. Like he would always shield her, always be there to care for her, whenever she needed it. She'd mistaken his physical strength for something else entirely. She'd been mistaken about a heck of a lot of things back then. She'd seen what she'd wanted to. That hadn't been fair on either of them.

'But this is just sex,' she said, after a beat. 'It doesn't mean anything. Okay?'

His response was to kiss her. Not a brushing of lips, but a proper, heart-squeezing, stomach-looping, knee-shaking, bone-melting kiss. The kind where his lips pushed hers apart and his tongue slid in and glided with hers, like some kind of erotic, tangly dance. When they reached the bed, he laid her down on it in the same motion that he brought his body over hers, his weight mostly held by his elbows, but just enough on Sienna to make her body throb with a hot, desperate need.

She knew this was a form of temporary delirium. Brought on by the heat and the beauty of the island, by the sense she'd carried for more than ten years that she and Aiden had never really had any proper closure, that somehow, what they'd been back then sort of deserved a better send off. But it was also just about desire.

She wanted him as much as she had as a teenager. That hadn't changed over time. She'd thought it had. She'd thought she'd outgrown whatever feelings she'd once had for him, but she was starting to recognise the merit of a 'chemical reaction' argument. Like adding heat to water and expecting it to boil, being near Aiden 'Walk Out On You' Carter just did something strange to her insides. And that was okay with her, because she wasn't going to be around him for much longer.

Surrendering herself to this was way easier – and more fun – than ignoring it.

Plans for revenge seemed so petty now. So unnecessary. He'd walked out on her, and she'd deserved better, but it was a long way in the rear-view mirror. There was no sense holding that grudge for the rest of her life.

She'd learned a lot from how he'd treated her. It had made her stronger. Harder. And it had shown her that she could cope with a hell of a lot more than she'd ever realised.

She hadn't needed him to protect her, in the end. She'd done a pretty damned good job of that, all on her own. She'd never rely on anyone else again.

His hands caught the flimsy material of her shirt and pushed it up her body. She wasn't wearing a bra, and the moment his palms connected with her bare breasts, his fingers tracing her nipples before squeezing them, so she convulsed. 'Aiden,' she groaned against his mouth.

'Too much?'

She shook her head, lifting her feet onto the mattress and arching her back. 'Not enough. Not nearly enough.'

She felt his smile against her mouth right before he kissed her, hard, heavy, desperate and demanding, only breaking away so he could push her shirt the rest of the way off her body, and then, so his mouth could drag over her collarbone, towards one breast, which he seemed determined to worship. His tongue flicked her nipple, then sucked it into his mouth, the warmth of him, the touch of his fingers on her other breast, the weight of his body, the way he smelled, like the beach and summer, and soapy, too, as if he'd just showered. She lifted her hips, so she felt his arousal through their far-too-many layers of clothing, and tilted her head back on a groan of exasperated need.

Her hands seemed to remember, belatedly, that they could explore, too, and she ran them under his shirt, over his back, feeling his smooth, warm skin, then pushing them lower, driving his fingertips into his shorts, curving over his buttocks – so hard and muscly, there was no mistaking this man's athleticism.

'God, Aiden, work out much?' she asked through pants of breath, as he transferred his mouth to her other breast.

She swore then, the pleasure almost blinding in its intensity.

'I could ask you the same thing.'

Something fluttered in her chest. Pleasure, because of his compliment. Pleasure she didn't want to feel. At least, she didn't want to feel it because of him. Not that kind of pleasure, anyway.

'Less talking,' she decided. 'More undressing.'

His laugh was hoarse. 'You've gotten bossy.'

She rolled her eyes. 'Opinionated and assertive, and neither of those is a bad thing.'

'Nope. Definitely not a bad thing.' He pulled away from her then, standing at the foot of the bed, looking down at her. 'You're really sure about this?'

She pushed up onto her elbows, staring at him, aghast. 'Seriously?'

He held his hands up placatingly. 'I was just going to say, before this goes any further, I should probably go get something from my room. Unless you happen to travel with a stash of condoms?'

She felt the colour drain from her face.

A sharp blade of panic sliced her to the core.

A condom.

Of *course* they needed to use protection. She would *never* ever risk accidentally falling pregnant to anyone, let alone Aiden. Just the thought of going through all that again turned her insides to ice.

'It's okay,' he said, moving towards the door. 'I'll be right back.' He'd obviously misunderstood her reaction. Or maybe he hadn't even clocked it. Either way, she was glad. She didn't particularly feel like talking about the precautions she always took. She was on the pill, and she always practised safe sex as well.

Because there was no downside to being extra, extra careful.

And a lot of downside in being careless, just once.

True to his word, he returned, so quickly she suspected he'd sprinted.

'I think you just set a land speed record...' she remarked, as he snibbed the lock on the door.

He shot a look at Sienna that made her blood turn to lava. 'I aim to please.'

'I really hope so.'

His smile was pure cocky confidence. BDE to the max.

'Now, the undressing,' he said, holding up a line of condoms as he strode back towards her, placing the packets on the bedside table before ripping his shirt over his head.

Her eyes devoured his chest. This time, she didn't bother trying to hide it. She ate up the sight of him, letting it nourish her hungry senses. His hands moved to his shorts, pushing them down, leaving his boxers in place.

'All of it,' she insisted, mouth dry as her gaze dropped lower.

'Opinionated and assertive?' he queried with a quirked brow.

'Damn straight.'

He pushed at his undershorts then, revealing an erection that was rock-hard and huge. She couldn't stop her eyes from devouring him.

'Your turn.'

'Wait. Stand there a minute longer,' she said. 'I just want to look a bit.'

He laughed, but the sound was strained. Nonetheless, he was a willing-ish model, taking a step back from the bed and putting his arms above his head in a weightlifter sort of pose, then turning around slowly, before strutting towards the door with an exaggerated hip wiggle and sashaying back.

'Had enough?'

She giggled. 'For now. Though you are an excellent model.'

'My agent will be glad to hear it.' Naked, he came back to the side of the bed and leaned over, bracing his hands on either side of her hips, his eyes locked to hers. 'Your turn.'

'Right. I guess that's fair.'

But she was nervous suddenly. Not about sleeping with him, but about getting undressed in front of him. Nervous about him seeing her naked, about being so vulnerable in front of him.

It wasn't like he hadn't seen her naked before. Nor did she have any hang ups about her body. It was just the crossing of a threshold she hadn't fully planned to step over. It was all happening kind of spontaneously, and yet, at the same time, it almost felt like it had been destined to come to this, from the minute she'd stepped foot on the same private island as Aiden.

With a slightly unsteady rush of breath, she pushed her skirt down, leaving her underpants in place. It might have been a double standard, but so what?

'You're beautiful,' he said, moving his body back over hers, never mind the cotton of her pants that were still in place. He pulled her lower lip between his teeth and wiggled it, before kissing her again, this time with one hand curving behind her head, fingers tangling in her hair as he lifted her a little, holding her there for his inspection, his tasting, his probing, desperate kissing.

And it was desperate. There was something in their kiss, in the way their bodies moved together, that spoke of two people being brought to a feast after a decade of famine. Sienna couldn't get enough of touching him, of feeling him, his skin warm and smooth, except where it wasn't, except where his chest was covered in hair or his arms. He was so hypermasculine, so absolutely alpha, it felt completely primal to lose herself to this.

'Christ,' he groaned, digging his fingers into her hips as he broke the kiss and pushed up to stare at her, a wildness in his eyes that was totally mirrored in her soul. 'I feel like I'm about to come.'

She arched a brow, snaking a hand down to his cock and wrapping it in her palm.

'Fuck, Mastrangelo. I wouldn't do that.'

She blinked up at him with wide-eyed innocence.

'Seriously, Sienna.' He pulled away, standing up and bracing his hands on his hips, his breathing coming out in a rush.

He reached for the condoms – to her immense relief – and opened one up with his teeth. His eyes held hers as he reached down and stretched it over his length, his eyes still on hers as he came back to the bed and slowly dragged her undies down her legs. Sienna shivered. Because he didn't move fast.

Nope.

Not fast, at all.

His palms seemed to inch over her bare legs, sending goosebumps trailing over her at the ghostly light touch, so she arched her back and writhed with hunger. 'Aiden, I need you.'

His smile was tense. Like he was holding on by a thread.

She totally understood.

Madness was spiralling between them, thick and heavy.

He dropped the scrap of lace on the floor and then stood again, to look at her. To really look. Just like she'd been feasting her eyes on him before.

'Where's my show?' he asked, a joke in his tone, as he nodded towards the door.

She laughed softly, though inwardly, she couldn't think of anything worse than leaving the bed, because it would delay what she now wanted more than she'd ever wanted any damned thing in her life.

'Okay,' she said, though, pushing up to sitting, then wriggling to the end of the bed and hopping off it. With the same exaggeratedly seductive swagger he'd employed, she wiggled her hips and walked towards the door, performing a pirouette there, before returning halfway across the room and posing like a supermodel in a shoot. One hand on her hip, then bending forward and blowing him a kiss.

He swore again, the word torn from him, and neither of them was laughing when he stalked across to her and dragged her body against his, lifting her this time to wrap her legs around his waist as he carried her not back to the bed, but rather, to the wall beside it.

Another curse, as he shifted her weight and positioned her so his cock was at her entrance, his strength an easy match for her weight, the wall helping support her as he moved his mouth to her breast and tormented it anew. It was Sienna who shifted though, pushing herself down, using the grip her heels had on his lower back to pull herself lower, to draw him deep – so, so deep – inside of her on a rush of need and hunger.

They both froze, going completely still as her muscles squeezed around him, and his length jerked inside. As she got used to the way he felt. Bigger. Different. New. The same.

'Sienna.' It wasn't a curse, but he said it like it was. He said it dirty and dark. Angry and delirious.

'Fuck me,' she implored, tilting her head back and staring at the ceiling. 'Please.'

He laughed then, but it was a strained sound, like he was barely, just barely, holding on, and she totally understood.

'Seeing as you asked so nicely,' he said, moving to kiss her, his tongue lashing hers as he began to thrust inside her, scuttling absolutely everything she ever thought she knew about the world into a thousand different directions. Nothing, and she meant nothing, made sense any more, and she wasn't sure she even cared.

16

'Oh my God.' Sienna's eyes flew open at the same moment she became aware of Aiden's arm thrown casually across her chest, and one of his legs entangled with hers. Of the fact they were both naked in her bed. As memories seemed to explode inside her brain like fireworks at a fair. 'Aiden!' She rolled over quickly, catching the moment he woke up in response to her plaintive cry. 'We fell asleep.'

He didn't look remotely concerned. 'Are you surprised?' His dark brows shot up and her stomach squished in on itself.

No, come to think of it. She wasn't. They'd spent several hours reacquainting themselves with one another's bodies. So much for an itch that needed to be scratched, she thought. This was more like the chicken pox, a whole-body rash that they couldn't get enough of rubbing down. Proof in point, just looking across at him now and she felt anticipation building inside of her in tingly, toe-curling waves.

Down, girl.

'You need to go.'

He glanced at her, then reached behind her for her phone. 'It's not even seven.'

'Yeah, but people will be up already.'

'So?'

'So,' she said, emphatically, 'they'll see you leaving my room.'

'I stayed in your room the night before last, and you didn't seem to care who saw me leave.'

'Yes, but we hadn't had sex then,' she pointed out, aware of the illogic of that.

'I don't have it tattooed on my forehead.'

'Yeah, but, we know. And if anyone sees you, and asks me, I'm going to have to make up an excuse, and I'm a terrible liar.'

'So, worst case, they'll know how we spent the night. Oh, *think* of the scandal! That two grown adults should have had consensual sex...' He clasped his hands to his chest in a gesture of mock outrage.

'I'm serious,' she said, but her lips were twitching with a need to smile.

'Who cares?'

She stared at him, bemused by his approach. Did he have a point? Was this even a big deal? People hooked up. So what? They were two consenting adults with history up the wazoo. So what if they'd done the horizontal mambo and everyone guessed it?

But, the girls. Sienna worried at her lower lip, trying to imagine how she could explain this to them. Them, who would be so worried about her. Worried she'd get hurt all over again. Worried she wasn't taking care of herself. Worried she was biting off more than she could chew. Or worse, excited that maybe this was the beginning of something big and exciting. That maybe she and Aiden had buried the hatchet and were about to become 'a thing'.

She shook her head. 'Bad idea.' She locked her eyes to his. 'This is Blake and Astrid's wedding. I don't want to overshadow that by getting people to speculate about what's going on with us. And people *will* speculate. Whether that's your mom, or Chuck, or the girls, and I really don't want to have to think about how to explain this to them.'

'What would you say, out of interest?'

'I just said, I don't want to have to think about it.'

'How about, "we had sex"?'

'For old times' sake,' she added, but with a roll of her eyes. 'Yeah, that'll placate precisely nobody.'

'And it's nobody's business,' he said, in a careless, relaxed kind of way.

She snorted. 'Since when has that stopped people from being concerned? Come on, Aiden. You're in the public eye. You've had a decade of being tabloid fodder. You know it's human nature to be curious, and even more so when it's someone you care about.' Her cheeks flushed pink. 'I mean they care about us, not that I care about you.'

'Naturally,' he said, but with a hint of something flattening the word.

'Okay.' She expelled a shaky breath. 'So, you'll sneak out of here without getting seen?'

'I mean, I'm not going to climb out the window, if that's what you're suggesting.'

'Heaven forbid. You might fall and break one of those very valuable legs of yours. I could do without incurring the wrath of your fans, believe me.'

'More like my team,' he said, with a grin.

She plucked at the sheet between them, eyes focused there, instead of on Aiden. 'You love it?'

He was quiet, like he hadn't understood the question.

She glanced at his face to find him staring at her with a hollowing-out sort of intensity. 'Hockey.' She cleared her throat. 'Do you still love it like you used to?'

'I guess.'

'You *guess*? Is a bajillion dollars and the adoration of puck bunnies and the bro crowd everywhere a little boring these days? Just gimme a second while I analyse the underwhelm of that.'

'Nothing to analyse,' he said with a crackly laugh. 'It's a job.'

'But... you always *loved* it.'

He frowned, his gaze focused now on a point beyond her shoulder, like he was stepping back in time. 'Did I?'

'You're serious?'

He didn't answer.

Sienna's lips parted. 'Aiden, you never could wait to get to the rink. When you couldn't skate, you and Blake used to just run at each other in the backyard. You were obsessed with all the teams, all the stats. You lived and breathed hockey.'

He nodded slowly, rubbing a hand over his stubbly chin. 'I guess I did.'

'And you don't now?'

His lips quirked downwards. 'I didn't say that.'

'You kind of did. I mean, not in so many words, but...'

His eyes lifted to hers, lancing her a little, but his own were laced with questions. Uncertainty. Doubt. Not emotions she readily associated with Aiden. 'I think it was probably more about escape than anything else. Maybe even about feeling in control. On the ice, I was in charge. I was good at it. I was strong.' He swallowed, throat shifting visibly. 'The worse things got at home, the more I craved that.'

'Control was important to you,' she murmured, nodding gently, because she could understand why.

'Hell, yeah.' He grimaced a little. 'Actually, if I'm being honest, that's something I didn't really understand about myself until...'

She waited, a sixth sense making her feel like he was about to say something important.

'Well, until you, actually.'

Her heart stammered. 'What do you mean?'

'You weren't the first girl I dated, but you were the first girl to make me feel like my feet had lost contact with the earth. The first girl to make me feel like I was floating away. The first girl to make me genuinely afraid that I would lose not just my control but also myself.' He moved closer, stroking her side, his features bearing a mask of genuine sorrow. 'I loved how being with you felt, but I hated it, too. It scared the hell out of me, if I'm honest.'

'Scared you?' she repeated, agog. 'You were *scared* of me?'

'Not of you, of how much you meant to me.'

'That's crazy. We were young and in love. I was supposed to mean something to you.'

'You meant too much.'

Her heart stopped stammering. It basically stopped beating. She felt an actual pain in the centre of her chest. 'What does that even mean?'

'It meant I was scared of what loving you could do to me.'

'You're talking in riddles. I don't get it.'

'I don't know if I ever told you what my dad was like, when things were okay. How much he loved my mom. How he doted on her. She was his queen. Until she wasn't. Until you've lived with that kind of... dark side of the moon phenomenon, you couldn't understand the fear of the flip side of love. But I've lived it. I've felt it.'

She swallowed, something jagging in her brain. And her heart. Some piece of a puzzle she hadn't even known she'd been holding all these years.

'You thought you were going to hurt me.'

'You. Any guy who noticed you.' He shrugged. 'It's a slippery slope.'

'But you're not your dad,' she said, simply, because it was true.

'Aren't I?'

Her heart was racing now. Her body ached. Her chest hurt. Her head was spinning. All the pieces were slotting into place. He'd left for his career, he's left to get his mom and Blake away from Ashbury Falls, but he'd also left because he'd been running from her. From his fear of hurting her.

He'd left, in part, because he loved her too much to take that risk.

She felt a tell-tale tingle at the back of the throat, threatening the onset of tears.

'You're not him,' she said. And when he didn't respond, she wriggled closer and cupped his face with her hands. She didn't know a damned thing beyond this: she had to get through to him. She had to make him understand.

'No. I've made sure of that.'

The words were vice-like. Iron. Control. Self-possession evident in each clearly enunciated syllable.

She stroked his cheek.

'How have you made sure of that?'

'I have my ways,' he joked, employing a thick, sort of Eastern European accent.

She shook her head. 'Don't push me away.'

His face sobered. 'Come on, Si. It doesn't matter. We shouldn't even be talking about this.'

'Why not?'

'Because it's going to stir up a hornet's nest neither of us wants to deal with.'

Her heart felt like it was dropping out of her body.

'I'm going back to New York. You're going home to Ashbury. We both have rich, full, complicated lives. So let's not drag the past into this. You're the one who said it was just sex – and you're right. It is. It has to be.'

It has to be.

This wasn't a choice for him. Their chemistry was the same as it had been all those years ago, and now Sienna wondered if other things were, too. Like her ability to get under his skin. To drive him crazy. To scare him, because of how much he might one day feel for her again.

It has to be.

He wasn't willing to risk it.

And nor was she.

Because they really were the same people they'd

been then, in all the ways that mattered, and Aiden was the one guy who could break her down and destroy her. She'd be ridiculously naïve to run that risk again. Particularly when he was saying, from the outset, that it wasn't what he wanted.

'Yeah, okay,' she said, forcing a bright smile, glad that the threatened tears hadn't eventuated. 'Secret sex,' she added. 'It's going to be way easier – and more fun – if we keep this between us.'

'Is that your way of saying you're not done with me yet, Mastrangelo?'

She glanced across at him. *Crap.* She'd totally been taking it for granted that they'd keep doing this for as long as they were on the island.

'I mean' – she infused humour into her tone – 'if you're busy, I can always see if Chuck's available...'

His eyes flashed to hers and for a second, she saw it. The intensity he was afraid of. Jealousy. Fierce, unmistakable. And she got it. She didn't for one second think he would ever, ever hurt her. He just wasn't wired that way. But she understood why he'd spent his adult life running from even being in that position.

And suddenly, his string of girlfriends made sense. Those short-term relationships, never serious, never long. Sienna had thought it was because he was a playboy, but she realised now he'd been running over baking-hot sand his whole life, doing everything he could to avoid putting down roots and getting close to another person.

She would have groaned, except Aiden was moving quickly, bringing his body over hers, kissing her until she was panting with need, and completely ready to surrender to him all over again. It might have been 'just sex', but she fully intended to make the most of having it – and him – on tap while they were on the island.

* * *

'Sienna?' She hardly heard the voice at first. Her whole body, her whole being, was in a whirling current of desire and satiation, courtesy of Aiden. Her cells seemed to be catching fire, one by one. 'Can I borrow your straightener? Mine just died.'

'Sienna.' It was Aiden, pushing up onto his elbows to stare down at her, his cock buried deep inside of her, his butt-naked body on top of her. 'Someone's at the door.'

'What?' she whispered, looking around and catching sight of them in the reflection of the mirror.

Her cheeks were flushed and their arrangement was most definitely NSFW.

'Your friend.'

Her eyes widened. 'Which friend? What?'

'Sounds like the blonde.'

'Bella,' she hissed.

'It's okay if you're busy.' Bella's voice warbled a little at the end, and Sienna guessed she was suppressing a laugh.

'I'm—'

Aiden moved then, and she had to bite down on her lip to stop from moaning.

Another thrust, and she felt her grip slipping. Her body was tingling all over, the beginning of her orgasm fast and intense.

'Oh my God,' she whispered.

'I'll come back,' Bella called, scuttling footsteps following her rushed escape.

'Oh my God,' Sienna groaned for a different reason now, arching her back and driving her hands through her hair, desperate to hold onto sanity and reality, even as she was falling apart, delightfully, deliriously, at the seams...

* * *

'Well, well,' Bella cooed, an hour and another orgasm later, by the coffee station. 'Don't you look like the cat that got the cream?'

Sienna felt heat flood her cheeks. 'Listen, Bella, about upstairs...'

'Don't worry,' she said. 'I borrowed a straightener from Cynthia – she's a peach.' Bella handed the coffee she'd evidently ordered for herself to Sienna. 'You look like you need it more.' She turned to the barista and placed another order. Sienna took a mighty grateful sip of the hot drink.

'I love you,' she said, closing her eyes as the caffeine infiltrated her body, bit by bit, reviving her from both sexual satiation and shock.

'I know you do.'

'But seriously, about this morning...'

'It's none of my business,' Bella promised. But her face clouded over a little with solicitousness. 'Just promise me you're being careful.'

'We are. I'm not going to risk anything happening, I promise.'

'I don't mean that.' Bella waved a slim hand through the air. 'This was meant to be a bit of fun. Flirty, casual. Easy. To teach him a lesson. But neither of you was meant to get seriously hurt in the process. That's still the plan, right?'

Sienna shook her head a little. 'I mean, I think any semblance of a plan whooshed right out the window within about twenty-four hours of getting to the island, don't you?'

'And why is that?' she pushed.

The barista handed over another coffee and they made their way through the crowd – which had really started to fill out, with the wedding now just one day away – towards the terrace. The air out here was warm and sweet, filled with the heavy aromas of citrus and lavender. They moved to an unoccupied table.

'I mean, the plan was pretty simple,' Bella continued. 'Unless you found it harder than you'd realised, to flirt with Aiden?'

'I think we've established flirting with him wasn't a problem.'

'But you were meant to flirt and walk away,' Bella reminded her. 'To teach him a lesson?'

'I know.' Sienna's glance dropped to her coffee. 'That's still what I'm intending to do.' She thought back to the way he'd insisted on that. *Just sex.* Neither of them had said 'meaningless', because it wasn't that, either. How could two people who'd shared so much ever have meaningless sex, anyway? 'I'm not going to get my revenge,' she said, lips pulling sideways. 'But the thing is, I'm not really sure he deserves it, anyway.'

Bella's perfect eyebrows pushed towards her hairline. 'What? Is this not the man we've spent almost a year wanting to burn in effigy?'

Sienna rolled her eyes. 'Not quite.'

'Okay.' Bella leaned forward, putting her hand on Sienna's wrist. 'But what happened? You thought he was the devil incarnate a week ago.'

She took another sip of coffee. 'I know. I've spent more than ten years thinking that. But maybe, I mean, what if I was wrong?'

Bella's expression was sceptical. 'Were you?'

'I think he had some pretty good reasons for wanting to get out of town,' she admitted.

'But to cut you out of his life so completely...'

'Yeah, I know. I guess... I guess I kind of understand even that, now.'

Bella let out a low whistle. 'Either this guy's got some magic excuse, or he's got a magic... something else entirely.'

Sienna's cheeks flushed but she grinned. 'Maybe both.'

'I see,' Bella said, sagely, after several beats. But Bella being Bella, that wasn't the end of it. 'So, what's the new plan?'

'There is no plan.'

'You're having sex with the guy who broke your heart and you've hated ever since, and you don't have a *plan* for how to *not* get hurt again?' Bella was whispering, but there was a screechy tone to her voice that made Sienna look around jumpily. Blake and Cynthia were out on the terrace, but far enough away, and deep in conversation, so she was pretty confident they hadn't heard.

'I'm not the same girl I was then. He won't hurt me.'

Bella looked far from convinced.

'We've talked about it,' Sienna promised. 'We've both agreed what we're doing, and when it will end. No hard feelings.'

Bella's expression didn't change.

'Back then, I thought we were in love, and going to, you know, grow up and get married. I thought he was my happily ever after. My knight in shining armour. Back then, he hurt me because I gave him enough of myself to make that possible. I will never make that mistake again, and nor would he. We know what we're doing, Bells. You can relax. I promise.'

'Okaaay,' she said hesitantly. 'Because I really would hate to have to kill Astrid's new brother-in-law,' she said with a joking grimace. 'But I'd do it, for you.'

Sienna grinned. 'Don't worry; it won't come to that. I know what I'm doing.'

'And that is?'

Sienna thought for a moment. 'You know, I think I'm actually having fun.'

Bella smiled, her eyes knowing. 'You deserve that.'

'Thanks. Now, I've got something else I want to run past you.' She glanced around, making sure they were still out of earshot. 'I was going to wait until after the wedding but... I'm too excited.' She sucked in a deep breath. 'I think I might have found a way to get to Horrible Harvey.'

Bella's brows shot upwards. 'You're kidding?'

She shook her head.

'Shall I get Olly?'

'Oh, God, yes. I can't think of anyone besides us who'll be more excited by the idea of finally getting that bastard back.'

When Bella, Olly and Chase joined her a short while later – Olly and Chase were seemingly inseparable – Sienna leaned forward, barely able to keep the excitement from her voice. 'Okay, so, here's what I'm thinking...'

17

He was surprised by how much he liked Chase and Olly. An artist and an author... not really his usual type of friends, but they were great guys, and he'd just spent more than an hour sharing breakfast with them, shooting the breeze.

They were both also as obviously, cloyingly loved up as his brother was, totally smitten by Bella and Paige respectively, so he'd also felt a bit like he was the odd one out, given his disavowal of serious relationships. He liked them, though, and he liked that they were now a part of Blake's orbit – by virtue of their close friendship with Astrid, and her besties.

And Sienna.

They'd been talking about the New York art scene when Bella had arrived at the table, cheeks flushed, barely glancing at Aiden and putting an arm around Chase's shoulders while asking Olly if he had a moment.

Chase hadn't looked at all concerned that his girl-friend wanted a minute alone with some other guy. If anything, he looked excited. 'Good news?'

'Maybe,' Bella had said, biting into her lip. 'Do you want to come, too?'

'Nah, this is probably best left to Olly...'

'No way, man. The more heads the better on this one.' Then, leaning closer. 'I know she'd want you to be involved. Come on.'

Then, Chase had turned to Aiden. 'Excuse us. Urgent, erm, wedding business.'

He nodded, watching as the three of them walked off, heads bent in conversation. Aiden took the op-portunity to catch up with some of the team, to sit and shoot the breeze like he always did. He'd been playing long enough to know he was a bit of an elder statesman of the game, that the younger players looked up to him. When he sat down and gave them the time of day, he could see the way it puffed out their chests, made them feel good. It was everything he and Blake had always said they wanted to give back to the sport that had saved their lives.

The morning passed and he was able to make a decent show of *not* spending a fair amount of his time casting his gaze around for a certain blonde to walk by. How could he be so desperate to see her again after having spent the night – and morning – with her?

Eventually, he made his excuses to the team, restless as all get-out, for reasons he couldn't explain. A walk seemed like as good an idea as any to burn off excess energy. Except, only a few minutes into his walk, bam...

He heard her before he saw her, and every cell in his body damn well told him it was Sienna, even prior to rounding the corner and finding her sitting on the grass lawn, looking out to the beach.

'You wouldn't believe it, baby. It's sooo pretty here. Hang on a sec.' She pressed the button on the phone, so the camera turned around, filling the screen with the pristine beach, the palm trees, the luscious nature of it all. When she flicked the camera back, the face she was talking to went back to prime position on the screen. A girl, a teenager, with a few spots and braces, grinned back at Sienna.

'Ohhh, I'm so jelly. Is it amazing? Is Astrid having fun?'

He knew he shouldn't be eavesdropping. Just standing behind a ficus hoping not to be seen. But curiosity was throbbing through him, along with some other things he really should have been getting better at controlling by now.

'She is. She's a perfect bride. Relaxed, happy, nothing's stressing her.'

'Soo good. Are you taking a billion pics?'

'At least a billion. Probably twice that.'

The teenager laughed. He knew it was Sienna's sort of step-daughter. He'd always figured Sienna had some kind of supercharged maternal gene, but seeing it in action now made an archaic part of him thunder and roar to life. A part of him he had subjugated a long time ago.

Not being like his father was high on his list of priorities.

Not having kids was there too.

Too risky.

Too terrifying.

If there was any chance he might end up out of control, he didn't want to risk having a child caught in the crosshairs.

But Sienna? She made this shit look easy.

No, she made it look... fun.

'What's the food like?'

'Ahmazing. I've eaten my bodyweight at least ten times over. There's been lobster and shrimp and these amazing chicken satay skewers that I can't get enough of. The breakfast bar has omelettes and crepes, and there are the juiciest sliders served with afternoon cocktails.'

'Oh, man,' Melanie groaned. 'You're making me hungry, and all we've got in the house is two-week-old bread.'

He saw the way Sienna sat a little straighter. 'Oh, yeah?'

'Don't worry,' Melanie immediately compensated with a bright smile. 'I had June's lunch leftovers. It was pasta bake. She hates pasta bake.'

Sienna made a soft noise that Aiden suspected he only heard because the wind was blowing his way.

'You know what? Could you do something for me, honey?'

'Sure.'

'Go over to my place and check the freezer. I'm 99 per cent sure there's a lasagne in there that needs to be eaten.'

Melanie shook her head a little.

'I mean it, kiddo. You know where the key is. Go

get it, chuck it in the oven at a low temp for a couple of hours, to make sure it defrosts properly and heats all the way through. You know how much you love my lasagnes.'

'I do, but I can't take your food.'

'Oh Mel, I'll let you in on a little secret.'

Melanie waited.

'I actually hate lasagne. I literally only make it because you love it. So you'd be doing me a favour, I swear.'

Melanie laughed. 'Okay, okay. You're the best, Sissi.'

'Nope, you are.'

'I miss you.'

'I miss you, too. So much. I'll be home in a couple of days.'

Something in Aiden's chest seemed to flap around. Or hollow out. He couldn't say for sure, only it was a new experience and he didn't like it. At all.

'Okay.' Melanie waved. 'Byeee. Love you.'

'I love you, too, honey. See you soon.'

She disconnected the call and sat with her elbows braced on her knees, staring out at the ocean for a few beats. Aiden took a step, to go over to her, but then heard the ringing of her phone. Not like it was receiving a call, but rather, as though she were making a FaceTime call.

'Yeah?' A man's face filled the screen. Aiden sought cover behind the ficus again – a somewhat ridiculous proposition given his size and frame, and the narrowness of the tree. He might as well try hiding behind a toothpick.

'Cory, you need to go shopping.'

'What?' The dude sounded like he'd just woken up. Aiden peered from between two thick, luscious green leaves, trying to get a clearer view of the man Sienna had dated seriously enough to consider his daughter her step-daughter.

'You have no food in the house.'

'Did Melanie call and tell you that?' he muttered.

'Not in so many words. She covered your ass, like she always does. But it was pretty obvious that she's starving. God, Cory. It's not brain surgery to go to the goddamned store and get your kid some fresh food. Hell, write a list, stick it on the fridge with a twenty and get Melanie to go shopping.'

'Can you give it a fucking break? I've just woken up, I've got a killer headache—'

She snorted. 'Are you hungover?'

'What the hell do you care?'

He saw her shoulder blades shift as if she were

rolling her head a little, trying to relax. 'I care about Melanie, and you know that.'

'She's not your kid.'

He wished for a thousand things in that moment. To see Sienna's face, to know how she was feeling. To be there with her, a protective arm around her shoulders. To reach through the screen and knock some sense into the other guy. The last one was why he stayed stock still, where he was, camouflaged by a tree.

'No, but she's yours. Start acting like you give a damn, or you're going to lose her.'

'Is that a threat?'

'She's old enough to start realising what a loser you are. Don't give her a reason to run away.'

'She'd never.'

'No, she'd never run away from me, but I don't know if the same could be said for you. Just... get your shit together, Cory. She deserves so much better than this.'

'You don't get to—'

'I mean, for God's sake. I'm away for *one week* and you can't even hold it together for her?'

He stared mutinously at the screen.

'Get it together,' she said again. 'I'll call Melanie

tomorrow. I'd better hear that there's milk and eggs in the fridge.'

'Yeah, yeah, okay. Whatever. Where are you, anyway?'

Sienna's shoulders shifted again, this time with an exhalation. 'It doesn't matter. I'll be home in a few days. Look after her until then, okay?'

'She's my kid...'

'Cory?'

'Yeah, okay. Fine. I'll look after her.'

Sienna disconnected the call and lowered her head onto her knees, her cheek pressed there as she stared sideways.

He could retreat. Tiptoe backwards, hoping the ficus kept him hidden. Or he could go and talk to her. Tell her he'd heard the conversation.

Or he could just stay hiding where he was indefinitely, he concluded with exasperation.

'I know you're there.' Her voice was a little louder, though it didn't need to be. He'd heard her fine.

She turned then, looking back at him.

'I didn't want to interrupt,' he admitted, straightening, feeling a little ridiculous.

'The tree wasn't exactly the best hiding spot for someone your size.'

'Yeah.' He shrugged. 'Sorry. I didn't want to interrupt but I just...'

'It's okay.' Her lips pulled to the side.

'So that's him, huh?' He strode over the grass and eased his large frame to the grass beside her, legs kicked out in front of him.

'Him?'

'The guy you dated after me?'

'Right, yeah. That's him. Cory.'

'Seems like a real catch.'

She laughed, but it was a sad, frustrated sound. 'Oh, yeah. I sure can pick 'em.'

He hated that.

He hated to be painted with the same brush as the other guy who was clearly a total drop kick.

'But Melanie is amazing,' she admitted, her eyes shifting to his and sparking with something that made his whole body tingle.

'So you stay because of her?'

'I'm not with him, any more,' she said.

'I mean, you stay in town. That's why you can't leave.'

'It's part of it,' she agreed. 'One day, when Mel's eighteen, she might want to go somewhere else and then, who knows? But for now, while she's there, I'm there, too.'

'What's his deal?' Aiden pushed, wondering at the kind of guy who could have a child and not take care of their most basic needs, like food.

'He's just a selfish prick,' she said, her smile more genuine now, even when it didn't quite reach her eyes. 'He's not intentionally mean or anything, and he's not violent, he just thinks only of himself and his needs. You can bet your bottom dollar he's grabbing burgers or whatever else he wants. He just wouldn't think to pick something up for Melanie.'

Outrage coursed through Aiden.

'I usually make sure their fridge is stocked, have her over for dinner a couple of times a week, you know. But God, it drives me crazy that he's so careless. Doesn't he realise how lucky he is, to have her?' Her voice cracked and something inside Aiden did exactly the same thing.

Her hollowed-out grief on that sentence was like a dagger to his chest.

Sienna didn't mention their baby, but it was there, right in front of them, like a visage of what could have been. What should have been.

Impulsively, he reached down and grabbed her hand, weaving their fingers together. She turned to look at him and something in his gut popped. He wanted to apologise again. To say sorry that he hadn't been there for her. But he wasn't sure she wanted to hear it. After all, it didn't matter how many times he said sorry, nothing would change the past. Nor how badly he'd let her down. All he could do was promise – himself, and her – that he'd never do that again.

* * *

'Okay, field trip time!' Paige said, waving a hand in the air to draw the attention of the guests. She stood shoulder to shoulder with Bella and Sienna. As bridesmaids, they'd organised today, each of them volunteering to go on a different boat and make sure the guests had a good time.

The whole group was on the island now. More than one hundred close friends, teammates, partners, children and family members, filling out the pristine white sand beaches of the private island. On the water in front of them, clustered around the jetty, sat four stunning boats, reasonably large in size, bearing Greek lettering down the sides. Sienna knew, from pre-wedding planning, that these boats had been chartered for the day, rather than using the smaller speedboat they'd come over on.

'You've all selected your activities. We've got a historic sightseeing tour in Athens – you'll be going with me, on boat one,' Paige said, into a megaphone, before turning her attention back to the clipboard (a clipboard Sienna would have put her last five bucks on Paige having insisted on) then pointing to the boat at the top left of the jetty.

'The art galleries of Athens are Chase and Bella,' she continued. Beside her, Bella waved and Chase grinned broadly.

'Boat two.' She moved her finger sideways. 'If you want to island-hop, with lunch in Lavrio – you're with Sienna.' Sienna waved a little hesitantly as Paige indicated the boat on the left side, closest to them, of the jetty. She'd committed to this *before* she'd realised that boats were as low on her enjoyment list as flying was. When the idea of sunning herself on the deck of some billionaire's yacht and feasting on chargrilled octopus had seemed like an *excellent* idea. Now, she eyed the bobbing crafts a little uneasily, and just hoped the seasickness bands Paige had magicked up out of somewhere would do the trick.

'As for the future Mr and Mrs Carter, it's rock climbing and cocktails on the other side of the island. Boat four will whizz you around there, unless you're feeling particularly energetic, in which case, it's an easy six-mile run.'

Someone let out a cheer. Her eyes filtered

through the crowd to where a selection of the Titans teammates was standing. A big guy with short blond hair grinned, flashing even white teeth, and beside him, a beautiful woman with fiery red hair shot him a look before sidling against him.

'Okay, I take it you're rock climbing. Everyone else, find your guide, or your boat, and have fun!'

'One last thing.' Astrid grabbed the megaphone. Blake stood beside her, one arm casually wrapped around her shoulders. Aiden was a little way to the left, wearing boardshorts and a shirt, big, muscular legs planted wide apart. Her stomach clenched. 'The wedding is tomorrow. Not until the afternoon, but nobody goes writing themselves off today. No hangovers, no broken bones, no face plants.' She seemed to be giving the Titans an extra hard look. 'A couple of cocktails and an afternoon, nap, fine. But by tomorrow, I expect each and every one of you to be happy and healthy. You hear me?'

There was a mumble of laughs, and then Blake shouted, 'Oy! You got it?'

'Yeah, yeah,' the Swedish guy from their team called out. 'We got it.'

'Okay.' Astrid smiled serenely once more. Sienna had to say, if that was the closest she came to a bridal freakout, then she was doing exceptionally well. 'Have fun, everyone!'

Astrid turned to the girls then and Sienna did her level best *not* to look over Astrid's shoulder, to where Aiden and Blake were locked in conversation.

'Thank you guys for playing mother hen for me.'

'Sightseeing around Athens? What a hardship,' Bella said with a lift of her brows.

'You know what I mean.'

'Don't worry. We'll make sure everyone gets back to the island in one piece,' Paige chimed in.

'I mean, there are tour guides. It's just some of those guys' – she thumbed towards the Titans – 'can be a bit of a handful. I know you ladies will know how to handle them.'

'In our sleep,' Sienna agreed. 'Don't worry, honey. We've got this. It's going to be an amazing day.' Out of nowhere, she felt tears stinging her eyes. 'An amazing weekend. Oh, God. I'm actually crying,' she laughed, fanning her face, so Paige put an arm around her waist and squeezed, and Astrid laughed.

'It's just a wedding,' she said with a shake of her head.

'It's been so beautiful,' she added, ignoring the twisty, turning, not-easy-to-understand feelings that were moving inside of her. 'All of it, Astrid.'

Astrid angled her face to regard the large mass of people who were moving off towards their separate boats. Four tour guides in matching uniforms stood with matching clipboards, writing names down as everyone boarded. Paige and Bella had worked as a team to coordinate this, too. Their organisation skills were a thing to behold.

'It really has been. Seeing our friends, from all different parts of our lives, and our families...' Her eyes shifted to her mother and her mother's partner, who were standing on the grass, waiting for Astrid. 'Spending time with family,' she corrected, smile wistful. 'I think that's been my favourite part. Even more than actually getting hitched,' she added with a laugh. Before Sienna could object, she held her hands up in the air. 'I'm kidding, I'm kidding.' She flashed a smile, but it wobbled a little, and they all understood why.

'You ready, babe?' Blake's voice cut across the group.

'You betcha,' Astrid said, reaching back for his hand.

'You know, you guys are kind of inseparable. I don't think I've looked for my fiancé once this week and not found her with one, or all, of you.'

'Yep, we know,' Paige said.

'We're a package deal,' Bella agreed.

'Uh huh. You might be marrying me, but you're inheriting three best friends.'

'I can live with that.' He pulled Astrid closer. 'Especially when they clearly love you so much they're happy to put up with all this madness.'

'We happen to love madness,' Paige promised.

'Yeah, it's kind of a part of how we met.'

'And don't I know it,' he teased, so Sienna glanced nervously over Blake's shoulder, to Aiden, who was now standing with his mother. Her heart ratcheted up a notch, as she contemplated that. Blake knew the truth of their plan. Sienna had been there when it had all come out. Even though he'd been sworn to secrecy, Sienna couldn't help worrying that it might not hold.

At some point, would Aiden find out that she'd been part of a revenge plot against him? Admittedly, a pretty funny one – that had been organised with the precision of a golden retriever marching band, but nonetheless, wouldn't it give him just a little too much insight into how messed up she'd been?

Or did he already know that?

Her mind was spinning like a top, refusing to settle in any one direction. She ground her teeth and tried to focus back on Astrid, but her own thoughts were too loud, making it almost impossible to hear anything anyone else said.

'Okay, ladies. So, dinner tonight, just the four of us, yes?'

Sienna finally lurched back into the present. 'Yeah, dinner,' she agreed, as they began to walk towards the jetty. It was only as she stepped foot onto the boat she'd been designated, she realised that Aiden 'Heartbreak' Carter was right freaking behind her.

18

'This suits you, you know.' Ten minutes after setting off from the island, she felt the moment he came and stood beside her.

She glanced to him, the sun bouncing off the Mediterranean and landing against his dark hair, glinting like onyx. 'Being a tour guide?'

He laughed. 'Relaxing. Sunshine. Island hopping.'

She pulled a face. 'I didn't even own a passport three months ago,' she pointed out. 'This is hardly my normal.'

'Nah, maybe not. But, like I said, it suits you, Mastrangelo.'

'I'll put it on my bucket list. Except I'm a little

short of billionaire friends,' she said with a small smile. 'Though I am warming to the whole boat thing. Maybe a bigger boat is what I need?'

'Bigger boat, less vomit?'

Her cheeks flushed pink at the memory of losing her lunch right at his feet. 'Well, that could have been the boat, or it could have been seeing you again,' she teased with saccharine sweetness.

'Great, so I literally make you sick?'

She laughed. 'Okay, it was probably the boat.'

'My ego is glad to hear it.'

'I have no doubt your ego is perfectly healthy.'

He pulled a face and she took pity on him, changing the subject.

'If you're keeping count, I also don't particularly like planes.'

His eyes scanned her face. 'I did not know that about you.'

'How could you? I'd never even been on a plane back then.'

'No.' He turned contemplative. 'That's true.'

He turned to look out at the water, which was crystal clear, even here, where they were deep and cutting through it at speed. The other guests milled on deck, in various states of relax and recline. Sunnies, sunscreen, smiles, some glasses of bubbly, some sipping coffee. Everything about the boat was sheer luxury perfection. No stone had been left unturned in planning the perfect wedding.

'And now?' he prompted, after a beat.

She looked at him, curiously.

'Do you travel much?'

She made a snorting sound, then forced a smile. 'I've travelled a bit, since meeting the girls. Just to catch up, when we can. Olly has a million air miles...' Her voice trailed off as she realised how revealing the comment was. Like the fact her financial situation was pretty damned tenuous.

His eyes narrowed. 'Otherwise you wouldn't be able to fly?'

'Well, I really don't like flying, anyway, as I said...'

'But you like seeing your friends.'

'Yes.' Her response was tight. She could feel him looking at her, feel the sympathetic answer he was formulating and she wanted to nip it in the bud. 'It's okay, Aiden. I mean, we don't all make ten million dollars a year, but I get by.'

Something shifted in his expression. A wariness. An uncertainty. He glanced down at her, eyes scanning her face. 'Once you have a million bucks to your name, it doesn't really make a huge difference.'

She laughed then. 'Spoken like someone with all

the money in the world and absolutely zero sleepless nights courtesy of a mountain of unpaid bills.'

'Is that what it's like for you, Si?'

'I'm fine,' she replied, stiffly.

'It's just... if you're stuck. I mean, if you're struggling, I could—'

She lifted her hand and clamped it against his lips. 'Don't. Don't say what you're thinking.'

His eyes didn't just look at her, but pierced her fully.

'I don't want your help,' she said, simply but forcefully. 'That's not what this is.' And with her striking blue eyes, she pierced him right back.

* * *

He felt it like a blade. The contemptuous, determined rejection of his spontaneous offer. Hell, he'd been beaten but good in his time. His dad had pounded on him as a kid, then he'd gone into a job that saw him regularly on the receiving end of some of the biggest defenders in the game, but he wasn't sure he'd ever felt such a precision sting as the way she'd just dismissed him.

Okay, he hadn't exactly thought it through. But suddenly, the amount in his bank account seemed utterly obscene. He hadn't wanted to correct her, but her figures were a bit out of date. It had been quite a few years since he'd 'only' earned ten mil per season. He was about to sign for a record-breaking amount. Add in what he made from sponsorships, not to mention the fact he'd partnered with a top investment guy in his first year playing pro, and Aiden was sitting on the kind of fortune that would have made his teenage self's eyes stream.

It would be the easiest thing in the world for him to throw some money Sienna's way. A million bucks? He wouldn't miss it.

Who even was he, that he could think like that? He knew he'd come a long way, he just hadn't really stopped to look back, and to recognise that. He'd come so far from his roots, he'd kind of forgotten what it was like to struggle. But as a kid, he'd known how hard it was for his parents to make rent, to pay the bills. Even going back to Ashbury to buy the house for his dad, he hadn't stopped to think about the rest of the town.

It had been depressing enough when he was a kid, then the biggest auto maker in the district had shut down. Meaning there were high levels of unemployment, not a lot of spare cash, and the whole place was suffering.

Suddenly, he imagined what it would be like for someone like him, or him and Blake, to roll up their sleeves and become Mother freaking Teresa to the whole place. Rejuvenate the main street, pour money into the school, the town facilities. To really make a difference to Ashbury.

His skin flushed hot then cold.

They'd never do it though. Their whole life philosophy had been about not going back. Apart from that one time, when it had been essential to go see his dad and sort out the house, Aiden had seen Ashbury Falls as some kind of personal Achilles' heel.

But how much of that was to do with Sienna?

And the fact he'd still been running from her.

No matter how many years they'd been apart, had he ever really been dumb enough to believe she was really just some woman from his past? Someone he'd once loved? Hadn't he actually known, on some soul deeper level, that seeing her again would unlock a door he desperately needed to keep firmly closed?

'Are you okay?' The antagonism was gone. So too was the hand that had been pressed to his mouth, and she was looking around a little self-consciously. Like she was worried someone would see them together. Like she didn't want to be seen with him. As though she were ashamed of him.

His gut rolled.

Everything seemed to slow down and then threaten to stop.

'Aiden, are you okay?' She spoke louder now, fixing him with a concerned look. Careful to keep her distance, though.

'Yeah.' His mouth felt dry. He stared at her almost as if he'd never seen her before in his life. Or as if there were many versions of her.

'I didn't mean to offend you,' she said, with the hint of apology in the lines of her mouth. 'It's just – we both know why that would never work.'

'Do we?'

'Come on.' She smiled, but it seemed forced to Aiden. 'I can't take anything from you.'

It was like another blow, right in the solar plexus. The woman he'd once loved, the woman he'd loved enough to walk hard and fast away from, rather than risk ever, ever hurting her, was telling him she wouldn't take something he could so easily give? 'It's just money.'

She pulled a face, and he knew straight away that he'd sounded like an insensitive ass.

'I just mean, I have money. If you don't, then let me—'

She closed her eyes, as if *he'd* hurt *her*. 'Please,

don't keep saying it,' she whispered then, before opening her eyes and glancing around at the other wedding guests. 'I really don't want to have this conversation with you.' Another smile, this time, tightly dismissive. 'Excuse me, I should go mingle. Bridesmaid duties, and all that.'

He watched as she walked away, beelining to Chuck Daly, who was all gleaming smile and popped collar, bronzed tan and sparkling eyes, waiting like a puppy dog for Sienna's attention. As she approached, she put her hand in the crook of his arm – no shame there, apparently – and guided him away from the group, locked in private conversation. Intimate conversation. Like they were old friends with a long list of secrets to spill.

She looked so damned gorgeous. He hadn't been kidding when he'd said that this suited her. She might have been a newcomer to the international jet-setting lifestyle, but she looked like she'd been doing it every day for the last ten years. Dressed in a pair of linen shorts and a cropped shirt that showed an inch or so of her slim, tanned midriff, wearing strappy flats that drew attention to her lean calves, with her shimmering blonde hair pulled back into a preppy, high ponytail, she looked... perfect. And he was clearly not the only one to think so, going by the way Chuck Daly was eating her up with his eyes.

Aiden looked away sharply, focusing on the distant landmass of the island, and recognising that it was an absolute metaphor – though he wouldn't have said so before this damned week – for his entire life.

* * *

He kept his distance because he somehow just knew she wanted him to. He played the part of Aiden 'Bigshot' Carter, shooting shit with some of the guys from the team who'd come along, or talking to some of the guests from Astrid's side. He'd never met them, but they all seemed to know who he was, and wanted to grill him on hockey. What it was like as a career, rumours about some of the other big-name players, random questions about ice preparation and training regimes. He ran the gamut of small talk, all the while doing his level best not to stare the hell out of Sienna, even when his stupid eyes seemed to have developed a mind of their own.

No matter how hard he tried, he found he just kept... looking at her.

Watching as she lifted a hand to her ponytail and flicked it over one shoulder. Or when she laughed at something that Astrid's uncle said, or almost lost her footing on an uneven cobblestone and Chuck 'Cut Your Lunch' Daly was right there to swoop to her rescue, wrapping an arm around her waist to steady her so Aiden's blood pounded in his ears so loudly it was like the ocean.

Her skin was a deep tan and she seemed to glory in the feeling of the sun on her. Several times, he saw her stop walking and tilt her face to the sky, as if basking in that small pleasure. Such a familiar gesture and like a bolt from the sky, he realised why.

He'd seen her do that before.

Memories wrapped around him like a boa constrictor, making breathing almost impossible.

On the way home from school, one of the first days of spring, when the sun had finally come out and the sky was clear, she'd stopped walking, put both hands on her hips and done exactly that. Back then, her hair had been unruly, even when she'd jammed it into a ponytail, and little bits of it had caught on the breeze and made the air sweet with the fragrance of her conditioner. She'd closed her eyes, parted her lips then sighed, and he'd looked at her then like he was now: like she was the damned embodiment of every single one of his dreams.

He groaned audibly and turned away from the

group, who had stopped to admire an ancient building. They were heading for lunch and afterwards, thank Christ, they were going back to the island, where he could get some time to himself. Away from harmless small talk and visions of Sienna morphing into the woman of his teenage dreams, threatening every shred of his equilibrium. How could he want to be around someone so much and also desperately need to get the hell away? What was happening?

He was Ice.

That was his name, his reputation. Hell, it was his whole freaking philosophy in life.

Feelings – bad. Control – good. Emotions – bad. The ability to walk away and not look back – excellent proof that you were in control.

Now *all* he could do was look back, and the overwhelming sense that he might have made the biggest screw up a person could make in their life – the kind that was impossible to fix – was now sitting in his gut like a lead balloon.

One more glance at Sienna as she laughed, and he felt the world tilt wildly off its axis.

Fuuuuck. In the end, it was the only word that could do justice to how he felt. And even that wasn't quite strong enough.

* * *

Given the lack of ice on this tropical island paradise, they settled for playing football instead. Titans, ex-hockey players, friends who just liked sport, gathered on one of the grassed areas near the house and set up for a casual evening game.

'Just don't get a black eye before the wedding,' Astrid warned, but she was grinning as Blake waved over his head and ran onto the field.

Aiden watched them, and felt it again. Just like he had on the boat. Jealousy.

Jealous, because Blake and he had been given the same cross to bear. And Aiden had always thought he'd been the one to sort his shit out, better than his brother, anyways. Blake who'd taken the opposite approach to Aiden – to ice his emotions – and instead felt *everything*. But it was Blake who'd finally put their shitshow of a childhood in the past, and was moving on with the love of his life. Blake was the one who looked carefree and blissed out.

Blake had been unafraid to reach for what he wanted with both hands and hold on, and never let go.

Blake hadn't run.

Not for good.

He'd faced his feelings and his fears, and he'd conquered the latter.

Whereas Aiden... his eyes shifted to Sienna, who was now huddled in conversation with the other three musketeers. For once, they weren't laughing and being silly, but rather, their expressions were serious. Thoughtful.

Astrid put her arm around Paige and drew her close. Paige smiled at her, but it was a strange smile. Haunted. Disbelieving.

He frowned, looking back to Sienna, who was holding her hands in front of her chest in a sort of prayer motion, looking hopeful. Worried. All the things. Then, Paige nodded, and they hugged, and laughed, like something miraculous had happened. He kicked his toe into the grass and looked away, bitterness flooding his gut as he felt completely on the outside of Sienna's life. She was a mystery to him in so many ways, and a part of him in others.

But the mysteries were something he was now finding impossible to accept.

He wanted to know her. To know everything about her. He wanted to see her and hear her, to just *watch* her go through life, achieving things because she worked so hard and gave everything her all.

The fact he'd already missed more than ten years,

hadn't been there for her when she'd needed him most, was the kind of ache he wasn't sure he'd ever not feel. Yet the future stretched before him, like a fork in the road. Go back to New York, his real life, his job, and the fact he was choosing every damned day to keep on running from his feelings and his fears. Or be brave, like Blake, and finally accept that against any and all probabilities and sense, he'd met his goddamned soulmate at sixteen, and the most important thing to him now, as a man approaching thirty, was to win her back at all costs. Because facing the rest of his life without her in it just didn't work for him.

To hell with his personal philosophy and his aversion to feelings.

Sienna was his. And unequivocally, he was, and always had been, hers.

* * *

'You look... not at all stressed,' he said to Blake, a couple of hours later when they were finally alone.

'Why would I be?'

'I mean, you're getting married tomorrow.'

'Yeah. To Astrid,' he said. The *duh* was implied.

Aiden shifted a little uncomfortably in his seat, reaching for the ice-cold beer and taking a drink, before cradling the bottle neck between his fingertips and thumb.

'You don't get it, do you?' Blake asked, leaning back in his own chair, one ankle crossed casually over the other knee.

'Get what?' Aiden tried to flatten the defensive note from his voice.

'What it's like to meet the one person you just know you need in your life. I'm not saying I couldn't live without Astrid. I'm just saying, I wouldn't want to. It's like, before I met her, I was running at maybe 40 per cent capacity. I wasn't... unlocked.'

Aiden threw his brother a quizzical look. 'Careful, bro. You sound kinda New Age.'

'I'm turning over a whole new leaf.'

'Yeah, I can see that,' Aiden said, serious again.

'You'll meet someone one day, and you'll understand what I'm talking about,' Blake promised, with all the smug indulgence of someone who secretly believed that they alone had found true love, and no one else would ever really know the sublime, soaring heights of their happiness.

Aiden grunted, turned back to the view of the

water, sipped his drink. Tried not to listen to his thumping, irritated heart. The same heart that had been shouting at him all day to stop being such an ass and wake the hell up.

'Unless you already have,' Blake inserted, a little too innocently to be without forethought.

Aiden threw him a glance then looked away.

Blake sighed. 'You're not gonna talk about it?'

'Talk about what?'

'The fact you're clearly as in love with Sienna as you were as a kid.'

Aiden bristled. His heart rejoiced. He continued to ignore it. But his stomach rolled and clenched and his eyes filled with stars and visions of a future he'd already discounted as impossible. A rosy future with a big old house, white picket fence and a town that he was single-handedly saving from desperation. The good he could do, with Sienna by his side...

'Come on, man. I've got eyes,' Blake continued.

'Yeah, well, I don't know what to say to that.'

'Why can't you just face it?'

Aiden sat a little straighter. His temples pounded. His certainty on the beach that afternoon that he couldn't let things go with Sienna again slammed into him, but he wasn't ready to admit it yet. It was terrifying. Too big. Too huge. Like a black hole of what ifs. 'You really have to ask me that?'

Blake made a noise. A groan. A sigh. All mixed in one. Then, he laughed. 'I don't believe it.'

'What?' Aiden couldn't quite keep the defensive note from his voice.

Blake visibly sobered. 'Ice is running scared.'

Aiden's spine couldn't have gone any straighter if he'd had a hockey stick pressed to it. He opened his mouth to deny it, but the words died before he could find them, because his brother was right.

'Holy shit, man. You're scared. You're scared like you've always been, that you're going to morph into him.'

Aiden turned to him quickly. 'What?'

'You told me. Once. Years ago. I remember, because it was like the most patently absurd thing I've ever heard in my life. *You* be like *Dad*? Me, yes, but not you.'

Aiden bristled. His voice though was perfectly calm. 'Just because I don't show what I'm feeling like you do, doesn't mean I don't still feel it.'

Blake's jaw squared. 'Feeling things isn't the problem,' Blake muttered. 'Feeling things is normal. Healthy. It's what you do with those feelings that matters. Dad never got that. He never learned to regulate. To take himself for a run or, I don't know, get a punching bag in the backyard, or a really good shrink.'

Aiden squeezed the beer bottle tighter. 'But he loved Mom.'

'So?'

'So how do you know, I mean, you love Astrid, but how do you *know*...'

'Because I'm not him. And you're not him either. That kind of violence, it's not genetic. It's not hard-wired into us. If anything, seeing what he was like, knowing what it's like to live with that fear, it's made us both the total opposite of him. I know when I'm getting pissed off. I feel it. Like a hum in my ears, and I know what to do, how to deal with it. Most of all, I know I would never, ever hurt Astrid, or anyone else. We're not him.'

Aiden dropped his head, staring at the ground between his feet, his breath burning as it tried to whoosh from his lungs. It was like being winded, or puffed out. He could hardly think straight. Sienna had said the same thing, but he hadn't believed her.

Or maybe he'd just been so determined to keep running from her, to close down the door of possibility to any kind of future with her, that he'd refused to listen.

But Blake knew him in a wholly different way to Sienna. And now, the past was wrapping around him like a patchwork blanket, memories of nights he'd spent with Blake, planning how they could fix everything, how they could make it better for their mom, how they could get away. They'd never once thought of turning to violence to hurt their dad. Even when all hell had broken loose and Blake had lashed out, it had been to defend Cynthia, not premeditated. They had seen the wreckage of their family and sought to do something good, not make everything worse.

They weren't him.

They had looked at him and known they wanted to get away from him. They'd chosen a different path.

And they'd walked it all these years.

His gut rolled.

Regret was a sinking pit of despair he skirted the edges of.

'It doesn't matter, anyway.'

'Why not?'

'Because she'd never take me back. Not in a million years.'

Blake considered that. 'Have you told her about me?'

Aiden shot him a look. 'The fact we're brothers? I think she's aware.'

'About the charges. About that night. About what would have happened to me if you hadn't gotten us out.'

Aiden took a sip of his beer. 'That's not why I left her.'

'You *had* to leave.'

'No, I didn't. I could have kept seeing her. We loved each other, man. The kind of love that would have survived a few years apart. I wanted to end it – that was nothing to do with you. It was... all the other shit. How I felt about her... the fact I *felt* anything at all...'

'Right, got it.' Blake nodded slowly. 'Like I said, you were scared.'

'Can we think of a different word? Like... avoiding commitment?'

'You were scared,' Blake replied, but grinned, in that brotherly teasing way.

'Fine. I was scared. I was terrified. I loved her so freaking much, the idea of ever being like him...'

'But you're not. We've dealt with that.'

'Yeah, and it's more than ten years later and she's still pissed.'

'Yeah.'

'Yeah?'

'I mean, I guess so.'

Aiden stared at his brother, long and hard, wheels turning. 'Hold up. Do you *know* something?'

Blake groaned. 'Nope.'

'Don't lie to me.'

'Don't ask me to spill Astrid's secrets.'

'Astrid's secrets?' Aiden stood up then, turning to face his brother, palm flat against his hip. 'Astrid's secrets, or Sienna's secrets?'

Blake blanched, then swore. 'Seriously, bro. Stop.'

'No, come on, man. This is my life we're talking about.'

'Yeah, I know. I know.' He dragged a hand through his hair. 'Just... hang on a sec.'

He pulled his phone out and started to type.

BLAKE

Hate to interrupt secret girls' business, but do you have a second?

ASTRID

Hmm, a second? Or a little longer... 🍆

Blake laughed.

'What?' Aiden asked.

'Astrid's just... being Astrid.' He went back to typing.

> **BLAKE**
> Love that idea, but my brickhead of a brother is here.

ASTRID
> Oh.

> **BLAKE**
> Yeah. So put that on ice for now.

ASTRID
> That's what she said.

Blake laughed again.

'What?'

'You don't want to know.'

Aiden nodded, anxiety spreading through him like the tide. Blake started typing again.

> **BLAKE**
> It won't take long.

Then:

BLAKE

It's about Sienna.

Her dots appeared immediately.

ASTRID

I'm on my way.

19

After a week of sunshine, on the morning of the wedding, it rained. It wasn't forecast, expected or ideal.

But when Sienna walked into Astrid's enormous suite carrying three cups of strong coffee, and one decaf for mum-to-be, and juggling a bag of pastries into the mix, it was to find her three besties locked in whispered conversation, apparently barely cognisant of a little thing like rain on Astrid's beach-side wedding day.

Something ran the length of Sienna's spine, something that made her shiver. Or worry. She stopped walking, as three pairs of eyes turned to look at her in unison.

'Morning,' she said, but a little hesitantly. She couldn't say why, but she was picking up seriously strange vibes off these women who she thought of as sisters. She placed the bag down on a table, realising belatedly that there was already an incredible spread of food courtesy of the island staff, so there'd been no need to pilfer the buffet.

'Hiya.' Bella smiled, but her cheeks were flushed. Guiltily.

'What's going on?' Sienna asked, handing out coffees.

'Just a... difference of opinions,' Paige explained, though the explanation was insufficient, because Sienna had no idea what that difference of opinion could entail.

'Can I help?' she offered.

'No,' Paige and Bella said.

'Yes.' Astrid overrode them. 'And as it's my wedding day, and I'm the bride, my vote counts double.'

'That would still make us tied,' Bella pointed out.

'So let me break the tie,' Sienna suggested. 'What's going on?'

Their lips compressed. A knock sounded at the door, and it pushed open. 'Make-up time!' a woman's voice called jubilantly into the room.

Astrid sipped her coffee, appraising Sienna carefully. 'Would you just give us two minutes, please?'

'No problem, beautiful.'

The door closed behind the cosmetician.

'Astrid?' Sienna tried to keep the impatience from her voice. It was, after all, her bestie's wedding day. But she didn't like the feeling that they'd all been talking *about her*. Even though she knew they'd always have her best interests at heart, it hurt to feel excluded, in any way, from this group they'd formed.

'We think you need to talk to Aiden,' Astrid said, carefully.

Paige nodded sagely.

'As in, today,' Bella added.

'I thought you had a difference of opinion?' Sienna said, to buy some time. 'It sounds to me like you're all perfectly in agreement.'

Bella pulled a face. 'In essentials we are.'

'There was some back and forth about how much we should strong-arm you,' Paige admitted.

'Or whether we should just manoeuvre a meeting between the two of you,' Bella said apologetically.

Sienna shook her head. 'I don't understand you guys. Why would you want to manoeuvre a meeting between me and Aiden?'

Paige and Bella looked at each other, then at Astrid, who held Sienna's gaze. 'He's in love with you, babe.'

Sienna stood stock still. No, that wasn't completely accurate. She almost spilled her coffee, so shocked was she by the most ridiculous, preposterous idea she'd heard in her entire life. She didn't know what was worse – hearing those words, or hearing them from the mouth of a woman who *knew* why it wasn't true. 'I'm sorry. *What*?'

'You should have seen him last night,' Astrid continued. 'Like some kind of wounded child bear. All confused and not understanding, trying to connect the dots and make sense of everything that's happened over the last, oh, I don't know, eleven years or so.'

Sienna closed her eyes against the surging rush of feelings. Feelings she absolutely didn't want to experience right now, on her best friend's wedding day. Feelings that were threatening to make her scream and rant and cry and hurl things around the room.

Anger.

Impossible, enervating anger.

Rage.

Disbelief.

Incredulity.

Fierce, all-consuming rejection.

How she hated him for this! How she hated him for being such a dense-witted fantasist!

'He doesn't love me,' she said, carefully, surprised she sounded so calm when her ears were ringing and her blood was pounding. 'And I sure as hell don't love him.'

Another look between the three, only this time, even Astrid succumbed, worry lining her pretty face. This was getting way out of hand.

'Anyway, this is *your* wedding day, and I absolutely refuse to have another word spoken about my one-time boyfriend. Okay?'

'But he's my future brother-in-law,' Astrid pointed out gently. 'And I promised I'd do this.'

Sienna's jaw dropped. 'He *asked* you to talk to me?'

'He—'

'So, let me get this straight.' The tenuous control she'd held on her temper was starting to slip. 'Not only does this asshole think he's in love with me, he's too screwed up to tell me that himself? What the actual hell?'

'He's not an asshole,' Paige said softly. 'We all agree about that.'

'Oh, well, I'm so glad *you* all agree,' Sienna said, slamming her coffee cup down then wincing with regret. This was Astrid's wedding day and she loved these women so damned much – she knew that to be mutual. This was coming from a good place. They just didn't understand.

'I'm sorry,' she said, as tears filled her eyes. 'I'm so sorry. I didn't mean to shout. I'm just – you have to understand. This is so completely a no-go zone for me.'

'But the other morning, you said you're having fun with him,' Bella pointed out gently, her expression softened with sympathy, as Astrid came up to Sienna and put an arm around her waist.

'I was having fun with him. That was the point. We both agreed it was just casual sex.'

'What?' Paige spat her coffee out, narrowly missing spraying the liquid across Astrid's stunning cream silk pyjamas. 'You're having sex with Aiden?'

There was no taking it back now. 'Yes. Just sex.'

Astrid, Sienna realised, already knew.

'He told you?' she demanded.

'Last night,' Astrid confirmed. 'Not in so many words, but it was obvious that... things have happened between the two of you.'

Sienna ignored the deep throbbing sense of betrayal. Her throat hurt with the force of unshed tears.

'Things we both agreed would mean nothing. He was very, very clear about that. We both were. He's got his life in New York, I'm in Ashbury Falls. Neither of us can – or wants – to move.'

'That's just geography.'

'No, it's a choice,' she insisted. 'And the whole sleeping together thing, it wasn't about starting everything up again. At least, it wasn't for me.'

'So what was it? And don't keep trying to tell us it was casual sex. We *know* you. That's not who you are,' Astrid said firmly.

Sienna's cheeks flushed.

'It was closure,' she said finally. Quietly. 'It was the goodbye we never got to have.' A tear slid down her cheek. 'It was an ending, only this time, we both knew it.' She sobbed. 'You guys, this is hard enough for me.' She sobbed again. 'I feel like I've been pulled in a thousand directions this week, and all I really want is to focus on you, honey. On your wedding. Your happiness. On you guys. But Aiden... it's just...' She cried properly now, and all three women came and wrapped her in a huge hug. She stood in the middle of them, feeling their love and support, knowing that even without finishing her sentence, they understood.

'It was a goodbye,' she finished, finally. 'That's all.' And she really, really meant that. She had to. To contemplate anything else, to even let herself start to dream, to hope, to want or imagine more, was a path she would *never* travel again. Not for all the money in all the world. Aiden 'Hockey God' Carter had proved once before that he couldn't be trusted with her heart and that was a lesson she'd never forget. She sniffed and sucked in a deep breath. 'Now' – she forced some sunshine into her voice – 'can we please just forget this and focus on our stunning bride-to-be?'

Astrid stroked her back.

'For now,' Paige said, gently.

'Thank you,' Sienna whispered, choosing to ignore the implicit promise of that phrasing. That they wouldn't let it go forever. It didn't matter. Tomorrow, she'd be off this island and away from Aiden 'No Future Here' Carter for good, and she couldn't freaking wait.

* * *

The day might have started with storm clouds but by mid-morning, when the make-up artist had finished and the hair wizards had arrived to work their magic, the sky had cleared and was once more a perfect shade of azure blue. Despite the whirlwind of activity happening around them, the four girls sat at the table and chatted like they didn't have a care in the world. They laughed, and they snacked, and it was just such a heart-healing day after the upset of that morning that Sienna could almost – *almost* – forget what Aiden had told Astrid.

Almost, but not quite. So every now and again, while the others were talking, she found her mind drifting over those words, lifting them up and shifting them around in her mind, studying them like a geologist might a rare and fascinating rock. But no matter how many times and in how many different ways she examined them, her feelings didn't change. Her anger didn't recede.

Besides, what did his claim to love her actually mean? He'd said the same thing when they were teenagers, and he'd still walked away from her. Had he really changed that much? Would she ever be able to let go of that hurt and trust him? And how could he even ask that of her? He might not have known, when he came to this island, how much his rejection had cut her. But he did know now. It wasn't fair of him to expect her to just set that aside and take some blind leap of faith towards whatever future he promised.

They were there to celebrate everlasting love, the promise of 'forever' that Astrid and Blake were going to make to one another, but the truth was, Sienna didn't know if she was capable of believing in it. Not for herself, anyway.

Astrid had chosen the most classically 'Astrid' wedding outfit imaginable. A stunning silky dress that was cut on the bias, so even though it sort of seemed to float to her ankles, it still hugged her hips and slim waist like a second skin. The dress dipped right down in the back to reveal delicate lace detailing on either side, satin buttons cresting over her backside. Astrid being Astrid, she'd teamed it with a boho plait, and a pair of cowboy boots, yeehaw. Not to mention a smile that just wouldn't quit.

There was not a single hint of nervousness for this bride.

Not an ounce.

She was vibrating with giddy joy, like every moment she'd lived on earth had all been building inexorably to this one moment.

And yet, as they moved out of the suite – assured that all guests had now assembled on the beach, ready for the wedding – Astrid took a second to grab

Sienna's hand and pull her back. Astrid the Bride-Chilla to end all Bride-Chillas had also been incredibly kind to the bridesmaids, letting them choose dresses in whatever style they wanted, so long as they were somewhere in the ballpark of the same palette.

Sienna had chosen a pale yellow – one of her favourite colours – and in terms of style, the dress was classic prom. Appropriate, given that she'd never been. It was fitted in the bodice, but flared at the waist, and fell to the knees. Her own hair had been pulled back into a low bun at the nape of her neck, and the make-up had been kept 'sun kissed and minimalist', or so the make-up artist promised.

'Love, just one sec, okay?'

Sienna had a sense of trepidation. 'Yeah?'

'Okay, I promise, this is the last thing I'll say about this today.'

Sienna craned her head, to see where the others had gone. She had a sinking feeling they'd known Astrid was going to bring this up again, and had made themselves scarce.

'Honey, your groom awaits,' Sienna said, aiming for humour.

'Trust me, he'll keep waiting,' Astrid said with serene assuredness.

'This is your wedding day,' Sienna groaned.

'Yes, it's my wedding day,' Astrid agreed. 'But it's not the most important day of my life.'

Sienna's eyes narrowed.

'Not even close. I love Blake, and he loves me. Regardless of what happens today, we're us, starting a family, a couple who loves each other very deeply. This is just... frosting. A bit of something extra to put on top of what we already have. Honestly, this isn't the most important day of my life but I truly feel like it might be yours. If you don't talk to Aiden, if you just let this go, if you keep fighting what I'm pretty sure you feel for him... I don't know if you'll get over it.'

Sienna closed her eyes, willing herself *not* to cry. Not to ruin the spectacular job the make-up artist had done.

'All I'll say,' Sienna whispered, 'is that if you really thought he loved me, it wouldn't matter whether I spoke to him today or not. Because love isn't transient. It isn't changeable. And it isn't temporary. You're describing a flimsy feeling, that will just go away if I don't say "yes" to him, right here and now. That's not love.' She forced a smile but it hurt. Oh, how it hurt. 'It's not love like you and Blake have, and it's not a love that's good enough for me.'

Astrid's eyes widened. 'I didn't mean—'

'It's okay,' Sienna promised. 'I'm okay. I just really don't want to think about Aiden ever again. He's been living rent free in my brain for way too long. I want to evict him – starting now.'

* * *

Two golf carts were being used to transport the bridal party from the house to the beach, and Aiden knew that the plan was for the golf carts to offload the passengers just out of sight, at which point the wedding coordinator would signal to the band, who'd begin to play 'Canon in D' as the bridesmaids walked down the aisle, followed, finally by Astrid and her mom.

He knew all the details, but when the music began to play, and he realised how soon he'd see Sienna, every part of him kicked into a very unnerving gear. He was more nervous than during the playoffs. More nervous than his first pro game. More nervous than he'd ever felt in his life.

Because last night, he'd come to realise something important. He loved Sienna. He'd always loved her. And he wanted to be with her. Not just for this week, but forever.

He'd told Blake, and Blake had told Astrid. Astrid had, by now, probably told Sienna.

Meaning that she *knew*. And the moment she stepped onto the sand, he'd *know* how she felt about it. Just by the way she looked at him, he'd know if she felt the same way. If she was open to feeling the same way.

He looked at his brother, who was grinning like a toddler at an all-you-can-eat dessert bar.

Paige walked down the aisle first, holding a small bunch of pretty wildflowers. He saw the way she glanced at her boyfriend, Olly, as she passed, and something twisted inside of him. Now that he'd opened his eyes to how he felt, it was like love was *everywhere*.

The classical strains filled the air. A moment later, Bella stepped out, gloriously elegant in a lustrous gold halter neck dress with a slightly more restrained bouquet of flowers. As she passed Chase – sitting beside Olly – she winked and he grinned from ear to ear.

Something shifted in his gut.

These were Sienna's friends. Her best friends. And he *liked* them. They were fun and sweet and kind, and the guys were cool. The kind of people he could actually see himself hanging around with, when his schedule permitted. It had been so long since he'd thought of having friends outside of his hockey team. Even then, Ice kept everyone at a distance except for Blake. He was professional. Untouchable. But with Sienna, and her friends, he found himself wanting to just *be*. Himself. Not Ice. Not Distant. Just... Aiden.

With the shift of movement in his peripheral vision, Aiden's gaze was drawn right to the back of the aisle again, as Sienna walked down, looking like some kind of princess. She held a simple bouquet of flowers, and her hair had some extra blossoms weaved through it, to form a sort of crown.

The whole bottom fell out of his world.

Yeah, he'd realised he loved her last night, but knowing that and seeing her now, it was like the world took on a whole new shape. Everything was bigger and brighter, glistening and glowing. Sparkling. Radiant.

Effervescent. Hell, he felt like poetry was bursting out of his pores. He felt like he might be able to fly.

If she'd just look at him. If she'd just turn to him and smile. Then, he'd know.

He'd know he hadn't ruined everything. He'd know there was still hope.

But she didn't look at him. And she didn't smile at him. She smiled, though. A serenely, beautiful, contented smile, for everyone *but* him, which slightly took the shimmer off the hazy euphoria he'd been feeling a minute earlier.

Blake made a sound, a gasp, a sigh, a something, and he glanced past Sienna, finally managing to wrest his eyes off her, to where Astrid was beginning to walk towards them. Her mother stood on one side of her, and their mother on the other, in a touching gesture that choked Aiden up as damn near much as it did Blake. One glance at his brother confirmed how overwhelmed his twin was. On his way back to Astrid, Aiden's gaze landed on Sienna, and found that she was looking at him, lips compressed. Not in a smile, but with an expression that was deliberately, carefully neutral. He smiled. She looked away.

His whole chest felt like it was about to split open.

Astrid reached the top of the aisle. Cynthia kissed her cheek, then Blake's, before taking her seat in the front row. Astrid's mom did the same thing. Then, Blake let out a low whistle. 'Holy shit, Twinkle Toes. You're hot.'

The whole crowd laughed, Aiden included. Sienna, too, he saw out of the corner of his eyes. A lump formed in Aiden's throat, and it didn't go away the whole ceremony. It wasn't just the fact his best friend in the whole world was marrying someone who clearly made him feel complete. It was that now, for the first time in his life, he realised that he wanted this for himself. That he deserved it.

That with the right woman, he could have this kind of happiness.

And there'd only ever been one right woman for him. His entire life, it had always been Sienna Mastrangelo, and it always would be.

20

'Mastrangelo, wait up.'

She stopped walking but instantly wished she hadn't. She'd made it through the wedding, the photos and most of the post wedding cocktail reception without being alone with Aiden. But right at the moment she decided to slip out and call Melanie, he followed her.

Grinding her teeth, the wave of anger she'd been surfing all day coming to the fore, she turned around, crossing her arms over her chest leaving her free to just stare at him.

'Hey, stranger,' he said, coming so close she thought he might actually do something stupid like try to kiss her on the cheek. But he didn't.

Thank God.

She didn't know what she'd do if he touched her.

Cry, punch him, or kiss him right back?

'Got a sec?'

'Well, we're at a wedding, so, not really.'

He looked around. 'As in, you're busy right now?'

She held her hand out, as if to say, 'what do you think?'

'I just want a couple of minutes of your time.'

She clamped her lips together, trying to bite back the angry retort. 'Why?' she managed to snap out.

He grimaced, dragging a hand through his thick dark hair.

She looked sideways, towards the ocean.

'Look, I need—'

She felt his finger on her chin and startled at the unexpected touch, as he guided her face back towards him.

'I need to tell you something.' There was urgency in his voice.

She closed her eyes. 'Please, don't.'

'It's important.' She heard the plea and ignored it.

'It's really not.'

'I realised something last night, something I think I've always known but never wanted to accept.'

'Don't say it,' she groaned.

'I'm in love with you.'

She swore, the curse a bitter recrimination, loud enough to push a bird in a nearby tree to seek flight.

'Damn you, Aiden,' she said, with more control. 'I said, I don't want to hear it.'

'Astrid told you.'

'Yes, Astrid told me. And where the hell do you get off putting this on her, of all people, on her wedding day? This is *their* day, not ours.'

'I didn't tell her, Blake did.'

'And how did Blake know? You told him, right?'

'We... were talking. I guess, yeah, I did.' His frown was a deeply etched line in his face. 'It kind of came out.'

'Is that supposed to impress me?' she demanded, crossing her arms over her chest.

His jaw dropped. 'I'm not trying to impress you, Si. I'm trying to tell you that I realised last night, I don't want to let you go. I don't want to wake up tomorrow and know I'm never going to see you again. I don't want this to end.'

'This? This?' She scoffed, half-laughing, in a manic, deranged sort of way. 'There is no *this*, we both agreed to that.'

A muscle ticked in his lower jaw. 'You're pissed.'

'I'm not "pissed". I am *furious. Livid.* So angry I

can hardly see straight.' She leaned close to him and jabbed a finger to his chest. 'How fucking dare you do this to me?'

His skin paled. 'Do *what* to you?'

'Take your pick! Think you can tell me you love me and that the past just magically goes away? Or do it on the day of my best friend's wedding? Or tell her before me so I'm left being goddamn ambushed?'

'That's not what I meant to happen.'

'Yeah, well, it did.'

'Okay, but listen,' he said, urgently, reaching out and putting his hands on her hips. 'I am in love with you. I have no answers about how this will work, where we'll live, what will happen next. All I know is I want you in my life. I can't lose you again.'

The last sentence was hollow, so desperate, it almost, *almost* got through to her. He sounded so genuine.

And maybe he was. Maybe on some level he'd really come to think he loved her, that they could make a go of this. Maybe he'd just got so caught up in all the excitement of Blake's wedding that he was fantasising about this kind of future for himself. Whatever. Sienna wasn't buying it.

'You don't love me.'

'I'm sorry?'

'An apology I might have accepted ten years ago, but I don't want to even hear it right now,' she muttered.

'I mean—'

'I know what you mean. I'm not interested. You. Don't. Love. Me.'

'Don't you think I know how I feel?'

'Nope.'

'You sound pretty sure of that.'

'Because I value facts over fantasy. Because I think actions speak louder than words.'

He stared at her, expression impossible to interpret.

'A decade ago, you did something to me that no one, and I mean *no one,* who was in love could ever, ever do.'

He blanched visibly. 'That's not true.'

'You dropped me like a hot potato.' Her voice cracked as she forced herself to admit the harsh truth to him. 'You dropped me like I was worthless.'

He shook his head. 'It's the exact opposite of how I felt.'

'It's easy to say that now.'

'Nothing about this is easy.'

'You think?'

They stared at each other, two people on opposite sides of the same divide.

'The thing is, I get why you did it. I get what you were afraid of. I get why you left town. I get all of that. I'm just saying, that's not the action of a man in love, and even though I understand it better now, it's definitely not the kind of thing I can forgive.'

His jaw dropped. 'I genuinely thought it was right for you, to end it like that. To make it a clean break.'

She wanted to push him. She wanted to push him so hard he fell backwards on his big, beautiful butt. She wanted to shove him because he was breaking her heart all over again now.

'And what? I didn't get any say in that?'

He clamped his lips together.

'You chose *for* me. You chose for us. And this, Aiden, this is what you chose.' She threw her hands up in the air in exasperation, tears now threatening and damn it all to hell if she'd let him see her cry. That was *definitely* not part of the plan. She dug her fingernails into the palm of one hand, staring at him with a mutinous expression.

'You're right.' His voice was soft, flooded with emotions. 'I did choose this, for both of us. And I'm standing here, right now, telling you it's a decision I regret with every single part of me. It's a choice I would undo a thousand times over, if there was any way to go back in time. I'm telling you, I made a mistake.'

She tried to channel her inner warrior woman. To think of Bella, Paige and Astrid and what they'd say to that. She tried to think of what she'd tell Melanie, if she ever wound up in the same situation. But her mind was spongy and her lips flubbed.

'And it took you this long to realise it?'

His Adam's apple shifted. 'It took me seeing you again to realise I couldn't keep pretending I don't feel this way. Out of sight, easy to put my head in the sand.'

She bristled. 'That's my point.' Now she jabbed his chest, and God, it felt good. 'You were *able* to put me out your mind and go on with your life. That's not love. That's *not love*.' Tears fell freely now, and she didn't bother to check them. 'Whereas I have spent the last ten years *hating* you for what you did to me, and simultaneously' – she stumbled a bit, drawing in a breath, a part of her desperately willing herself to stop talking, but she didn't – 'missing you so much I couldn't think straight.'

He stared at her, but there was a look of hope on his face, almost a smile on his lips, so she shook her head angrily.

'No, you don't get it,' she growled. 'That's not a good thing.'

'But doesn't that tell you that you're not over me?'

'I know I'm not over you,' she muttered. 'I'm not an idiot. Do you know how I met those girls?' She thumbed towards the reception, still in full swing.

'At an airport.'

'Yeah. At an airport, where we drank way too much prosecco and talked about our worst ever exes, and made plans to get revenge on them.'

'What?' She could practically see the gears of his brain turning. With the slight guilt of someone throwing their best friend under a bus, she didn't see any way through this conversation without revealing the truth of the Karma Club. He needed to understand.

'The guys we really, really couldn't ever forgive.'

He was frowning, still connecting the dots. 'You mean, me?'

She closed her eyes, screwing up her courage, and hoping Astrid would forgive her for this. 'That's what Astrid was doing in New York. She was meant to be screwing up your life, not falling in love with Blake.'

His eyes widened. 'You sent *Astrid* to get revenge on me?'

'Not mean revenge. Not, like, stabby murder or whatever. More like giving you a taste of your own medicine. To reel you in and cast you adrift... which was damn stupid now I come to think of it.'

'How so?'

'Because you'd have to have a heart capable of breaking for the plan to have worked.'

'I see.'

She refused to pander to the pain in his gaze. So what if her words stung? He'd hurt her far more.

'She turned me orange,' he muttered.

'Yes.' Sienna nodded once, remembering the fake tan incident with a hint of amusement, despite her splintering heart.

'The chilli!' His eyes widened, and she halfway felt sorry for him.

'Yep.'

'She gave me diarrhoea because of you?'

She bit into her lower lip, fighting an urge to defend both herself and Astrid. But Aiden wasn't waiting for an answer. He dragged a hand through his hair and said, 'That's why Astrid came to New York? The real reason for her article was to get back at me?'

She didn't want to get bogged down in that though. In any event, Astrid had written an incredible article that did everything she'd promised: she'd rehabilitated Blake's image, and in the process, she'd rehabilitated him. 'My point is, you were the worst ex of my life, Aiden! I didn't get over you. I didn't move on. I've never moved on. And I don't know what that means—'

'Don't you?' he interrupted, gently, moving a little closer towards her.

She took an abrupt step backwards, talking over him. 'This week wasn't about a fresh start.'

'Then what was it?'

'Fun. Nothing. Closure.' She searched around for the right word. 'It was an end, not a beginning.'

'I don't believe you.'

'That's your prerogative, but I'm not lying to you.'

'Sienna—'

'Please, stop,' she begged, trying – and failing – to channel her friends' inner-strength.

He was quiet, his lips forming a mutinous line.

'I'm grateful for this week. I'm grateful for seeing you again, for talking to you. I think we both under-stand each other so much more now, and whatever we were back then, our relationship deserves that.'

His jaw throbbed visibly.

'I understand why you left. I even understand why you cut me out the way you did. But I'll never trust you again. I don't want to trust you. Don't you see, Aiden? You hurt me because I let you. I gave you my heart, and that gave you all the power. I'll never do that again.'

'But this week—'

'Has been sex. Not for one second have I wanted anything more from you than that.'

He blinked, like he couldn't quite make sense of that.

'I'll never trust you not to hurt me, even though I understand it wasn't your intention.' She sobbed. 'And without trust, what kind of love is there?'

'Sienna.' His voice was rough, as if dragged from deep inside him. 'I'm not the same guy I was then.'

'Nor am I. I'm completely different. You broke me, and I've turned myself into someone else. Someone different. Stronger.'

'Sienna,' he groaned, taking another step forwards.

'No.' She moved away from him again. 'It's over, Aiden. Once and for all.'

'Don't shut the door on this.'

She made a deranged sound. 'You did that. The door has been closed ever since. This week doesn't change a damn thing.'

'It could if we wanted it to.'

'But I don't. I want to go back to my real life, and forget all about you. The thing is, none of it really made sense to me. I couldn't understand why you left. Why you didn't answer my calls. But now I know, now I understand, and I've had a chance to make my peace with it, I think I might actually be able to forget about you.' Now it was Sienna who put a hand to his chest. 'It really is over, Aiden. And for the first time in a long time, I'm okay with that.' She forced a smile. 'I'm more than okay. I'm finally free.' And then, she turned her back and walked away, before he could see the tears streaming down her cheeks.

* * *

A bridesmaid could hardly desert the wedding, even if she was completely and utterly mentally spent, so she took a scant few minutes to tidy up her face, settle her nerves, chug half a glass of bubbly before rejoining the reception, focusing all of her attention on Chuck Daly, who'd become unwittingly, the newest recruit to the Karma Club.

It helped to have something concrete to focus on.

To think about getting revenge for Paige, finally. The last ex the club had to seek revenge on.

Because, she supposed, they'd done what they'd set out to with Aiden.

Ridiculously.

Having days ago given up on the very juvenile idea of making him want her and then walk away, in the end, that was exactly what had happened. Only it hadn't just been fun and flirty. It hadn't been harmless. She could say with absolute certainty that her rejection of Aiden had hurt him. Deeply.

She believed he did, in fact, love her on some level.

Maybe he always had, but not enough.

Not enough to make it work.

Not enough to even try.

What if something happened in a year's time, where he had to choose between Sienna and something else? Another predicament where he felt like he had to leave her? She'd never feel safe with him. She'd never feel secure. Because she'd felt both those things in the past, she'd felt totally lulled into a false sense of security, and he'd ripped it right out from under her.

Bouncing back from that had been no mean feat.

'So, what do you think?'

'I think your last name should be Machiavelli,' he said with a carefree grin, and no idea that Sienna's never-fully-recovered heart was currently experiencing fresh stress fractures. 'That's a pretty well-cooked plan.'

'Well, I had help,' she assured him. 'There were a couple of other evil geniuses at work.'

'Hmm.'

'So?'

'I'm willing to help you,' he said quickly. 'It doesn't cross the line, as far as I'm concerned, and God knows the bastard deserves it.' Having heard the full story, which Paige had authorised Sienna to share, Chuck had been a very serious, very angry version of his usual self. 'Why don't we have lunch next week, to go over the finer details?'

'Erm, because I won't be here next week.'

He laughed. 'No, you'll be in Ashbury Falls, right?'

She was surprised he remembered the name. 'Right.'

'A place I'm dying to see after hearing Aiden's five-star review of it.'

She rolled her eyes. 'Funny, the tourism board went a different direction, in the end, to asking him to be spokesperson.'

'Funny,' he agreed, with a wink. 'I've got business

nearby. It's no hassle to come to you. You can buy me a burger in the local diner.'

'Ha. I happen to work in the local diner, I can probably score you one for free.'

'Ah, I always love a girl who can hook me up with a freebie.' He leaned forward and squeezed her hand, then slipped a business card over the table. 'We could go for a run afterwards?'

'It's too hot for a run at lunch time.' She pulled a face.

'Fine, we'll make it dinner.'

'I'm not running after eating a burger.'

'Shame.' He grinned. 'I'd like a chance to whoop your ass again.'

She rolled her eyes. 'You wish.'

He shrugged, then looked over her shoulder. 'Someone's waiting for you.'

She turned, glancing in the same direction. Aiden was hovering a couple of feet away.

Her heart stammered then pounded into her ribcage.

Her smile slipped.

Not because she didn't want to see him, but because it was all so heart-hurtingly hard.

'I'll see you next week.' He kissed her cheek. 'It's been nice meeting you, Sienna.'

'You too.'

Sienna sat very still, composing her fluttering nerves, until Aiden came to crouch beside her, his face wearing an expressionless mask.

'Hey,' she said, a little self-conscious and breathy.

'Hey,' he repeated. 'I wanted to say goodbye.'

She glanced at him sharply then.

'I'm going to hitch a ride with Blake and Astrid tonight, rather than leave in the morning.'

Sienna's jaw dropped. 'They're going on their honeymoon.'

'Yeah, but the boat's taking them to Athens first. I'm going to stay there – not with them, obviously – then fly out in the morning.'

'Oh.'

'I've got negotiations, and stuff...' He tapered off. 'But that's not why I'm leaving, and after last time, I'm going to be completely honest with you.' He swallowed hard. 'I just can't be here with you. Not because I don't want to be, but because it's too hard. Being near you, loving you, knowing how much it's never going to happen. I need to get away.'

'I get it,' she whispered, closing her eyes. 'It's how I've felt for years, but I could never get away from you. You were everywhere I looked. Every nook and cranny in Ashbury is the beginning and end of our love story. You're everywhere, even when you're nowhere.' Her eyes glazed over. 'I get it.'

'This is so fucked up,' he muttered, but stood, face resolute. 'I'm sorry. If you don't believe I love you, at least believe that. Please.'

Her mouth gaped. She nodded. 'Okay.'

'Okay.' He reached down, as if to touch her shoulder, but pulled his hand away at the last second. She thought she heard him swear again. 'I'll see you—' He broke off with a shake of his head. 'Goodbye. Just... please take care of yourself.'

She nodded again.

He turned and walked away, and not ten seconds later, her three best friends in the whole world descended on Sienna and wrapped her in a huge hug. She didn't need to be the only one taking care of herself. She had the girls, and she knew she always would.

21

Routine was good. Routine was important. Sienna leaned into it hard when she got back to Ashbury Falls and tried to pick up the threads of a life she'd been convinced, only eight or so days ago, she could absolutely never leave.

She buried herself in study, work, visitations with her dad when the prison permitted, spending time with Melanie, tolerating Cory. She did all the things that had meant so much to her before and tried to ignore the fact that so much of it seemed shallow now. Not seeing Melanie or her dad, but everything else.

Or not exactly shallow, perhaps monochromatic.

Dim.

Dull.

Hollow and hard.

She felt a thousand things and nothing. She felt burned and cold, all at once. Almost a full week after getting home, and halfway through *When Harry Met Sally*, there was a knock on her door. For the briefest second, she imagined it might be Aiden and her heart went into total overdrive, but of course it wouldn't be Aiden.

They'd said their goodbyes.

She'd made it clear she didn't want to see him again.

And what a liar she'd been.

Her preservation instincts had taken over. She was too scared to take a risk on him. On anyone. That was the problem. But if she looked into her heart of hearts, she knew what she'd see there. She knew how she felt about Aiden.

And it didn't matter what she'd said to him: there would be no getting over him. Not now, not in a year, probably not ever.

She wrenched open the door without checking to see who was there – and her heart lifted. In profile, they were so similar, that for a millisecond, she actually thought it was Aiden. But then, Blake turned to face her properly, and smiled, and there was no mis-taking which brother had come to see her now.

Particularly not with Astrid just behind him.

'Guys?' Sienna looked from one to the other. 'What are you doing here?'

'We came to see you, silly,' Astrid said, leaning forward and wrapping her arms around Sienna. Her basketball tummy pressed against Sienna, and without thinking, Sienna put a hand down and patted her friend's bump.

'But you're on your honeymoon.'

'We were on our honeymoon,' Astrid corrected. 'Blake's got pre-season.'

'You're meant to be away another week.'

'Okay, fine.' Astrid held her hands up, glancing at Blake. Sienna realised they were hovering on her doorstep, and stepped backwards to silently invite them in.

They followed her into the hallway, and it was Blake who shut the door.

'We need to talk to you.'

Sienna's heart dropped. 'Guys—'

'I know, I know. Blake told me I shouldn't get involved.'

Sienna glanced at the other Carter twin.

'And he's probably right. But you need to understand—'

'Come on, honey,' Sienna groaned. 'We really don't need to rehash this.'

'It's not rehashing,' Blake said, after a beat. 'Astrid's right. I did say we shouldn't interfere, but I was wrong. There's stuff about Aiden you don't know.'

Her lips pulled to the side and after a brief pause, she moved deeper into the living room. The newlyweds followed and she gestured for them to take a seat. Neither did.

'Tell her,' Astrid said, gently.

Blake nodded once, dragging a hand through his hair. 'Look, I'm not proud of what I was like back then. When we were kids. You probably remember...'

She thought back to Blake Carter, and the teenager he'd been. A heart of gold, but with a lot of rough edges.

'I was skating around trouble for a while. On the edges of a group of friends that were pretty messed up. But I was always okay – Aiden made sure of it. He kept my nose clean. Until one night...' His voice tapered off and Astrid reached down to lace their fingers together, squeezing his.

'It's alright, babe. This is Sienna.'

His throat shifted as he nodded.

'Look, I did it out of self-defence. Or defence of Mom.'

'Did what?'

'I hit him.'

'Aiden?'

'No. That bastard of a father of ours.'

Sienna's lips formed a perfect circle. 'Okay...' She frowned, still not sure how this connected to her in the slightest. 'But that was a long time ago—'

'No, Sienna, when I say I hit him, I mean I hit him. Hard. And I didn't stop, not until I was sure he wasn't getting up.' He shook his head. 'I wasn't thinking. I was just... so angry. So sick of living in fear.'

Sienna shook her head a little, sympathy washing over her. 'You're a good guy, Blake. That was just one night, one act. And your dad survived.'

He ground his jaw. 'I almost ruined everything.'

She frowned. With their father?

'Our college scholarships – everything. The whole fresh start we'd been working towards since we were boys, the chance to get out of here. I put it all in jeopardy...' he choked out.

She saw Astrid squeeze his hand again.

'The cops drew up charges. I would have gone away, Sienna.'

She hated the thought of that. Blake wasn't a criminal. He wasn't violent. He had been reacting to an awful circumstance, protecting a woman who'd suffered too much at the hands of a violent, sadistic asshole.

'But Aiden fixed it,' Astrid said, her eyes boring into Sienna's.

Sienna's heart did a strange twist.

'Aiden made it all go away. He came to a deal with the college team, and our coach negotiated with the cops so I could plead down to a misdemeanour. But we had to leave town.'

Sienna's heart thumped against her ribs.

'We had to get out of here. That was the deal. Aiden saved me from going to prison, but he did it by leaving you, Ashbury, everything behind.' He took a step towards her; Astrid followed. 'Everyone calls him Ice, like he's too cold to feel a damned thing. I'm probably the only person on earth who knows the truth. He froze his feelings the night he left you, because without you in his life, he had no need for them any more.'

'Blake, please,' she said, her voice wavering with the force of her emotions. It wasn't that she didn't want to know this, it was that she couldn't quite work out how to process it.

'I just need you to understand that for ten years, I've lived with the guilt of this. I kept hoping he'd move on, fall in love, meet someone else. Be less Ice. Be more like he used to be. Be alive like he was when he was with you. But the first time I've seen that version of my brother in a long time was on the island, with you. It's always been you, Sienna. And if I hadn't been such a monumental hothead, everything would have been different.'

'You can't blame yourself,' Astrid whispered.

'But I do.'

'You shouldn't,' Sienna said, holding onto her emotions with difficulty. 'Aiden did what he needed to get you out of town, out of trouble, but he still chose to cut me out of his life.'

'He spent all our lives protecting me. That's a hard habit to break.'

Her heart twisted, because Blake wasn't wrong. Confusion seeped into her.

'We agreed not to tell anyone about this,' Blake said. 'Our coach advised us not to stir it up, initially. But you had to know...'

'Yeah,' she whispered, knowing that was true, too. She'd deserved to know back then. Maybe if she had, his leaving wouldn't have stung quite as much.

But maybe she'd have fought to keep him in town. Maybe she'd have convinced him to stay. Or take her with him.

And then she remembered something else he'd said, about how he'd needed to focus everything on the game, and that she somehow threatened that.

'I think he had other reasons for leaving me, Blake. You need to let any guilt you're carrying go. Aiden made his decision—'

'I made it for him.'

She sighed. 'He's a big boy—'

'He wasn't, though. He was a scared kid, just like I was. He ran away. From our father, from the shit-storm I'd created, and from the kind of love that was way too much for him to know what to do with. If you'd seen him like I've seen him these last ten years, you'd know I'm right.'

Her heart dropped down to her toes. 'Maybe,' she said, because she couldn't have this conversation any more.

'I mean it—'

'I think she gets it,' Astrid said, gently, dropping Blake's hand so she could put an arm around Sienna's waist. 'You okay, love?'

Was she okay? *Was she okay?* Of course she wasn't

okay, but there was no way in hell she was going to let her best friend have that on her conscience. So she forced a bright smile. 'Yeah, of course. Thanks for coming to tell me. Did you guys want to stay for something to eat? I've got cake in the fridge...'

'Our car's waiting,' Astrid demurred. 'We're heading to the airport to catch a red eye to New York.' She hesitated. 'Don't suppose you want to come with us?'

Sienna's heart went into overdrive. Fly to New York? To see Aiden?

Everything exploded inside of her, like a whirlwind of colour and sound, but she shook her head, quickly dismissing the idea. 'I can't. But I'll come visit soon, okay? We've got a baby shower to think about.'

Astrid's face showed disappointment, Blake's concern. 'But you could—'

'She'll work it out,' Astrid said, turning back to her newly minted husband.

She could tell Blake wanted to argue but after a beat, he shrugged and said, 'Okay, Twinkle Toes. If you say so.'

* * *

When Chuck came to visit the next day, Sienna was still obsessing over every detail of her conversation with Blake and Astrid. It was almost impossible to push it out of her mind, but somehow, she managed to at least make a passable effort of doing so. When they ate a light lunch, they talked about their Harvey plan. And afterwards, when they watched a movie, she made a point of laughing at the right places, and looking like she was paying attention. But when they went for a run – which Chuck managed to talk her into after all – Sienna felt her mind falling back into a rut, going over everything Blake had said, driving her crazy with the insistent thoughts.

As they approached the old dam and evening began to wrap around them, they stopped running, and Sienna was glad. She needed a reprieve from the whirlwind of her mind. 'I used to come fishing here, as a kid,' she said conversationally; she just needed to say *something*.

'Yeah? Catch anything big?' He held his hands wide, and she laughed.

'More like this.' She held her forefinger and thumb up.

'Mmm, tasty,' he laughed.

'Right?'

'I can see you as a fisher.'

'A fisher?' She forced a grin. 'I'm not so sure about that.' She sat down on the long grass and rubbed the space beside her. Chuck collapsed onto it, reminding her, briefly, of Aiden. He was big and burly like Aiden, but with a lot more of the Silicon Valley suaveness about him.

Aiden was raw.

An unpolished diamond.

She knew which she preferred. Her heart popped. She ignored it.

'I used to come here with him,' she said, softly, almost to herself.

'Aiden?'

She nodded, glancing across at Chuck. 'A million years ago. At least, that's what it feels like.'

Chuck rested his elbow on one knee, and gave her the full force of his megawatt attention.

'What was he like back then?'

Her heart hurt.

'He was...' She sought the words that could do him justice. Words that encapsulated what she'd thought he was, and what he'd become. Words that captured the knight in shining armour she'd thought he was, and the heartbreaker he'd morphed into.

But none of it would form properly in her mind. Because Aiden *had* been a knight in shining armour, just not for her. He'd put it all on the line to save his mom and Blake. And from his stupid, messed-up perspective, he'd even left her for her own sake. To save her from him. Having seen Blake beat their dad to within an inch of his life must have been terrifying for Aiden. Aiden who needed to believe they weren't like their father, who needed to believe they could be different.

And then he'd had proof that maybe they weren't.

So he'd left to protect her, so that he'd never hurt her. Just like he'd said.

Because he'd seen enough hurt in his life.

A tear slid down her cheek.

'Oh, babe.' Chuck reached out and put an arm around her shoulders, drawing her to him. 'That's no good.'

'I know. I'm sorry.' She dashed away her tears.

'Don't apologise.' He stroked her shoulder. 'But why are you sitting here, crying over a guy who is so obviously in love with you?'

She considered that carefully. 'Because I don't want to be with him.'

'But you love him.'

It wasn't even a question. How transparent was she?

She shook her head anyway. 'It's not that easy.'

'That's not an answer.'

'Well, I don't know how to answer. It's just, complicated.'

'So?'

'You're annoying me now,' she said on a half laugh, half sob.

'I'm just saying, if it's complicated, what are you going to do about it?'

She stared at him.

'Lots of things are complicated in life. In my opinion, they don't get any easier by pretending they don't exist.'

She turned away from him and stared at the dam, with the little pinpricks of light reflecting off it, thanks to the stars and inky-black sky.

'Didn't you guys break up way back when?'

She nodded stiffly.

'And yet you're still in love with him, and he's in love with you.'

'So what?'

'So what makes you think you're not still going to feel like this in another ten years' time? Twenty?'

She turned back to Chuck, her heart racing now.

'You get one life. One.' He lifted his finger for emphasis. 'If I was you, I'd ask myself if this is really how I want to spend it.'

She swallowed, the question suddenly super-seding everything else that had been swirling around in her mind for over a week, over a decade, every hes-itation and doubt, every long-held feeling of hurt and blame. And suddenly she was standing, her lungs filling with air as though she was preparing for a marathon.

'I need to ask you another favour, Chuck. I know I already owe you a whole big bunch—'

'Name it,' he invited.

And so, she did.

* * *

When Blake had moved out of their penthouse, Aiden had thought he'd miss him. After all, they'd lived together all their lives. They were twins. He might be a grown-ass man but he'd got used to having his bro around.

But coming back from the wedding to the blessed peace and solitude of their apartment – alone – had been the biggest fucking relief of his life.

Unlike the journey off the island and into Athens, Aiden no longer had to pretend to be fine. He no longer had to pretend to be Ice. He no longer had to act like he had his shit together, which he absofuck-inglutely did *not.*

Here, surrounded by the comforting darkness of their place, he could sit and... brood.

Brood like the devil. Brood in a way that made Heathcliff seem like Pollyanna.

He stared out at the twinkling cityscape, feet planted wide on the floor, arms crossed, and gave into the weight of desperate disappointment that was making it hurt to breathe.

He leaned into it. He let it wash over him fully.

No more pretending he didn't feel.

Even if he wanted to, he wasn't sure this partic-ular disappointment was something he could just pick himself up and move on from.

He'd fought this for so long.

But now that his eyes had been opened to what his heart had properly known since leaving Ashbury Falls, he felt completely powerless against the long, snaking tendrils of the past. They were reaching out for him, all the time. When he least expected it, bam! It was like being sledged in the face.

Sienna, as if in slow motion, turning to smile at him, that first time they'd walked home together. Of-fering to help with his English homework. Making him laugh with a stupid impersonation of one of the teachers at school. Looking like she was about to cry when she was locked out of her house – her dad had been on a bender and Sienna didn't have a key. He'd sat on the step with her for hours and eventually taken her to the local diner for a burger, when it had become obvious Nico Mastrangelo wasn't coming home any time soon. He'd almost invited her back to his place – which was a gamble, because he never knew what mood his own dad was going to be in, but Nico had swerved into the drive around the same time they had. That was probably the first night he started to feel like she'd climbed right in under his skin.

It wasn't a long walk from the school to her place. A single mile shouldn't have taken much more than half an hour. But they'd stretched it out to an hour, walking slowly, stopping often. And hour by hour, day by day, she'd breathed something into him he hadn't known he'd been missing. She'd become a part of him.

But it was more than ten years ago.

Ten years.

He was a different man now. Hell, he was a *man*, whereas back then, he'd been a *boy*. Little more than a kid, trying to find his way in a world that was frequently terrifying thanks to their dad. He'd built a career for himself, a name, made a fortune, mentored kids from all walks of life.

He'd dated other women.

He'd slept with other women.

He'd laughed with them. Talked with them. Walked with them.

But it had never been like it was with Sienna.

And even knowing *that,* he'd still been able to fool himself into believing that it was just because his mind was idealising that time in his life. Minds had a habit of playing tricks, didn't they? And there was something about looking back to those days that was filled with the golden light of adolescence. Something that must have made everything with Sienna seem sweeter and more idealised than the reality had been.

He'd clung to that – taken reassurance from it – all these long, lonely, Ice-control years, until he'd seen her again on the island. Until she'd opened her mouth and that voice that had been flooding his dreams so often was right there, and it was just exactly like he remembered. Whatever she'd breathed into his soul way back when was still between them, and he was just as addicted to it.

To her.

Because he loved her.

The kind of love that didn't just go away.

The kind of love you couldn't fight.

The kind of love that was real, and lasting. And worth fighting for.

He groaned, dropping his forehead against the cool glass of his penthouse's floor-to-ceiling windows. Fighting for?

Hadn't he done that?

He'd told her how he'd felt and she'd made it so abundantly clear that there was no way in hell she'd give him a second chance, even if she felt the same way. It was a question of self-preservation. Didn't he have to respect that? Didn't he have to let this go, even when it hurt like hell?

Let her go?

Those three words swirled through him.

Tormenting him.

Half a question, half a statement. Sometimes he knew it was what he had to do, other times, he wondered, and hoped. Maybe there was a way around this?

But then he remembered the look on her face, the way she'd stepped back from him as if she was *terrified* of what loving him back might mean for her, and it had been an absolute death knell to his own hopes. All this time, he'd been scared of hurting her.

He'd run from her for precisely that reason, yet he'd hurt her anyway.

And in a way that had shaped her into adulthood.

You're the ex I couldn't get over.

* * *

For days, he followed the same pattern, telling himself eventually, if he got back into his groove, it would all start to hurt less.

He ran ten miles in the mornings, went to the club gym and did sixty-minute weight sessions followed by another block of cardio. He watched that cooking show on Netflix everyone was raving about, with the guy who swore all the time. He went to bed early, hoping it would mean he'd get a good night's sleep.

He prepped for pre-season training to begin. He told himself this was his life – the same life he'd had before the wedding – and eventually he'd feel like he belonged in it again.

But no matter how much he told himself that, he still felt the growing, aching, expansion of a black hole in his chest.

He still felt lost at sea. Adrift.

And his anchor was all the way back in Ashbury Falls, determined to never see him again.

There was no solution to that. No magic fix. He just had to accept it and learn to live with the pain.

* * *

Aiden 'Man Mountain' Carter hadn't become a man mountain by accident. Even as a teenager, he'd pushed his limits constantly. His height he couldn't really control, but the rest of it was sheer willpower and determination.

Nonetheless, as she stood in the back of the gym and watched him lift the bar of weights, so every muscle in his body pulsed and vibrated, his face taut from the effort, sweat running down his shirtless back in rivulets from the monumental all-body stamina it took to hold the thing at shoulder height, her mouth went dry, and her gut clenched up.

She'd known he worked hard but this was next level.

She couldn't hear him grunting, or panting, because the music in the gym – some kind of thrasher metal – was up way too loud, but she could see the way his lips were parted, his fierce concentration as he stared at himself in the mirror and presumably counted or whatever it was he did to know that he'd pushed himself just the right amount.

Afraid of startling him and having him drop the thing on his feet, she stayed exactly where she was, where the security guard had let her into the gym, wincing a little at the barrage of heavy beats thrumming around them.

Though Sienna had hated bothering Astrid and Blake on their honeymoon, a quick text explaining the situation had resulted in Blake pulling strings – immediately – to get VIP access to the clubrooms and gym of the training grounds. Chuck had happily let her hitch a ride back on his private jet, and had spent a lot of the time going over the mechanics of flight in a way that finally seemed to unclog something she'd been holding onto for years. Or maybe it was just that for the first time ever, she was so excited about where she was going, and who she was going to see, that she almost forgot to feel terrified.

Even above the decibel-bending level of the music, she heard the metal hit the ground and saw the way his whole body seemed to tighten up in relief at no longer holding the thing. He stood still, staring at himself, frowning, sweating, for several seconds and then went to pick it back up again, so she knew that if she didn't move now, she'd have to wait all over again.

And she didn't want to wait any more.

She was completely done with waiting.

'Aiden.' Her voice barely made a dint in the song.

She had no choice but to walk over to him. To grab his attention, before he picked up the bar again.

The second she stepped out, his eyes flicked to hers in the mirror and his expression turned into something anguished. Something awful. Something that ripped her heart out of its cavity and made the whole world spin too fast.

Just like the way he turned to face her, as if his mind might have been playing tricks on him in the mirror, showing something that didn't exist.

You're in every nook and cranny of Ashbury Falls.

Was it possible that he was just as haunted by her as she was him?

'Sienna.' She couldn't hear him say her name, but she read it on his lips.

With fingers that weren't completely steady, she pointed to her ears, and he nodded jerkily, striding across to a sit-up bench and grabbing his phone to flick off the music, then a towel to wipe his sweaty face and torso. He did not put on a shirt, she noticed, but rather slung the towel around his neck before walking back to her, his expression now one she was more familiar with – neutrality. Cautious, careful nothing. Ice.

'Hey.' His voice though was filled with all the feelings he wouldn't show. In that one single syllable, she heard hope, surrender, pain, need. All the emotions that were a part of her, that she intrinsically understood.

'Hey.'

They stood several paces apart, just staring at each other. With the absence of his metal music, the silence in the gym was deafening.

'You're here.'

She pulled a face. In any other circumstances, she would have made a joke. Like, *no shit, Sherlock*. Or, *yes, I'm aware, Captain Obvious*. But it wasn't any other circumstance. This was a huge circumstance. Quite possibly the most important circumstance of her whole life, and she wasn't going to ruin it by being flippant.

'Yeah. I've got a bone to pick with you.'

He nodded, but his brow furrowed, like he didn't understand.

'You're angry.'

She nodded, took a step forward. His whole body was perfectly, utterly still, except for the rivulets of perspiration that ran down his delicious torso.

She felt like she'd been jammed full of electricity. Her whole body was reverberating with a power source she couldn't place. But she had to get through this. Everything that had seemed murky and incomprehensible was now perfectly, crystal clear.

'How come you didn't tell me about Blake?'

He opened his mouth and stared at her.

'The police. The charges. The reason you had to leave town.'

His eyes shuttered behind thick, dark lashes, like he wanted to hide himself from her. Like he was desperately seeking his defensive structures.

'Blake and Astrid told me,' she muttered. 'I shouldn't have had to hear it from them.'

'Yeah.'

Anger exploded in her chest. Anger at all their wasted time. Missed opportunities. At the cruelty of life, backing Aiden into just the kind of corner that had taken him away from her.

'Damn it, Aiden. You should have told me.'

A muscle jerked in his jaw. 'Yes. I should have. But at the time, I just wanted to get us out of Ashbury. And you were...' He dragged a hand through his hair, frustration evident in every line of his body. 'You were too much.'

'Too much?'

'Too much risk. Too much feeling. Too much of everything. I'd never wanted anything like I wanted you. Not hockey. Not safety. Nothing. But I didn't have the liberty of thinking just of myself, Si.'

'I know that. I get it. I understand.' Tears built in her eyes and she moved towards him then, quickly: one step, two steps, until they were toe to toe, and she pressed her hand to his chest, feeling a wall of tears threaten. 'The thing is, I was wrong, on the island.'

He made a growling sound. She didn't know what it meant. Agreement? Disagreement? Surprise?

She ploughed on.

'Last week wasn't closure. It wasn't an ending. It was another chapter in our story.'

He stared at her without speaking, without moving.

'It's a story we started a long time ago. Once upon a time, a boy met a girl and fell head over heels in love. And when they broke up, it ripped her apart.'

'It ripped him apart too,' he said. 'He just didn't understand what he could do about that. He was in denial.'

She nodded slowly. 'Until he saw her again, ten long years later.'

'And he realised he was just as much in love as ever. More so, for having lived through so long without her.' Now Aiden stepped forward. 'He realised that there is no greater sight on earth than her face, on the pillow beside his, first thing in the morning. No greater feeling than being able to reach out and just take her hand. No greater sound than her laugh.'

'And she realised that being afraid of something isn't a good enough reason to avoid it. I was so scared of letting you back into my heart Aiden that I fought it, tooth and nail, the whole time we were on the island. Which was stupid. Because you were there, just like you always have been. Just like you always will be.'

His jaw shifted as he ground his teeth.

'I don't want to live the next ten years of my life in Ashbury Falls, missing you, wanting you, knowing that this time, I'm miserable because I walked away from what you were offering. I don't want to spend another day of my life missing you. I love you,' she said, half-holding her breath as she waited for his response. She felt like the bravest woman on earth. She felt like a freaking superhero. She felt – terrified and amazing, all at once.

'What?'

She flattened her smile. 'We love each other – and I get that now. I love you and you love me.'

'We do?' He, on the other hand, looked shocked, and incredulous. 'I mean, I know how I feel, but I've spent the last week pretty damned sure that you don't – and would never – love me again. So, I just... need a second to understand...'

'What's to understand?' she asked. 'It's the most straightforward thing in the world, really.'

'Sienna.' He shook his head. 'Are you – is this part of your whole revenge thing?'

She blanched. That he could think that made her bitterly regret ever agreeing to the whole damned scheme, even when it had been responsible for mending four broken hearts.

'Because I get it, you know, and I'm here to be pranked if you need to get it out of your system, but is there any chance you could choose something less barbed than pretending you feel something for me you don't?'

She actually laughed, then. She couldn't believe it.

'I probably deserve it, I just don't think... I don't think I can take it.'

She stopped laughing. Her heart splintered. This big, macho, man mountain of a guy was admitting his vulnerability to her. She was his weakness. She was his everything. It was something she'd never take for granted. She lifted her hands and cupped his face, her fingers splayed wide, her body finally now pressed against his. Her chest rose and fell with the force of each breath.

'You don't deserve it. Aiden, you hurt me back then, but I forgive you. I know why you did what you did. You acted out of love for your family, you even acted out of love for me – out of a mistaken belief that you could hurt me. You thought that a clean break would save me from pining for you. You thought I'd move on with my life, and that I'd be happy. You thought you'd be the only one who was suffering. I understand all of that, and we both need to let it go now.'

He shook his head slowly, a look on his face that was gruff and frustrated. 'It's been so long. I've missed you so much—'

She talked over the top of him. 'I love you. It's not a prank, it's not a joke, it's not a thing but the damned truth. I have loved you since the first day we walked home together, and I will love you every day for the rest of my life. I don't know what that means. Or how this all works. But I realised I couldn't spend another night without you at least understanding that everything you say you feel for me, I feel for you, too.'

'You love me,' he said, and finally, he smiled, like he actually, really believed her.

'Just kidding,' she said, poking out her tongue, but when his smile slipped and was replaced by a look of ice-cold shock, she shook her head. 'That was so mean of me. No, I'm serious. I love you. God, you are really touchy about this.'

'Do you blame me? I've lost you once before because of my own stupidity and now you're dangling this carrot in front of me, and I am just so shit-scared I'm going to say or do the wrong thing and you'll disappear.'

'I'm not going anywhere,' she promised. 'At least, not tonight. Ashbury is my home, and this is your home. I know we're going to have to work out a lot of the details later. All we need to know, for now, is that we want to work that stuff out. Together. That we want to try this again.'

He dropped his forehead and inhaled deeply. 'More than you know.'

'I find that impossible to believe.'

'But you're staying for now? For tonight?'

She nodded, her heart lifting.

'Maybe two nights?'

She laughed. 'I have a job, you know...'

He groaned. 'Let's cross that bridge when we get

to it.' He wrapped his arms around her waist and held her tight to his chest. 'Do you have any idea how happy you've made me?'

She groaned, and lifted onto the tips of her toes, removing her finger and replacing it with her mouth – a much more effective and enjoyable way to silence him. Their kiss was slow at first, tentative, tasting; or maybe it was more of a promise? A pledge that they were going to give this another go and this time, it was for keeps. Which Sienna knew, from the moment their eyes had met in the mirror and she'd seen how utterly devastated he was, that they would both fight for their relationship, no matter what. Because they'd seen the alternative. They'd lived it. And they knew, without a shadow of a doubt that they were stronger, happier, and better together.

'God, I love you,' he said against her mouth. She swallowed those words up and buried them deep in her chest, the warmth radiating through her like nothing she'd ever known.

* * *

Sienna hadn't come to New York for any reason besides seeing Aiden, but when, the next morning, the WhatsApp chat exploded with a flurry of messages, her whole world burst into technicolour.

PAIGE

Olly is meeting with a publisher in Manhattan this afternoon. We land in a couple of hours. Who's around?

BELLA

Meeeeeee! Yipppeeeeee!

ASTRID

Count me in.

BELLA

What? Aren't you off being honeymooned?

ASTRID

Pre-season. And morning sickness. Which FYI can last way past the first trimester if you're super lucky. We'll have a babymoon.

BELLA

Nawww.

PAIGE

Sienna, don't suppose you can hitch a ride? We miss you!

SIENNA

Actually...

She lifted the phone up and snapped a photo of the panoramic Manhattan skyline she could see from Aiden's massive bed. Beside her, he rolled over at the audible click of the camera.

'Please, no photos. No autographs.' He grinned.

'I bet you say that to all your groupies.' She sent the message to the girls.

BELLA

OMG! You're here! Why didn't you tell me?

SIENNA

I just flew in last night.

PAIGE

OMG! Yay! Where shall we meet?

That afternoon, Sienna arrived at the diner Astrid had suggested with cheeks that were flushed pink from the warmth of the day, and the way she and Aiden had spent the better part of the morning: thoroughly re-acquainting themselves with one another, and talking about their shared future. Their hopes, dreams, plans, and what would come next for them. It was all so perfect, she literally couldn't stop shining like a moonbeam.

The others were already inside, heads bent together, as Paige spoke. Sienna took a moment, paused on the sidewalk, just to look at them. To see them. Her best friends, her sisters, her soulmates.

Inside the restaurant, the low murmur of diners enjoying their meals made a background hum as Sienna weaved through the tables to the Karma Club. Funny, when they'd initially thought about karma, it had been about avenging the men who'd wronged them, but now she saw it for what it really was: four women who'd been hurt in the past learning to love again, to heal their hearts and find comfort in true friendship. That was the true karma, the true just desserts.

'Ladies.' Sienna grinned as she approached the table.

Astrid squeaked, her eyes shiny, and Paige let out a squeal.

'Ahhh! I didn't think we'd get to see each other again so soon!' They were oblivious to the way other patrons turned to look at them, as they fell into a four-way group hug.

'I know, I know, me neither.' Sienna sobbed with happiness.

'Why are you here?' Bella asked. 'And how long are you staying?'

'Just another night,' she said. 'I've got to get home to work and Melanie. But...' She let the word hang in the air a moment, until Paige made a noise of impatience.

Sienna laughed. 'I have a feeling I'll be coming and going a fair bit. You know, my boyfriend happens to live around the corner.'

'Boyfriend?' Bella frowned, at the same time Astrid let out another squeak and Paige said, 'Oh my God, no way!'

'You guys worked it out?' Astrid said, smiling, but with a gentleness to her tone, because she'd been witness to both Aiden and Sienna's heartbreak.

'We worked it out *a lot*.' Sienna winked.

'You and Aiden?' Bella clapped her hands together. 'It worked!' She turned to the others. 'We really are very good at this.'

'Very good at what?' Sienna prompted.

'Pulling strings. Getting people what they deserve,' Paige said.

'What are you talking about?'

The four of them sat down, and Sienna looked from one to the other with bemusement, as they began to explain, all talking over each other, how from the minute Astrid got to know Aiden, she knew that he and Sienna weren't done. That he was just as hung up on Sienna as she was on him. 'But the trick was getting you both to see it,' Bella said.

'We knew you wouldn't take our word for it,' Paige agreed with a nod.

'You very nearly didn't even take his word for it,' Bella added.

'That's true.' Sienna sipped her drink, shuddering to think how awful it would have been to have disregarded her instincts and not gone to Aiden. A life without him in it suddenly seemed incredibly, desperately wrong. 'So you're telling me the whole "flirt with him to make him pay" was a set-up?'

'Well, I mean...' Paige flushed. 'If we hadn't suggested it, you'd have spent the whole wedding week ignoring him.'

'And we couldn't bear to think of you as two ships in the night,' Bella added.

'We just didn't want you to miss the opportunity to get to know him again. He's such a great guy, Sissi, and he never got over you. You both just needed a chance to see each other again, to work it out...'

Silence fell as Sienna processed that.

'Are you mad?' Paige asked.

'Mad?' Sienna repeated, with a shake of her head. 'Mad? I'm literally the luckiest woman on the face of the earth. I have a second chance with the only guy I've ever loved, and it's all because of the best friends a woman could want. I just have no idea how to count this many blessings...'

'Don't count,' Bella advised. 'Just sit back and enjoy.'

Which was exactly what Sienna intended to do, just as soon as she'd meted out the final piece of karmic retribution to Horrible Harvey. There was a special piece of justice on his horizon, he just didn't realise it yet...

22

JUST DESSERTS WHATSAPP
GROUP. 14.35 CDT.

SIENNA

Are you guys here?

BELLA

In the locker room. Where are you?

SIENNA

On our way.

PAIGE

Is Astrid with you?

ASTRID

I'm here.

PAIGE

So this is happening?

SIENNA

Aiden and Blake have got the worm on the hook.

PAIGE

Gross. But accurate.

ASTRID

So gross.

BELLA

And Chuck?

SIENNA

He's in the box. Says he doesn't need to see him squirm, it'll be enough to know we've nailed him.

BELLA

Okay. Let's do this.

ASTRID

Be there in five.

The away team locker rooms for the Titans' game against the Chicago Arctics was completely deserted, except for the Karma Club. The team wouldn't start arriving for another hour or so, giving them plenty of time to complete this final revenge quest.

Sienna was a tangle of nerves, hope and anxiety.

She so desperately wanted to thread this needle for Paige. God knew the other woman deserved it. Except, at some point, it had stopped being about Paige. Whether it was falling in love with a guy as sweet and kind as Olly, or just an inner sense of peace and calm, her need for revenge had lessened day by day, to the point where she was almost the least invested in this of the group.

The thing was, it wasn't just for Paige.

Horrible Harvey had form for this, and if they didn't act, he'd keep doing what he'd been doing all his adult life.

Revenge porn was the lowest of the low, especially when it was perpetuated by a guy who had the computer skills to make sure he was never caught by law enforcement.

She thought of Chuck, and the team of cyber ninjas he'd engaged to help them fight the good fight, and her heart lifted. He'd been such a good friend through all this. Hanging out with him, when she was in New York, was something she always looked forward to. And even though she hadn't fully decided to accept his job offer, the prospect was growing more and more tempting by the day.

Sienna's phone buzzed.

AIDEN

Showtime.

'You guys, they're nearly here.'

'Ohmygod.'

'Don't worry. It's almost over,' Sienna promised.

The women moved to the assigned spot, where they were hidden from easily being seen, but still able to look out. Sienna crouched beside a heavily pregnant but incredibly nimble Astrid. This woman made ballerinas look like oafs – she was some kind of freaky, super-breeding princess. Sienna could hear her breathing so hard that she had to reach out and squeeze her hand to remind her to be quiet.

Astrid pulled a face.

'Not bad.' A male voice reached them and when Sienna looked up at Paige, she knew it was Harvey, because of the way Paige's lips were pressed together so hard they'd turned white-rimmed. They'd had to ban Chase and Olly from being anywhere near this guy – Olly in particular. He might have been diffident with a capital D, but he'd made no effort to hide how much he wanted to be let loose on the guy who'd been such a monumental dick to his girlfriend.

'When do the rest of the team get here?'

'Soon. The bus pulls up in about an hour.'

'I thought it was a whole team meet and greet?'

'Yeah, it is, if you want it to be.' Aiden shrugged carelessly.

'That's what I won at the auction.'

Sienna hid her smile. Thanks to Paige, they knew Harvey was incredibly competitive, so setting up a charity auction with a Titans 'meet and greet' package as the prize had been one thing. But getting Chuck to bid on it as though it were the only thing he could possibly want in life had been the perfect bait. Harvey hadn't been able to resist the chance to one-up his professional rival, nor to show the gathering of East Coast elites just how much money he'd made from his tech empire.

'So you did,' Blake murmured smoothly. 'Okay, we can wait for the whole team, if you'd like. We just thought this might be a bit better if it's just the three of us. Up to you, though.'

'What might be better?' Harvey's voice was all bravado, but Sienna was sure she heard the slightest quiver. And who could blame him? The guy spent most of his time hunched over his desk and had the physique to prove it. Here he was being confronted with two huge, buff hockey players. It was only natural he'd feel a hint of panic.

'To show you this.'

Blake grabbed the tablet they'd left on one of the seats, and turned the screen on. They'd linked the audio to the locker-room speakers, so it came out loud and clear.

'Hey, that's me,' Harvey said.

'Shhh.' Aiden lifted a finger to his lips exaggeratedly. 'You'll miss the good part.' With Harvey's attention focused on the screen, Aiden glanced towards the towel rack the girls were hiding behind and risked a wink.

Nah, you don't let them know. Women get crazy uptight about that kind of shit, but deep down, they love it, even if they won't admit it.

Bella put her arm around Paige's shoulders and pulled her in for a hug. Sienna, crouching down, could only pat her foot, but she did so, because she needed to comfort their friend.

'Is that legal?' A man's voice came over the speakers, responding to Harvey's bragging.

Chuck had roped another Silicon Valley friend into taking Harvey to lunch and getting him to spill the beans. It had been a precision operation, thanks

to Chuck and his contacts. For legal reasons per-
taining to consent and recorded conversations, Sienna had made sure the lunch took place out of state.
Usually, she'd have felt bad about that – in her opinion, people should always consent to everything they
did that affected them – but this was Harvey the Horrible, and it was one of the rare instances where two
wrongs absolutely made a right. Or something like a
right.

*Who gives a shit? You and I know how to bury this
kind of thing without having our fingerprints on it.*

'And then you put it on the internet. Why?' the
voice volleyed back.

Because I'm the boss. It was almost psychopathi-
cally self-assured. *I call the shots. No one walks away
from me until I'm ready to let them go.*

It was damning; they'd heard enough. Blake
stopped the recording.

'There's another twenty minutes of that,' Aiden
said.

Harvey was whiter than paper. He looked satisfy-
ingly awful.

'What the hell is going on?' he asked when he
was able to speak, some moments later.

'You screwed with a very good friend of ours,'

Blake said. 'Someone sweet and kind, who deserved a hell of a lot better than to cross paths with you.'

When Sienna looked at Paige, she saw her eyes were moist and the smile she shot back was wobbly.

'She's fine though. In fact, she doesn't ever give you a moment's thought, these days. But knowing you were out there, doing this to other women, she decided to act.'

'And we decided to help her,' Aiden added.

'So, you set me up?'

'Hell, yeah, and I'd do it again and again and again. It's not even in the same ballpark as what you're doing.'

'Fuck you,' Harvey said, storming towards the door.

'You don't want to meet the team?' Blake asked, grinning.

Harvey looked like he was going to vomit or pass out.

'Oh, you should know something,' Aiden started, but then, out of the corner of her eye, she saw Paige moving, a fire in her eyes that warmed Sienna's belly and shot goosebumps over her skin.

Aiden, Blake and Harvey all sensed her at the same time, turning towards the motion in the corner.

Harvey blanched.

'You should know something,' she said, a little softly at first, so the three other women moved like a wall of support, coming to stand beside Paige without touching her. Just letting her know they were there. They literally had her back, and always would. She cleared her throat and tried again. 'That tape isn't just for your ears.'

Harvey was frozen to the spot. Sienna could just make out a bead of perspiration forming on his brow.

'Oh, no. Why waste such good filmmaking?' she said, taunting him with a line he'd once thrown at her. 'We made sure your mum got a copy, and your sister.' She smiled serenely.

He went from white to grey.

'But it really was too compelling to limit just to family.'

He reached for the doorjamb. 'So, we also sent digital copies to your board, and just to be extra sure the message got out there, we sent it to the DA, and two national broadsheets.'

Paige's smile was slow and half-manic, and Sienna couldn't blame her. Finally, they had outmanoeuvred a guy who'd made it his life's work to hurt women, to embarrass them in the most defiling, vicious way.

'You picked on women who didn't know what you were like. Women like me, whose only mistake was trusting an asshole like you. But you're done with that now, Harvey. You're going straight to hell.'

'Pretty sure he's going there by way of prison,' Astrid whispered, pressing a hand to her basketball-round stomach.

'Even better,' Paige said.

'Now, if you don't mind, get your ass off the grounds.'

Harvey didn't move. He couldn't. He looked from one, to the other, to the other, gawping like a fish.

'Get the hell outta here,' Aiden said, taking a step towards him, and that did it. Harvey turned and stormed out of the room, and they all knew he wouldn't get far. The walls were closing in for Harvey and there was no way he'd be able to escape the consequences – societal, legal and within his family – for his awful, demeaning actions.

'Good riddance,' Paige said.

'Are you okay?' The girls formed a circle around her, hugging her tight.

She was laughing though, while tears streamed down her cheeks. 'I'm better than okay. I'm elated. I'm relieved. I'm vindicated. I'm – it's over.'

Sienna nodded quickly. 'And Chuck is doing everything he can to have those videos removed. It's painstaking but he's got a team working on it.'

'I can't believe it. You guys really are my guardian angels.'

'We're each other's,' Astrid assured her, and Bella nodded.

'And you're pretty good sidekicks,' Paige called towards Aiden and Blake, who were still standing by the door, as if they were bouncers in a nightclub, bracing for Harvey's return.

* * *

He didn't return though.

After that day's game, which the Titans won 7-2, Chuck group called them to say that Harvey had been arrested, and also removed from his own company.

They were giddy with excitement and relief, and their celebrations would go down in history as some of the best of all time.

* * *

The next day, Chicago O'Hare Airport

Unlike that cold and blustery, snowed-in night, Chicago was now a picture of autumn beauty, with a crystal-clear sky and flights streaming in and out of the airport, all on schedule.

And four women, who'd met on that fateful night, found themselves back at the airport, accompanying the Titans back to New York. But first, they had a little reminiscing to do. So, leaving the team to the first-class lounge, they slipped out and retraced their footsteps to a familiar bar, with its familiar décor, and the signed picture of Aiden 'Love of Sienna's Life' Carter behind the counter, and found, to their surprise, that despite being busy with a lunchtime rush, 'their' table was available.

They swooped on it, sitting silently and staring at one another, as if they almost couldn't believe how much had happened and changed since that night.

The same waitress who'd served them back then appeared. 'Can I get you ladies anything?'

'Prosecco,' they said, in unison.

'A bottle,' Bella clarified.

They all laughed, then Astrid added, 'And a mocktail.'

'This is strange,' Sienna said, looking around, shaking her head a little in wonderment. 'We're here, and yet, everything is so different. I don't recognise the woman I was back then.'

'No, nor do I,' Paige admitted.

'Honestly, meeting you guys changed my life,' Astrid said.

Bella nodded. 'I couldn't have imagined how fateful that drunken chat would be.' The waitress placed Astrid's mocktail, an ice bucket and three glasses in the middle of the table. Sienna set about filling the glasses. 'I don't just mean because it's how I met Chase, but obviously that too. It's more... you guys.'

They all looked at one another and nodded. Sienna felt a lump form in her throat.

'I never had a sister,' Sienna said. 'I never understood what that bond was like. But if I had, I guess I imagined it might have felt like this.'

Bella nodded. 'But better, because we chose each other,' she said.

Emotions were strong. They sat quietly, each reflecting on the importance of this friendship.

'To us,' Bella said, lifting her glass into the air.

'To Just Desserts, and our crazy little Karma Club,' Astrid added.

'To living our best lives,' Paige chimed in.

'To best friends,' Sienna murmured.

'Forever,' they all said, and laughed, as they clinked their glasses together for what was most definitely not the last time.

* * *

As their glasses emptied, the diner had filled, so there was a line of people at the bar, and not a spare seat in sight. The Karma Club barely noticed – they were still riding high on their success. But then a woman walked past, flustered, eyes darting across the restaurant, and in her hand, she held something Sienna instantly recognised. She sat a little straighter.

'You guys, look.'

'What?' Astrid lifted a hot chip towards her lips but paused, midway. 'What is it?'

'Look!' Sienna pointed, and the gesture caught the attention of the flustered woman.

'Ohmygod.' Paige's jaw dropped. 'The *flyer*.'

'It's funny,' Sienna murmured, thinking back to that fateful night. 'I watched that woman with the magenta hair handing out leaflets, and I wondered what her criteria was for who received one. Like, it wasn't everyone. She was very selective.'

'And she selected us,' Bella said, with a small nod. 'Well, actually, she selected my kinky friend Diedre, but *she* selected me.'

'We were meant to meet,' Sienna said, leaning forward and putting her hand out. Each of the women put theirs on top, supportive. Agreeing.

Astrid's eyes filled with tears. 'Yep.'

'But look.' Now it was Bella who pointed across the restaurant, at another woman who was clutching a flyer, looking totally lost and stranded in manic air-port hell. 'She's been working her magic again.'

'You guys,' Paige said. 'Are you thinking what I'm thinking?'

In answer, Astrid lifted an elegant hand in the air and waved it around, gesturing first to one of the women, and then another, beckoning them over.

'Heya,' Astrid said, when they reached the table. 'Did you want our seats?'

The women looked from one to the other. 'Oh, we're not together,' the shorter woman with thick glasses demurred.

Paige smiled serenely. 'Neither were we. Don't let a simple thing like that get in the way of a good time.'

The women looked unconvinced, but the four original members were already standing, their hearts warm with being able to pay forward their good fortune – and hoping that these women's lives might even be changed in the same way theirs had been.

'Hi, I'm Monica,' Sienna heard the woman in the green hat say, as they walked away from the table.

'Mary-Beth. Where are you heading to tonight?'

As they reached the door to the packed diner, two more women walked in. 'There are a couple of seats at that table,' Bella offered. 'Just over there.'

And when they glanced back at the table they'd recently occupied, it was to see Mary-Beth and Monica locked in conversation, laughing about something.

Sienna reached down and squeezed Astrid's hand; Astrid looked at her and smiled. Everything was just as it was meant to be.

* * *

The following Christmas. Ashbury Falls, NC

'Is that them?'

Aiden peered out of the window and shook his head. 'They'll be here soon.'

'I know.' Sienna smiled. 'I'm just excited.'

'Me too.' Melanie grinned from where she was curled up on the sofa, a small red ribbon around her plaited hair. Though they were no longer neighbours – Aiden and Sienna had moved into the big, beautiful house they'd always walked past (the one Aiden had all but promised he'd make Sienna hers when he could) and were painstakingly restoring it – but Melanie was still a regular fixture in their lives. If anything, the house was closer to the school than Melanie's, so it was easy to stop in on her way home, to share the news of her day or grab a sandwich. Being so close made it easier for Sienna to be away from home, which she frequently was. At least when she was there, she got to spend lots of quality time with the girl she loved like a daughter. 'I can't wait to finally meet them.'

Sienna scrunched her nose. 'You've met my friends.'

'But not, like, all together, at the same time. He says it's like nothing I can imagine.'

'He, being Aiden?'

Melanie nodded, and Sienna laughed softly. 'Well, *he* is not wrong.'

Sienna took a moment to turn slowly and take in the lounge room. It was the first room they'd fully finished re-doing, carefully returning the historic charm of the place, while updating the wiring and features to make sure it was safe and modern. The bedrooms had been renovated just enough to make them comfortable for this weekend – when the original Karma Club crew, plus the honorary members (including Chuck) were coming to stay, and Sienna couldn't wait to play host and show them her town. Though she hoped they'd forgive Aiden for having hidden remote-controlled crickets in all of their rooms. He'd laughed, when she'd told him the truth of that noise, especially when it had been a part of what had driven them back together, but he'd sworn he'd get his own revenge, when the time was right... which apparently it now was.

In the end, Aiden hadn't hated coming back to Ashbury Falls. Everything he'd felt on that score had, they'd decided, been about running from how much he loved Sienna rather than the place itself. Now that he'd accepted his feelings, Ashbury Falls had earned a different place in his heart. Though his father was the only dark spot on their horizon, they rarely saw him. He'd given up on going to church, and from what they heard, he seemed to be in a committed relationship with a bottle of liquor, each and every day.

He was beyond help, beyond redemption, and they had agreed that they'd just let him do him.

Living well was their best revenge, anyway.

Coming back to Ashbury, Aiden had been determined to do something about the way it was morphing into a town with no hope and no prospects. Bit by bit, he'd started investing in the place. He now co-owned the diner, the hardware store, and was in talks with the Titans about co-funding an ice rink in town, on the basis that Aiden and Blake would personally run recruitment and training sessions for talented young kids like they'd been.

They split their time almost equally between New York and Ashbury Falls, with the exception of the odd trip to the UK, to catch up with Paige and Olly. Though they also did their fair share of trans-Atlantic travel, with Paige never wanting to go too long without face-to-face time with her girls.

Sienna was always careful about Aiden's generosity. She'd worked so hard all her life, and asserted her independence wherever possible. But in one way, she'd allowed him to help financially – as a loan. He'd hired an incredible team of lawyers to work on her father's case, and Sienna had every reason to think this would be his last Christmas behind bars.

Not only that, they'd been so impressed with the briefs Sienna had put together that they'd asked her to intern for them over the summer.

She'd agreed, for the experience, but Chuck's offer was still very much in her mind.

It was no bad thing, she considered, to have such great possibilities, and she knew that whichever she chose, it would be right for her, because she'd work hard, and because she deserved to succeed.

Since that fateful night in Chicago, Sienna had done a lot of thinking about life, and families. Melanie wasn't her daughter, and yet she occupied that space in her heart. Cynthia wasn't her mother, yet Sienna truly loved her as she would have her own. And her friends – well, they weren't family, but they were every bit as dear to her as family ever could be. There wasn't a thing she wouldn't do for them, and knowing that loyalty and love was reciprocated made her feel as though she was going through life with the biggest and best support network anyone could ever want.

Christmas magic was heavy in the air, but Sienna didn't need it. She had everything she'd ever wanted, and then some.

Just desserts had been served to all – it was just

very lucky that they'd happened to deserve the happiest of endings imaginable.

* * *

MORE FROM THE KARMA CLUB

Another book in the Karma Club Series, *The Puck Stops Here*, is available to order now here:

    https://mybook.to/PuckStopsBackAd

ACKNOWLEDGEMENTS

In order to write books, I have to feel the magic of the story. It needs to completely absorb and consume me, to sweep me away with every twist and turn, so that all I want is to lose myself in the words that are forming on the page. This has rarely been so true for me as it was in writing *Settling the Score*. This book is the fourth in our beloved Karma Club series, and the world Amy Andrews, Pippa Roscoe, Rachael Stewart and I built, over Zoom calls and email, became incredibly special and real. Our characters – Paige, Bella, Astrid and Sienna – are serious girlfriend goals. Creating their friendships was a true delight.

An enormous acknowledgement of gratitude is owed to Boldwood Books, and particularly Megan Haslam, for championing this project. On a personal note, Megan and I have a long working history together. She acquired one of my earliest manuscripts and over the years, we've worked on dozens of books together. I have learned so much from her, so the chance to bring her into the Karma Club world was an absolute blessing. Beyond Megan, the entire team at Boldwood have been incredibly professional and joyous to work with. Their innovative approach to social media marketing and storytelling has been so much fun. Thank you to the team for the hard work, diligence and professionalism in giving our books the best chance to find their way to readers.

I am ever grateful to my husband and kiddos, who continue to tolerate the fact that I am frequently in the room without actually being present, because in my mind, I'm inhabiting the worlds of my characters. Not only do they tolerate this, they celebrate my achievements, and beam with pride with the release of each of book.

Finally, my biggest thanks is saved for you, the reader. While characters come to life in my mind when I'm writing a book, it's through you and your imagination that they continue to exist, to be adored, and remembered. I hope you take Sienna and her besties into your heart, as I have mine, and that their stories continue to bring you joy for a long time to come.

ABOUT THE AUTHOR

Clare Connelly is the bestselling author of more than one hundred romance novels, and has sold more than four million copies of her books worldwide. Clare is also the co-founder of the How to Write Academy, and the co-writer of the Karma Club series from Boldwood Books.

Follow Clare on social media here:

- facebook.com/clarewriteslove
- x.com/clarewriteslove
- instagram.com/clarewriteslove

ALSO BY CLARE CONNELLY

The Karma Club Series

The Payback Plan by Amy Andrews

How to Get Even by Pippa Roscoe

The Puck Stops Here by Rachael Stewart

Settling the Score by Clare Connelly

Boldwood
EVER AFTER

x♡x♡

JOIN BOLDWOOD'S
**ROMANCE
COMMUNITY**
FOR SWEET AND
SPICY BOOK RECS
WITH ALL YOUR
FAVOURITE
TROPES!

SIGN UP TO OUR
NEWSLETTER

HTTPS://BIT.LY/BOLDWOODEVERAFTER

Boldwood

Boldwood Books is an award-winning fiction publishing company seeking out the best stories from around the world.

Find out more at www.boldwoodbooks.com

Join our reader community for brilliant books, competitions and offers!

Follow us
@BoldwoodBooks
@TheBoldBookClub

Sign up to our weekly deals newsletter

https://bit.ly/BoldwoodBNewsletter

www.ingramcontent.com/pod-product-compliance
Lightning Source LLC
Chambersburg PA
CBHW010658100726

47900CB00010B/2709